Secrets Beneath the Vows

Nora Kensington

Published by Nora Kensington, 2024.

Copyright © 2024 by Nora Kensington

All rights reserved.

No part of this book may be reproduced, distributed, or transmitted in any form or by any means, including photocopying, recording, or other electronic or mechanical methods, without the prior written permission of the publisher, except in the case of brief quotations embodied in critical reviews and certain other noncommercial uses permitted by copyright law.

This is a work of fiction. Names, characters, places, and incidents are either the product of the author's imagination or used fictitiously. Any resemblance to actual persons, living or dead, events, or locales is entirely coincidental.

For permission requests, please contact the publisher at: nora.kensington.author@gmail.com

Prologue

Dell

The room is in complete darkness, the heavy curtains blocking the sunlight because nothing about my father had to do with brightness, sunny days, or joy.

I see his dead body, outlined in the dim light of the suite, but I don't approach just yet.

Somehow, I knew it would be like this, that he would leave without saying goodbye. Silent in death as he was in life.

My father's existence was marked by pain.

First, the tragic loss of my grandparents.

Then, the woman he loved.

And as if fate didn't think he had enough trials, Lee, my brother, was taken from us too.

Now, all that remains of the Westbrooks are me, London, and Vernon.

No.

There's also the promise I made to him to never allow a descendant of the enemy to take control of the company my great-grandfather founded, and to fulfill it, I will do whatever it takes.

I walk over to his bed and notice that he is holding a photograph between his fingers.

Did he know he was dying? Was that why he made me promise to fight against the Seymours, or was last night just another of the many when he must have missed all those we lost?

I turn on the lamp and am not surprised to see one of the images is of my mother with Lee in her arms.

A memory, two pains, and losses intertwined.

The other is the hateful photo that haunted both him and me our whole lives.

I keep it in the pocket of my blazer to later put it in a safe.

I will look at it from time to time to remind myself to feed the hatred I feel for the Seymours.

Chapter 1

Evelina

Moscow

The smell of vanilla cream fills the air as I finish the cake I need to deliver tomorrow morning.

They say those who work with sweets quickly get tired of them. That's not the case for me. I've been surrounded by sugar since I was a child, as Grandma was considered the best baker in all of Moscow.

With a magical touch for sweets, she provided wedding cakes for the Russian high society.

And yet, she died with nothing. Not even a roof over her head, which had always been her dream.

The memory makes me sad, but at the same time, it motivates me because I know what I need to do to change the end of our family story.

Work, fight, never give up.

My grandmother made the mistake of loving the wrong man.

Every Volkova before me, without exception, fell in love with scoundrels and ended their lives without fulfilling their dreams, living in the shadow of partners who never valued them.

Grandma married a gambling addict who always cleaned out all the savings from the house, taking every penny that came in.

It was like trying to put out a forest fire with a bucket from the beach, as she used to tell me.

I don't have many memories of my grandfather because, although my brother and I lived with our *babushka* since we were little, Grandpa was never home, which, now that I'm an adult, makes me wonder if he was cheating on her with other women.

I decorate the cake with a few extra roses than requested because I think whoever ordered it "skimped" on their desire for flowers. When I'm satisfied, I hand it to my assistant so she can store it in the fridge until tomorrow, at delivery time.

Each cake I finish is like a silent tribute to Grandma. I think she would be happy to know that I managed to pay off our debts and get our lives back on track. Maybe, in another year, the café will even start turning a profit.

"Evelina, have you noticed some strange men hanging around the shop?" Katya, my employee, asks.

I check the sidewalk through the cracked glass of the window, which I intend to replace soon.

"Look around us, dear. The whole neighborhood is strange, just like its residents."

"Yeah, you're right." She chuckles. "Must be my imagination."

The door opens, and a customer enters with what I assume are her two children. They are all redheads and look alike.

She clearly isn't Russian because I hear her speaking to the kids in English without an accent.

The woman is well-dressed, so I wonder what she might be doing in a neighborhood like this.

To start my business, I had to set up the café here. It was the only property I could find with an apartment on the second floor that fit my budget. However, I hope that soon I will be able to move.

"Good afternoon, I would like three slices of..." she pauses and glances at a magazine, which confuses me "*medovik*? Is that the name?"

"Yes, *medovik* is a honey cake. Are you American?" I ask in English.

"I am."

"Could you explain how you knew I sold *medovik*? " I say, smiling and pointing to a table for the three of them.

There are only two in my establishment because there isn't room for more.

"I saw it in a travel magazine. They were raving about your sweets."

"What? But I only opened three months ago!"

"You can check for yourself."

She hands me the magazine, and before I start reading, I tell Katya to get the three slices of cake the customer wants.

"What are you going to drink?"

"My boys will have milk. What do you recommend?"

"Coffee or black tea."

"Coffee, then."

I wait for my employee to serve them before I read the article.

"A little piece of heaven on an unassuming street in Moscow."

"Amidst the grandeur of the Russian capital, where historical monuments enchant us with their beauty, hidden in a neighborhood of dubious safety, lies a small and cozy candy shop with a unique and irresistible flavor."

"Excuse me," I say to the customer, placing my hand on my chest, feeling emotional.

I see Katya serving them and only then gesture for her to come closer to me.

"Recently, I had the opportunity to visit this hidden gem in the middle of an ugly street, and as a food reporter, I was completely fascinated by the discovery of this treasure.

The shop, Slastyona, offers an experience that transcends the simple act of eating; it's a dive into rich Russian cuisine.

The owner, Evelina Volkova, welcomed me with a smile and told me she follows her grandmother's old recipes.
The establishment, though modest in size, is a must-visit for sugar lovers.
The medovik, in particular, a honey cake with several layers of thin dough and condensed milk cream, is so delicious that I'm still dreaming about the taste.
What also impressed me was the passion and care with which Evelina talks about her work.
My visit to Slastyona was much more than just a stop for a sweet treat. It was a journey to the heart of Russian tradition.
If you are in Moscow, this little shop is a must-see."

At the end of the article, there's a photo of the man.

"That's the gentleman who came here the week we opened! He was a food reporter," I say, leaning on the counter with wobbly legs from excitement.

"The shop was featured in a magazine. Soon, we'll have a line of customers!" Katya says enthusiastically.

"You think?"

"I'm sure, boss. We're going to get rich!"

"Hummmm..." We hear the customer and her kids moan as they savor my sweet. "My God, this is sinfully delicious!"

I smile at Katya, and when a few minutes later the American prepares to leave, I ask if I can take a photo of the magazine because I want to frame the article.

"Keep it; I can buy another. And you can be sure I'll recommend your sweets to all my friends."

"Thank you so much!" I say, escorting them to the door, but at the same time thinking about how many chic Americans will come to this place for dessert.

As soon as I return inside the shop, my mind still lost in dreams of a better future, I realize something is wrong just by the expression on Katya's face.

"What is it?"

She makes a grimace of disgust.

"Your brother is on the phone. He said it's urgent."

Chapter 2

Evelina

"No, I'm not going to lend you money again. You know perfectly well that I'm still paying off Grandma's debts, Pyotr."

It's a small lie. I've already paid them off, but I can't tell my brother the truth or he'll bankrupt me.

"You were in a magazine, Evelina! How can you be so selfish?"

"Selfish? Surviving by working honestly is now called selfishness? And how do you know I was in the magazine? I just found out myself."

"You might not believe it, Evelina, but I care about you. I'm always in the loop about what's going on in your life."

I roll my eyes and see Katya's face, just a few steps away from me, twist into a frown because I think she overheard what my brother said.

My employee has never seen the good side of Pyotr, which even I must admit has long since disappeared. All she knows about him is that he treats me like an ATM with an endless balance.

I've sworn to myself many times that I wouldn't help him anymore because he's heading down the same path as our grandfather, getting into gambling debts.

Unfortunately, I can't lay my head peacefully on my pillow imagining him getting beaten up by loan sharks or worse men, so I always end up giving in.

Pyotr is the only family I have left. I don't have anyone else. More than not wanting to be completely alone, I fear that something might happen to him.

Every night I pray for God to put some sense in his head so we can move on with our lives. My brother is a handsome and intelligent man. It's a shame he wastes his brain scheming to deceive me or take advantage of me.

"I don't believe you," I finally respond. "You never call to see how I'm doing. You only come to see me when you're in trouble."

At first, saying something like that would make me want to cry. My brother and I were best friends until adolescence, but something happened along the way that made him completely lose his way.

My grandmother used to say it was bad company, but I suspect it was more than that. The fact is, I no longer recognize the man who is two years older than me as my childhood partner, confidant, and protector.

Every time he shows up, I know I'll have trouble ahead.

"I'm trying to change," he says, his voice saddened, and I hate that my foolish heart fills with hope because this isn't the first time I've heard that.

"How?"

"I want to go back to school."

"You're already an adult, Pyotr. What do you plan to do? Become a full-time student at twenty-one? And how do you think you'll support yourself during that time?"

"You're so negative, Evelina."

"No, brother, I'm practical. As you know, I had to take care of Grandma when she got sick" I don't finish: while you were living it up with your friends all over Russia without even remembering that we existed "so I don't indulge in dreams. Or rather, I have dreams, although they might not be as colorful and light as yours. To me,

an ideal world is one where I don't have debts and can run my shop, closing the month with the accounts in the black."
"What if I help you?"
"What?"
"What if I work for you?"
"You know as much about cakes and sweets as I do about mechanics. What's really going on, Pyotr? Because you're never going to convince me that you called me because you missed me. Especially after you mentioned an article that until a few minutes ago, I had no idea was published."
"You know what? Forget it, Evelina. There's no way to talk to you. All you think about is money and advantages."
"I can't believe you said that to me."
"Don't play the victim. None of what I said is a lie, and if one day I show up dead somewhere, I hope you're haunted by your own selfishness forever."
He hangs up the phone without saying goodbye.
"He hung up on me."
"I don't know how you can be surprised, Evelina. Your brother does nothing but create trouble and make you sad."
"He's getting worse, Katya. It's as if he's entered an emotional downward spiral. I see him crumbling in front of me like a house of cards."
"He's not crumbling in front of you, boss. I'm sorry to say this, but the brother you knew as a child has been gone for a long time and..."
She stops as we both hear the shop door open and a man who looks like he walked straight out of a comic book about villains enters.
"Can I help you?"

He doesn't answer me, and an uncomfortable sensation spreads through my chest, especially when I see his eyes scanning me from head to toe.

I think Katya feels the same way because she steps in front of me, blocking him from seeing me.

"Unfortunately, we're closing, sir. If you want any sweets, you'll have to come back tomorrow."

It's a downright lie. There are still a few hours until we close, and although the display cases are currently empty, we have a stock of sweets in the fridge at the back of the shop.

"I don't want any sweets," he says, before turning his back on us and leaving without saying another word.

In that instant, my employee rushes to put up the closed sign and locks the door.

When she returns to my side, her face is pale.

"I don't think it's a coincidence that this man came in the same day your brother called, Evelina."

"What are you insinuating?"

"It's not an insinuation, it's intuition."

"I don't understand."

"For days, I've seen strange men lurking around the shop. At first, I thought it was just my imagination, but after that guy came here shortly after Pyotr called... I think this time he might have gotten involved with really dangerous people, boss."

Chapter 3

Dell

I throw the newspaper my personal assistant, Colton, handed me about ten minutes ago into the trash, wishing it was the head of that son of a bitch, Seth Jasper Seymour.

"He has to be behind this," I say.

Colton, much more a friend than an employee, shrugs.

"And what difference does it make who tipped off that gossip column, Dell? Is it a lie? Weren't you having sex with an exotic dancer on your yacht at the last party?"

"So if she were an Italian princess, would it make a difference? That's ridiculous."

"You know it would, because with an Italian princess, the media would think there might be a chance of you marrying her, and that would satisfy your 'watchers.'"

I know he's referring to the Tempus Board, the company that has belonged to my family for generations.

"What I do with my personal life is no one's business."

"The board of directors of the company you insist on keeping as CEO disagrees."

I stand up and walk to the window, turning my back on him and thinking about what he's saying. I know he's right. The Tempus Board, founded by my great-grandfather, is made up mainly of men in their eighties, married, who are also fathers and grandfathers.

For them, it doesn't matter how rich I am and that Tempus is far from being my main business; they want someone at the helm who has impeccable behavior. Preferably married with children.

If I didn't have this thorn in my side called Seth Jasper Seymour, I wouldn't care who sat in the CEO's chair of the company, but I know that even if, like me, Tempus isn't his main focus, the grandson of my late grandfather's partner will make it a point to take the role if I leave it vacant, just to torment me.

"Risking sounding repetitive, why can't you just let it go?" Colton asks.

I can't tell him the truth: that I will never allow the grandson of a former friend who betrayed the man I loved so much to usurp a position that, I know, he only desires to win this war that has lasted for generations.

As much as I hate him, I have no doubt the feeling is mutual.

While I stand in front of the window, I take the pocket watch from inside my suit, the first from Tempus, made by my great-grandfather when his workshop was still functioning in a tiny shed in his backyard.

The company he founded represents not only the most sophisticated in terms of watches but also showcases meticulous engineering. The watches we produce are precise and unmatched. Much more than timekeepers, they are crafted with passion, elegance, and destined to become a true legacy for future generations.

Each piece is assembled by craftsmen who employ a combination of traditional techniques and cutting-edge technology.

Unlike most watches that feature more beauty than quality, ours are handmade, true works of art where every detail is checked.

They are traditionally produced only in gold and platinum, and just a couple of years ago I succumbed to the fact that women want more than metal; they desire sparkle, so we added diamonds and some other precious stones to the women's models, depending on the type of watch.

Since its founding, Tempus has dedicated itself to the art of high watchmaking, and this tradition has been extending through generations in our family.

Although my brothers and I have never made the company our main focus, I would be dead before I let it fall into the hands of a traitor's grandson.

"You don't have much time to make a decision."

"Decision?" I refuse to accept what I know he's talking about.

"I'm not the enemy here, Dell. The opposite is true. I see you as a brother, and that's why I'm telling you your time is running out." He pauses, and I hear a chuckle. "I swear I didn't try to make a joke about the name of your family's watch brand."

I turn to face him.

"That's not funny."

"What do you plan to do? They made it clear what they want to keep you at the helm of the company."

"If it weren't for Seth, I'd tell them all to go fuck themselves."

"I know, but I'm also sure that as soon as you step down, if you act impulsively against the board, Seth will take your place. It's the logical order. He's the second-largest shareholder of Tempus, and as far as we know, he has an impeccable reputation."

"Impeccable my ass! The only difference between us is that I don't hide my girlfriends in the basement."

"Well, we're making progress."

"I didn't get the joke."

"Up until a week ago, you called them 'friends.' Now you refer to them as girlfriends. Or rather, ex-girlfriends, because as far as I know, you're single at the moment. What I'm trying to say is that maybe, with a little luck, soon you'll find one you'll label as fiancée, and then, wife."

"I don't want to marry anyone."

"As we've discussed before, it doesn't have to be a real relationship. Just real enough to get the Tempus Board off your back."

"The woman will be my wife for a year. I'm going to bring a stranger into my life to satisfy the outdated eccentricity of a bunch of lunatics who think a married man is more respectable than a single one."

"In your case, there's no denying it would be. At least for a year, you would need to keep up appearances, which you haven't bothered to do until now."

"I'm not going to apologize for fucking when I feel like it. I'm thirty-two. I've never deceived a woman into believing I'd promised her anything other than good sex."

"I'm not going to argue with you. I know the idea of having to find a convenience wife to keep your CEO position pisses you off, but there's no way out. Have you looked through your contact list to see if any of your exes would fit the role?"

"That was the first thing I did, and I'm sure it would never work. The most reliable woman who wouldn't ask anything in return for taking my name and putting a ring on her finger is my secretary. Too bad she's sixty-eight and has been married for fifty."

He laughs, the bastard.

"Maybe I have a tailored solution."

"What's it about?"

"I'll explain. From my point of view, all your problems will be solved with my suggestion."

Chapter 4

Evelina

A Few Days Later

"I'm so sorry, sir, but we've already closed the register." I hear my employee say, and even from inside the café's office, without seeing who arrived, I know something is wrong.

Her voice sounds frightened.

I glance at the rolling pin resting on a chair a few steps away, made of solid iron, a gift from Grandpa to Grandma, as she often found herself alone in the old shop she owned. Even though he wasn't around to save her if necessary, at least he had that much care.

Grandma didn't like guns or knives, but she wasn't a damsel trapped in a castle needing to be rescued either.

We never lived in the upscale part of Moscow, and I've seen her threaten abusive neighbors and customers who wanted more than her cakes because my grandmother was a beautiful woman.

I try to sharpen my hearing, listening to the sounds from the shop, but now I can't hear anything.

I think about what she asked me the last time my brother called: if I hadn't noticed strange people hanging around the shop.

Katya noticing this on the same day Pyotr called feels like bad news.

It wouldn't be the first time my brother got involved with "very wrong" people, but in all the other instances, he kept them away from me.

"If one day I end up dead somewhere, I hope you're haunted by your own selfishness forever."

My God, Pyotr, what have you gotten yourself into this time?

With trembling legs, I reach for the rolling pin and hide it behind my body.

I'm naturally optimistic, and despite feeling uneasy about the sudden silence, I walk to the front of the shop, certain that Katya chased away the intruder, since I'm sure we put up the "closed" sign about half an hour ago.

My heart races to my throat in a fraction of a second, however, when I see they've lowered the shop's gate and pulled down the curtains, but what sends me into a panic is that a huge man has one arm around Katya's neck, and a gun pointed at her head.

Another man is watching the entrance of the shop, perhaps just in case a customer tries to lift the gate and enter.

"What's happening here?" I pretend to be oblivious because the men look too well-dressed to be common thieves.

Behind my body, my hands are sweating so much I fear dropping the rolling pin.

"Your brother owes us," the man holding Katya captive says, turning my nightmares into reality.

"My brother sent you here?"

"No, he said you were the guarantee that he would pay us."

"Please, sir, could you let my employee go? I can't think straight seeing her with a gun to her head."

He stares at me for a while, and just as I begin to believe he won't heed my request, he shoves Katya into me. With only one arm, so I won't have to drop the rolling pin, I embrace her.

"Shhh... I'm so sorry. I'll take care of this."

"It's not your fault; it's that unfortunate brother of yours. You don't deserve this, Evelina."

"Whether she deserves it or not," the giant growls, "is not our problem. Pyotr owes us and has disappeared. It's better if you pay us. You don't want a visit from our boss, girl."

"Boss? Who is your boss?"

He ignores my question, and without any ceremony, points the gun at my face.

"You have two weeks to get us what your brother owes."

"I don't owe you anything."

"Are you stupid or something? Didn't you understand that your brother put you and this shit of a shop up as collateral?"

"My shop? Look, sir, if I weren't about to faint from nerves, I'd almost be able to laugh. If you didn't notice before you came in, this is a small business. I can barely close the month in the black. Whatever Pyotr told you, he lied."

"Too bad for you, then, for having a shit brother, because our problem now is with you. Pyotr has vanished, and we can't find him anywhere. Incredible how he managed to escape with a broken leg."

I widen my eyes.

"Broken leg?"

The man gives me a wicked smile.

"Fifteen days."

"What?"

"That's the time you have to get the money. And I'm being generous."

"How much money are we talking about?"

"There's no point in telling you the exact amount because interest accrues daily, but let's say it's around fifty million rubles."

"My God, that's more than half a million U.S. dollars!" Katya, whose mother was born in the United States, quickly calculates.

"How could you lend so much money to Pyotr? He has nowhere to drop dead!"

"We didn't lend it. It was the interest. Initially, he only owed us five hundred thousand rubles."

Which means about fifty thousand dollars.

"How long has my brother owed you?"

He scratches his head with his free hand, the gun still pointed at me.

"Six months?" he asks the other loser guarding the door.

"Eight."

I want to scream at the miserable bastard that nowhere in the world could a debt grow so much in such a short time, but I think better of it since the barrel of the gun is still aimed at me.

"I have fifteen days?" I try to put on the sweetest and most neutral voice in the world while inside, I want to cry.

I thought my life was finally getting back on track, but now, I have no choice but to run. There's no way a bank would lend me that much money.

Besides, even if by some miracle I managed to gather the amount, who guarantees that Pyotr isn't also in debt to other people?

"Yes, fifteen days," he repeats, but I notice a mocking smile because we both know there's no way I can get that amount.

"And what happens if I don't pay?"

"Then you'll be his."

"His?"

"The boss's. The new toy of the boss. Until he gets tired of you."

Chapter 5

Dell

"You must be going crazy!" Vernon, my younger brother, growls when I tell them Colton's idea. "Your hatred for Seth is getting out of control, Dell."

"Out of control?" London, the middle brother, scoffs. "Both of you have lost your sense of proportion a long time ago."

"I made a promise to our father. A Seymour will never be at the helm of Tempus. The company our great-grandfather founded belongs to the Westbrooks."

"The only Seymour you need to worry about is Seth. Lazarus never cared about his share in the company, and I'm sure if it weren't for Seth's stubbornness, he would have sold it to us, just as his younger sister, Lois, would have done."

I feel an involuntary muscle contraction in my neck as I think about what I discovered yesterday.

"Actually, LJ and Lois transferred all their shares to Seth."

London doesn't hesitate.

"We'll do the same with you. Of the three of us, you're the one who feels the most resentment toward the Seymours."

Because it was I who my father asked, near his death, to swear that this cursed family would never be in charge of our company.

"It won't matter. Even if I numerically have more shares than all the Seymours combined, the Board is unyielding. I have no choice but to present a wife and impeccable behavior for a year."

"Those old bastards..." London irritably responds because perhaps, even more than I and Vernon, he has an allergy to the word marriage.

"It's a means to an end. If it's imperative for Dell to stay in charge of Tempus, I see no other alternative."

Our youngest brother is the most practical of the three of us.

"Okay," London says. "But marrying a stranger is going too far."

"There's no such thing as 'going too far' when what's at stake is preventing that bastard from usurping what is rightfully ours," I say.

"We both agree on that, but why do you need to choose a wife from a catalog?"

"It's the most practical way."

Vernon laughs.

"At least you can be sure she's pretty." He seems to think. "Being hot, in fact, is more important to me. I've been with gorgeous women with whom I had zero chemistry in bed."

"Who?" London asks.

"Kiss and don't tell," Vernon jokes.

I roll my eyes.

There must be something seriously wrong with the men in our family. There are only two things that matter to us: work and sex.

No, in my case, there's the certainty that I will fulfill the promise I made to my father, no matter the cost.

"Do you even know who she is?"

"I haven't checked the website yet," I say, referring to a "catalog" of convenience wives for the elite, presented to me by Colton, "but I definitely don't want one from the American continent. I prefer a woman who only wants to have an adventure and then disappear from my life."

"You'll need to draft a careful contract; otherwise, she might want to take everything from you in court," London says.

"That won't happen. First of all, because I don't intend to consummate the marriage. This way, I can annul it later. I also plan to create a generous prenuptial agreement so she can live comfortably when it's all over. Furthermore, she'll have to accept a confidentiality agreement. She'll never be able to mention my name for the rest of her life."

"I can't imagine why a single woman would agree to such a contract, a fake marriage where you won't even have sex. And speaking of that, how do you plan to resolve this issue? Because I doubt you can go a year without fucking."

"As for your first question: a woman who agrees to marry a stranger would do so for money, of course. And about going without sex, there's no chance in hell that's happening. I've thought about it. I'll be discreet. I'll put that in the clause."

London bursts out laughing.

"As discreet as when you fucked that exotic dancer, which is precisely what got you in the mess you're in now?"

"Go to hell, London."

"He's not entirely wrong, brother. I wouldn't doubt that the Board would put someone to watch you."

I pull at my shirt collar, feeling suffocated.

The idea of having someone in control of my life drives me crazy.

"So let me see if I understand," my younger brother continues. "You're looking for a woman who comes from a good family, broke, I suppose, otherwise she wouldn't accept something like this, who isn't from the American continents, and who will agree to all your terms in the contract?"

"The way you talk, it sounds like I'm buying someone."

"No, he's not buying. I'd say the word 'rent' fits better."

"You both can go to hell."

"I'm just curious." Vernon defends himself. "I can't imagine being in your shoes with such a short deadline to find a wife."

"I'll manage. That's not what I'm worried about."
"Then what is?"
"Getting back at Seth. He's the one who set me up."
"You're referring to the incident with the exotic dancer?"
I nod in agreement.
"And what do you plan to do?"
"Turn his life into a hell."

Chapter 6

Evelina

"I don't want to hate my own brother, but it's becoming harder not to."

We've both been terrified since the day those men were here. They haven't returned to the shop, but I feel constantly watched, and if it weren't for Katya's courage, who despite her fear comes to open the café with me every day, I don't know what I would do.

I've been to practically every bank in Moscow, and when I mention the amount I need for a loan, the managers barely hold back laughter in my face. Who could blame them? If I were in their shoes, I wouldn't lend even a third of that to a woman who only has a small shop that was just starting to break even.

I also tried to get in touch with my brother, but his phone goes straight to voicemail. I wish I could say I hope he didn't offer my shop as payment to those scoundrels, but I know him too well. This isn't the first time he's gotten into trouble, and I know it won't be the last. I'm afraid that one day he won't be able to escape the clutches of those dangerous men.

I feel a chill of fear when I remember the man insinuating that they broke my brother's leg.

You're a fool, Evelina. How can you still care about him when Pyotr has put your life at risk?

"If you can't hate him, Pyotr, I'll do it for both of us," Katya says, pulling me back to reality.

We hear a trash can fall over as we sneak through the alley behind the café, and we both jump in fright.

Since I was threatened, Katya won't let me sleep in my apartment above the shop anymore. In fact, I'm gradually moving my things, carrying bags with essentials like tonight, for example.

She hasn't gone home either. We're staying with an old neighbor of her deceased mother, whose address no one knows.

It's not ideal, but it keeps us alive, at least. And we still have the advantage of being able to save money until we can leave. We'll run away together.

Thinking about leaving my life behind makes me very sad, especially now that the shop has started to gain a reputation, but the alternative, staying in Moscow and risking it, is far too frightening.

I keep waiting for that man to show up and attack us. I haven't been able to sleep well at all.

Katya has come up with a plan, and it's only for this reason that I haven't completely lost it yet.

I didn't want to come to the shop anymore, and that alone says a lot about how frightened I feel because the establishment is my pride and my life.

However, my friend, who at this moment can think more clearly than I can, said I would need every penny I could save. After the article in that magazine, our revenue tripled, and sometimes there's even a line at the door.

What we've both noticed, however, is that even with the café full and it being clear to any passerby that it's profitable, no one has shown up to collect from me.

Of course, it could be that what I make in an entire day would be a drop in the ocean compared to the debt my brother has accrued. Katya, however, came up with another theory: that the boss of the men who threatened us doesn't actually want a payment.

From the moment she raised this hypothesis, I feel my nerves jump under my skin because I can't forget the words of those thugs.

"And what happens if I don't pay?"

"Then you will be his."

"His?"

"The boss's. The new toy of the boss until he gets tired of you."

"Regarding what you told me, if the man to whom Pyotr owes knows that I will never gather the money in time to pay him, and that I'm also in his hands..."

"What about it?"

"If that's the case, if you're sure I would never have the amount in the time he gave me, why not just come and get me?"

She wraps her arm around mine and urges me to walk faster. The alley is dark and smelly. A sinister place for two women to walk alone at night, but we always prefer to exit through the back of the shop in case someone is watching us.

The night is cold, which is not unusual for early autumn, so I zip up my jacket while trying to keep up with her steps, because Katya is very tall.

"Do you really want me to tell the truth?"

"Yes."

"Because I think he might want to play with you. To give you a false sense of freedom until the moment he comes to take you."

I feel the snack I had an hour ago turn in my stomach.

"To do something like that, that man must be sick."

"I have no doubt about that, Evelina. Tell me the name of a decent man who would accept a human being as payment for a debt?"

"Don't get me wrong. I was sure they weren't decent people. I remember that idiot with a gun to his head perfectly. What I'm saying is there's a higher level of cruelty in someone who plays with another's fear, and..."

We reach the corner of the alley, which leads directly to the main street, about fifty meters from my shop's entrance, and Katya squeezes my hand, interrupting me.

"Stay quiet."

"What is it?"

"I think someone is breaking into the café."

"What? Breaking into the café?" I repeat like a robot.

"Look and see for yourself!"

She pulls me so we can hide behind a parked car.

Now we have a perfect view of the front of my shop, as well as of a black car with all four doors open and men, also dressed in dark clothes, jumping out.

It feels like I'm witnessing a horror movie, except after what happened in the café when we were threatened, I know the risk we're facing is very real.

"What are we going to do?"

"Wait a little. Maybe they just want to check if you're in the apartment above the shop."

A tremor runs through my body, and it has nothing to do with the cold wind. I'm in a panic.

We stay silent, watching them almost without breathing. I watch in shock as one of the men, with an ease that clearly comes from years of practice, manages to unlock the iron door of my shop and lift it up. Three of them enter while two stand at the car door, as if keeping watch.

Not even five minutes pass before the men come back, irritated. One of them kicks a trash can on the sidewalk and curses loudly.

Then they return to the car without even bothering to close my shop.

I only realize I'm crying when I feel my cheeks wet.

I've worked multiple jobs, sometimes three shifts a day, to pay off the debts from when my grandmother was sick. There were still some gambling debts left by my grandfather. Today, they're all paid off.

In the months I kept the café open, my brother would occasionally show up asking for some money because he was "in debt to someone." Sometimes I'd give, sometimes I truly didn't have it, so I'd tell him a flat no.

I'm naturally optimistic and was sure that over time the shop would prosper, but I don't need to be a genius to understand that this will never happen. I can't go back there anymore because those men are after me.

We're still crouched down, hiding like two criminals, but Katya hugs me.

"I'm so sorry, my dear."

"They didn't even close the door again. By the time dawn breaks, the shop will have been ransacked."

She doesn't try to comfort me because she knows what I'm saying is a fact, so she just lets me cry for a bit.

"What we just saw, in my opinion, looks like an attempt to kidnap you, Evelina. They wouldn't respect the deadline. They came in the middle of the night to take you. I know you love this shop, but you can't go back there anymore, dear."

"I know."

"You have no idea the hatred I feel for your brother right now."

"You've never liked him."

"No, I've never liked him because he reminded me too much of my father: a womanizer. Pyotr followed the example of your grandfather, from what you've told me about him. He's a user of women, Evelina. A man who will never mature because he's convinced the world owes him something and that everyone must cater to his whims."

I nod in agreement because at this moment, I can't think of him as my brother but as someone without character who puts himself before anyone else. The fact that we share the same blood and he's my older brother hasn't stopped him from dragging me into his shady dealings without me even suspecting a thing.

"I don't know where to go."

"I do. I saw this coming, Evelina. I'm thirty-five and have dealt with my fair share of scoundrels over the years. I didn't like your brother the first moment I laid eyes on him, but forgive me for saying this, Pyotr is just a selfish jerk, not dangerous. The men he owes, however, in my opinion, are part of the Bratva."

"What?"

"They are..."

"I know what Bratva is. What I'm asking is why you think these men are in the mafia."

"I'm almost certain, actually. Remember the man who was guarding the door the day they broke into the café?"

"I remember."

"Well, he had a tattoo of rings on the fingers of both hands, which means, in 'mafia language,' that he's a convicted criminal."

"And how do you know this?"

"I had an uncle, long dead, who was a soldier in the Bratva, so I know the symbols. What I'm trying to tell you, Evelina, is that this time your brother has gotten involved with the wrong people. As I told you before, we need to get out of Moscow."

"I know what we discussed, but until now, they were just plans."

"Not anymore. I have an idea. We'll leave from here to Saint Petersburg, and from there, we'll drive across the border to Finland."

"And what will we do when we get there?"

"I had plans to move there in the near future, dear. I have a friend there. You'll come with me, and then we'll figure out what to do."

"I'll never get a visa in time for us to escape. They won't let me cross the Russian border into Finland without one."

"I knew being a bit of a flirt all my life would come in handy," she says, drying my tears. "I have an ex who happens to work at the Consulate. Trust me, Evelina, it will all work out."

Chapter 7

Evelina

Finland

Two Weeks Later

"I won't take long."
"Be honest, am I being the annoying older sister?" Katya asks.

"No."

"Then why do you look like you want to run away from home all the time?"

"I'm feeling a little anxious, and walking helps me calm down. I'll just take a quick stroll," I smile "to make you two more comfortable."

I kiss her cheek, and after putting on my jacket, I leave the tiny apartment, which barely fits a couple, let alone a "third wheel" me, in this case.

About fifteen days ago, we arrived in Finland. As promised, Katya worked her magic and not only got a passport made for me at lightning speed but also secured a visa for me to come to Finland.

Twenty-four hours after we set foot in Helsinki, when we were already staying at the home of a childhood friend of Katya — who has now become her boyfriend — and a little paranoid that those men might have come after us, we saw on a Russian news broadcast that the entire building where I kept my shop exploded.

I was sleepless that night, simultaneously thanking God that no one was injured in the explosion since my apartment was the only one in the building, and the two shops flanking it were unoccupied.

In any case, Katya and I were certain that those men after me were truly dangerous and that I had irritated them greatly.

I begin to walk through the city streets, oblivious to the people around me.

I need to leave Finland. Not only because I'm interfering in my friend's relationship with someone who, she has already confessed to me, was her teenage crush, but also because the longer I stay here, the more I put their lives at risk.

I heard them say they wanted to backpack and travel around Europe. Right now, that would be the safest thing for both of them, because if those men really are from the mafia, I'm sure they won't leave me in peace. I grew up hearing stories about the Bratva — or would it be better to say stories about how I should never get in the way of the Russian mafia — as they were cruel and people for whom a human life was worth very little.

My grandmother had a real horror that I or my brother would fall into the crosshairs of the Bratva, and look where I ended up.

I look up at the sky and wonder if she can see the mess her grandson got me into. I hope not. Grandma did her best to make sure we both became decent people. If Pyotr decided to take the path of evil, it's not her fault.

I notice that the weather is starting to turn, as if it's going to rain, and I'm irritated that I didn't check the forecast.

Getting caught in a rainstorm and catching pneumonia will just be the cherry on top of all the crap that's been happening in my life.

I prepare to cross the street because there's an awning on the other sidewalk to protect me when I hear a screeching halt in front of me and a woman's scream.

Only my quick reflexes allow me to reach her in time and prevent her from falling, hitting her head on the curb.

"You idiot, can't you watch where you're going?" I yell in Russian because I'm at my limit and I don't care if the driver understands or not. "Are you alright, ma'am?" I ask, now in English.

I help her stand up carefully because she's very small and looks fragile.

"My God, you must be an angel sent from heaven!"

Even though she's speaking English too, I can tell she must be French because she has a more melodic accent. I've always been good with languages and can usually guess people's nationalities.

"It wasn't your fault. The driver acted irresponsibly," I help her back on her feet.

She must be around seventy years old, has completely gray hair, and a face like a movie star from the 1940s. A classic beauty, as my grandmother would say.

"Yes, I know. That man makes the car a weapon. Damn Helsinki. I never liked coming here."

Despite my previous concerns, I laugh at her grumpiness.

"Are you sure you're alright? Didn't twist your ankle when you almost fell?"

"No, my girl. It will take more than a four-wheeled assassin to take me down."

"Well, in that case, I think you should hurry, wherever you were heading. It looks like it's going to pour."

"You're not Finnish," she says, furrowing her brow.

"Neither are you."

"No, I was born in Marseille, France."

"And I in Moscow. Nice to meet you, my name is Evelina Volkova."

"I'm Fantini Poulain."

We hear a thunderclap, and I worry that if she runs to take cover from the rain, she might fall and hurt herself.

"Nice to meet you, Mrs. Poulain," I say, offering my hand in greeting. "I'm not trying to be rude, but I strongly advise you to find shelter before the storm starts."

She smiles at me.

"I have a better idea. Let's go to that café across the street and get something to eat. That way, we'll both be protected from the storm, and I can properly thank you for being my savior."

I look at the woman, considering the invitation. I soon conclude that I have nothing to lose. I don't want to return to Katya's boyfriend's apartment just yet.

"If the invitation is sincere and not just because you feel obligated to repay me in some way, I'll accept, thank you."

I help her sit down in the café as soon as she removes her coat. We arrive at the establishment just as a heavy rain starts to fall.

"I think we'll be here for at least the next hour, so Evelina, you have plenty of time to tell me why you seem so sad."

"Do I seem that way?"

"My dear, I've been around long enough to know when someone has a broken heart."

"It's not about love; it's about my brother," I confess, giving up on pretending I'm okay. The woman seems to possess a crystal ball.

"Good afternoon, what can I get you?" a smiling waitress asks us, and I feel a tightness in my heart when I remember my shop.

I don't even know if I'll have to face legal consequences for the explosion. It's another thing that's been haunting me.

Katya's boyfriend, who is a lawyer here in Finland, told me no, since my lease expired a day before I left Russia, and my contract stated it would be automatically canceled in case of a delay. Since both my apartment and the shop, which used to be an old restaurant, were rented fully furnished, there was nothing of mine left there, except for kitchen utensils and some clothes. Furthermore, I paid an additional fee for building insurance, so I believe my landlord will be fine.

In any case, as soon as possible, I'll try to research this. I'm already being hunted by the mafia. I don't want to be a fugitive from the police over debts as well.

"What do you suggest?" Mrs. Poulain asks.

"If you're looking for something sweet, I recommend our *mustikkapiirakka*."

"What is that?" she asks.

"Blueberry pie," I respond instead of the waitress because with nothing to do in this country, I started researching local recipes.

I will never give up on my dreams.

I need to believe that what's happening is temporary. I will get my life back on track.

At the same time, I wonder how I will feel safe in any future moment in Moscow.

The Bratva controls a good part of the country, although Katya explained to me that currently, the real power in Russia lies with the Brotherhood, a dissident arm of former Bratva members who founded their own organization decades ago due to disagreements with the Bratva's principles.

Katya even knows the name of this other mafia's Pakhan: Yerik Vassiliev.

Only if the Brotherhood decimated the Bratva, which I think is unlikely to happen, since both organizations have coexisted for many years with the Bratva accepting "second place," might it be safe for me to return to Russia.

"Yes, that's right," the waitress says, bringing me back to reality. "Mustikkapiirakka is the traditional Finnish blueberry pie. It has a crunchy crust and a filling of fresh blueberries, combined with a layer of sour cream or yogurt. It's delicious."

"My God, I'm salivating," Fantini Poulain says, making me smile.

"Yes, it's delicious," the waitress agrees. "I also suggest a scoop of vanilla ice cream on top, and to drink, Glögi."

"Glögi?" Fantini and I ask at the same time.

"Yes. Glögi is a typical drink from my country. I'm assuming neither of you was born in Finland," she says, smiling.

"No. I'm French, and she's Russian."

"Well, as I was saying, Glögi is made with grape juice, spices like cinnamon, cloves, orange peel, and chopped almonds. It's usually served on colder days, but with this rain today, I think it will be a perfect accompaniment to the pie."

"Tell me what this drink is similar to," Fantini asks.

"Glögi is reminiscent of mulled wine."

"Hmm... wine!" my new friend says, licking her lips. "That's exactly what I want. And you, dear?" she asks me, and I nod, as if agreeing with the waitress's suggestion.

"I have both alcoholic and non-alcoholic versions. What do you prefer?"

"Non-alcoholic," Fantini and I respond and burst into laughter because it seems coordinated.

As soon as the waitress goes to the back of the café with our orders, the Frenchwoman says:

"There you go. I knew that beneath your sad expression, there was a ray of sunshine. You're beautiful, Evelina, and now, can you share with me what's making you so unhappy?"

I grew up learning to be cautious around people. My grandmother, though good to the last strand of hair, never let anyone take advantage of her, so trusting others immediately isn't in my nature. But in retrospect, I wasn't put in this situation by a stranger, but by my own blood.

What do I have to lose?

I take a sip of the glass of water that has been served to us and look at Fantini over the rim as I do it, because I'm trying to buy time.

I trust my intuition, and it tells me that the woman I saved from getting hurt is someone good.

"It's not a short or pretty story."

"All good stories worth hearing have their share of drama, my dear. If you're willing to open up, I want to hear it."

"You..."

"You can call me by my first name."

"You already know I'm Russian, but what I need to tell you, you might not believe. I'm a baker, or rather, a cake artisan, as my grandmother liked to say, specializing mainly in wedding cakes."

She tilts her head to the side.

"So that's why you knew what the mustikkapiirakka was."

"Yes. I've been in Finland for two weeks and got bored, so I decided to research local recipes."

"Right, I think the profession suits you. Now tell me, what is a Russian baker doing in Finland when she clearly doesn't want to be here?"

I take a deep breath because I hate having to lie to myself, but a stranger will never believe me if I tell her about the mess my life has become.

"I'm fleeing from an abusive ex-boyfriend," I say, and remembering what the men did, exploding my shop, I add. "He's a bit psychotic."

Chapter 8

Evelina

"An abusive ex-boyfriend?"

"Yes," I reply, feeling even more embarrassed for lying, because the sophisticated woman looks like a noble who has never heard the word "abuse" in her life.

"Tell me. Who is the unfortunate man? What did he do to you?"

My God, what now?

The problem with lying is exactly that: once you start, you're caught in your own web.

I decide to twist the truth, and while I think about what to say, I look around a bit paranoid, as if one of the Bratva men is about to storm the café right now.

"It's like living a horror movie in real time. And I swear I'm not trying to be dramatic."

It's easy to say this because God knows how frightened I've been feeling. Lately, anything scares me. The other day, the bathroom faucet in my apartment started dripping, and in my mind, I was sure someone had broken into Katya's boyfriend's house.

"Are you telling me you're in danger?" She takes my hand across the table.

"I am. Are you sure you want to hear the whole story?"

"Absolutely."

My intuition tells me that maybe Fantini Poulain can help me get out of Finland and perhaps even hide in France for a while. She seems genuinely concerned about me.

"My older brother, Pyotr, and I are orphans. We were raised by our grandparents. No, actually, by my grandmother, because Grandpa rarely stayed at home. My grandmother was the greatest wedding cake baker in Moscow, although she never received the recognition she deserved, mainly because my grandfather spent all her profits from her orders on gambling debts."

"The worst kind of man. I bet he was handsome and charming too."

"Yes, he was. He died young, however, when I was still a girl. The fact is, I think we, the Volkova women, have a knack for picking the wrong men."

"You too?"

I shrug.

"I didn't have time to date. I was more focused on being a successful baker."

"Go on."

"As we grew up, my brother and I drifted apart because instead of choosing to follow my grandmother's teachings, he increasingly became like Grandpa. He skipped school, lied, drank when he wasn't even of age. Little did we know that was just the tip of the iceberg. He went down such a bad path that he dropped out of school, and I think, though I'm not sure, that he used or maybe even still uses drugs too."

"God, that must have broken your grandmother's heart."

"Not really. She wasn't healthy enough to see what her grandson had become. He barely visited her anymore, and when he did, at least he bothered to show up clean and shaven. To sum up part of the story, even at that time, my brother would come to ask me for money since I was the one managing the cake orders. My grandmother taught me the trade from a young age."

"Money for what?"

"Debts, as I mentioned. He said he owed loan sharks because he needed to eat, dress, have a place to live, and had no other means but to borrow money. Anyway, for a while, I agreed and helped him as best as I could. I feel like an idiot, but he is my only brother, and until everything went wrong in his life, we were best friends."

"Oh, what a tragedy, my dear."

"Aren't you going to ask me what you think went wrong?"

"What?"

"Usually, people who know the story of Pyotr, especially his change in behavior, ask me this question. I even question it myself sometimes."

"No, my dear. I'm not going to ask. I've lived long enough to understand that two people can have the same background, upbringing, receive similar blessings or face similar sacrifices, and yet none of that guarantees they will walk the same path."

"I sometimes feel guilty. It's as if there was something I failed to do, you know? I wonder if I loved him enough."

"You told me your brother is older, Evelina. He made his own choices."

The waitress arrives and serves us the pie and drinks, and for about five minutes, we eat in silence, savoring the sweet.

"Keep telling your story, Evelina. Part of my greed has already been satisfied," she says, after wiping her lips with the napkin.

"My grandmother died less than a year ago. I was never one to spend much, and despite having some debts from her prolonged illness, I also saved some money. When she finally rested, I gathered the courage to fulfill her dream."

"Dream?"

"Grandma once owned her own candy shop, but my grandfather's constant gambling debts forced her to close the doors and work from home. She would start every month in the red, you know? Owing a lot along with the shop rent, employees... anyway, it became impossible to keep the business."

"I don't like your grandfather, even though he's already dead."

"Look, I guarantee you, if he were alive, even being a scoundrel, may God have him in a good place, you would like him. There wasn't a living being who didn't love him."

"As I told you a little while ago, the worst kind of man. He doesn't even allow us to hate him."

I smile and take a sip of the Glögi.

"I managed to open the shop. I was terrified, but I have a friend, Katya, who was also my neighbor and had a small business, so she helped me. Before long, the shop started to become a success. Eventually, my brother would call or show up asking for money. I couldn't always help him."

She gestures as if zipping her lips to keep herself from speaking ill of Pyotr, and I smile.

"Less than a month ago, an American came to my shop. She found her way there after seeing a report about the café in a magazine."

"Wonderful!" she exclaims, clapping, but then I think she remembers that if everything had gone well, I wouldn't be so upset. "What happened?"

"Pyotr called the same day and asked me for money. I didn't have any because I was nearing the end of the month and needed to pay the bills. As always, he told me he was in financial trouble, but do you know what happens to people who keep making the same mistake?"

"They end up tiring us out."

"Exactly. It became easier and easier to say no to him because I felt used, you know?"

"Yes, of course. Totally understandable."

And now comes the big moment, Evelina. You'll need an Oscar-worthy performance.

"So, a few days later, when the shop started getting more and more orders," I say, pausing, mortified at having to deceive her. "I think I forgot to mention that the abusive boyfriend I told you about is my brother's best friend. I found out that the two of them were involved in gambling debts, and I decided to end the relationship once and for all. He pretended to accept it but kept pressuring me to get back together just a few days later. On top of that, my brother said he needed money to pay off a debt he had incurred."

"And how much was it?"

"The equivalent of about half a million US dollars."

"Jesus!"

Again, my sixth sense tells me to stick to the story about the fictional boyfriend and not my brother's illegal activities.

"But that wasn't what was really scaring me; it was the constant 'visits' from my ex-boyfriend to my shop, as his tone became increasingly threatening. I started planning to flee at the advice of my friend and employee."

"But wasn't that a bit of a drastic decision?"

"No, because he was genuinely frightening me. Katya arranged for us to come to Finland. As I told you, I arrived fifteen days ago. Shortly after we started living here, we saw on the news that my shop had been blown up."

"My God, my dear. The man must be crazy!"

"Yes, and my current situation is: I can't go back to Russia. I don't have money to keep hiding in Europe, and I also shouldn't stay with my friend and her boyfriend because the longer I'm here, the more danger they are in because of me."

She seems to think for over a minute, then leans back in her chair and crosses her arms.

"Do you believe in miracles?"

"I used to, but I've been a bit faithless lately."

"Well, I think that's exactly what happened today. Our meeting wasn't a coincidence, Evelina. I have the solution to your problem, and you will have one for mine."

"I don't understand," I say.

"First, let me tell you a bit about myself. I've never been married, but I'm a romantic."

"So why...?"

"I don't believe in fidelity. Or rather, in fidelity until death do you part and all that nonsense. Maybe because I myself am sure that I could never be faithful. The fact is, I have an agency for arranged marriages."

"What?"

I'm sure I didn't hear her right. An arranged marriage agency? Who does that these days?

"I can explain."

"Thank you, because at the moment my brain short-circuited. First, I didn't think something like that existed. What's confusing me, however, is that when I combine the information you just gave me with the fact that you said we are the solution to each other's problems, I can't reach a common denominator."

"Understand that when I talked about a convenience marriage agency, I wasn't referring to love. Quite the opposite. I unite people in delicate situations who need a temporary partner solely for, as the name suggests, a matter of *convenience*."

"Well, a business arrangement then? That doesn't sound so scary anymore. When you said convenience marriage, I pictured a woman covered up to her neck being forced by her father to marry a heartless man."

She laughs and takes a sip of her drink.

"Nothing like that. I unite interests, not hearts."

"And why did you say you could help me?"

"First, I need to warn you how my business works, and if you think it fits into your future, you need to pay close attention to the fine print of the contract, figuratively speaking."

"I don't think that..."

"Before you refuse the proposal, listen to what I have to offer because I'm certain that you and this client of mine are heaven's answer to what the other needs. I came to Finland specifically to look for a candidate who sent me her résumé a few months ago. She seemed perfect for this client... until I got here."

"What happened?"

"A baby happened. She forgot to mention the 'detail' that she was a month pregnant when I accepted her résumé. Two days ago, I asked her for a recent full-body photo because I got suspicious since she hadn't attached one at the time of application, as required. She only responded with evasions. When I met her this morning, the pregnancy was undeniable."

"Why..."

"She lied?"

"Yes."

"You wouldn't guess?"

I shake my head no.

"My clients are millionaires, Evelina. In fact, most are so rich that there's no classification possible for them. It's likely she thought she could seduce the future convenience husband and pin another man's child on him."

"My God, she wanted to pull a scam on the fake husband?"

"Far beyond that; it would be a breach of contract. For the fake marriage to work, it's essential that there is no... um... *consummation*, my dear. Once that happens, annulment will no longer be possible."

"And how long do they stay married?"

It's her turn to shrug.

"Six months, a year. It varies a lot depending on why they need a wife."

"And it never happens the other way around? A woman needing a husband?"

"There has only been one such case. It went very wrong. The woman fell in love with her fake husband, and he pretended to reciprocate. As soon as they consummated the marriage, he filed for divorce and took everything she had."

"Goodness!"

"My power is limited, Evelina. I deal with adults who have a contract in front of them. If they choose to break it and then regret it, the consequences can be severe."

"And you have a client who thinks he could be perfect for me? As I told you, I don't plan on getting married."

She smiles.

"Trust me, I'm sure he doesn't either. To give you an idea, he's never shown himself, only contacted me through lawyers, so I assume he must be someone powerful."

"And why do you think we are perfect together?"

"Both of you need an urgent solution: he needs a wife; you need to escape, from what I understand."

"And what else?"

"Neither of you is interested in love."

"But will I have to live with him?"

"I'm not sure yet. I only received a draft of the contract he wants the convenience wife to sign. The main item is absolute confidentiality. That is essential."

"And what would I gain from this?"

"That's where you come in, my dear. Besides a generous sum of money that will make you financially independent for the rest of your life, you'll also gain a Green Card. I doubt that this ex of yours, who's been stalking you, will cross the world to find you. Sure, it's likely you may never be able to return to Russia, but let's be honest, Evelina, whether with or without a convenience marriage, do you think you could do that? Your ex-boyfriend, by blowing up the shop, showed clear signs of mental disturbance and malice. You would be dead if you were in the shop at the time of the explosion."

"I don't think I can go back to Russia anytime soon, at least, but marriage seems like a very drastic solution."

"I'm not trying to sound harsh, but what options do you have?"

"Not many," I admit.

"So, what's stopping you?"

"To be honest? It sounds too good to be true. First of all, and I apologize in advance for the rudeness, I don't even know if you're who you say you are."

She gestures with her hand for me to wait a moment and pulls out her phone. She types something and then hands me the device.

I'm shocked when I see photos of Fantini with celebrities from all over the world and even with members of the British royal family.

"Forgive me, but if you're so rich, why do you need to work arranging marriages for billionaires?"

"I'm not rich; I have a noble surname and influence. Power and money are not the same thing. I'm an expensive woman and I like luxury. By organizing convenience marriages, I get the best of both worlds and can still live the life I deserve."

"And the men who hire you trust you because you're one of them."

"Exactly. If this kind of agreement were to leak, everyone would lose. And that's exactly why, because this particular client is so special and demanding, you are the ideal candidate. You will never betray him, go to the newspapers to talk about this arrangement, because if you do, it will send a bright signal for your ex to come after you."

"Even if I accepted, this man wouldn't want to be with me knowing that I have a lunatic chasing me."

"That can be arranged. It's likely he will put you in a beach house, with bodyguards looking after you, and you would only need to go out when necessary. One year, Evelina, and you will be rich and able to live in America forever."

"No one gets a Green Card in a year. I've researched this. It's a type of visa where the couple must stay married for at least two or three years for it to change from temporary to permanent."

"For ordinary people, that's probably how it works, but my client is not an ordinary man. What do you say?"

I bite the inside of my cheek, thinking.

"And how will I know if he's not a lunatic?"

"Because by the time the contract is finalized, I will have checked him out. He doesn't want to show himself now, but he will appear at some point."

I take a deep breath, knowing that the decision has already been made. What she's offering me is the answer to my prayers.

"He will have to guarantee my Green Card, as well as my financial independence. He can never touch me, and because of that, I want to have an independent lawyer to review the contract. Of course, he will send me the money to pay him."

She smiles.

"You're smart, Evelina. That's fine. And what else?"

"I need you to check if there are any pending issues in my name due to the explosion of my shop. I don't want to be sought by the police."

"I will take your demands to him. I'm not saying he will accept, but I think there's a good chance he will."

I feel a heavy weight stir in my stomach because I suddenly realize that the offer she's made is my only way out.

However, I'm not going to beg.

"Okay."

"I'll stay in Helsinki until we sort this out. I'm extending my stay because of you. I intend to speak with my client tomorrow."

"Why the rush?"

"He has to get married as soon as possible, according to what he told me."

Chapter 9

Dell

New York

The next day

"I would like to ask you gentlemen to answer something simple," the son of a bitch Seth Jasper Seymour says, standing in front of the room where the entire board of *Tempus* is gathered.

The bastard points to the screen that has just risen, showing a drop in stock prices over the last six months, and it becomes clear to everyone, by the date, that they began to lose strength precisely during the episode when I was caught with the exotic dancer.

The Board of Directors of *Tempus*, composed of men, some of whom date back to my grandfather's time, listens attentively as the jerk narrates the graphs. The miserable seems very comfortable demonstrating the company's losses.

"Presenting only graphs related to losses means nothing. You need to put the current scenario into a global context," I interrupt him, opening a folder in front of me that my advisors and I have been working on for the past few weeks. I take the first sheet and shake it. "Perhaps if you had delved deeper into your analyses, Seymour, you would have seen that, overall, stocks worldwide experienced a loss of zero point eight percent during that same period. Thus, your claims are, at the very least, frivolous."

Of course, I know that what Seth is presenting has nothing to do with the fact that he hasn't studied the financial market lately. Even though I hate him, I know he's not stupid—far from it—and like me, he knows the world is going through a phase of financial instability. What he did was manipulate the data to paint me as the villain in our stock losses.

He doesn't get angry. Or at least he doesn't show it. I think either of us would prefer to die than let the other see that we've been hit by a blow.

For several seconds, he stares at me. Then he looks away, focuses on the Board again, and smiles. He turns to the graphs on the screen.

"Yes, Westbrook, I'm aware of the drop in stock prices worldwide, but in the case of *Tempus*, particularly, we know *what caused* that drop."

He turns to me, and when our eyes meet, despite maintaining a neutral expression now, I can see that Seth is smiling inside.

And it's in that moment that I understand.

It was him. The bastard paid the woman who's causing me so much trouble. He hired the dancer to convince me to fuck outdoors.

I watch the man I've hated my entire life, more than any other of the Seymours, perhaps because he, like me, takes our grandparents' feud seriously.

I feel a tick that makes my jaw clench, and it is the result of the anger that spreads through my blood at this moment.

"Continuing, as you can see, gentlemen, our stocks were high in the first quarter of this year until a mass sell-off began, "coincidentally," right after some sensationalist articles about the personal life of the current CEO of *Tempus* hit the media, which, as you know, led to a drop in their individual prices."

"I don't see how questions raised about my personal conduct would affect the solidity of this company. We need to focus on facts, not intrigues."

Across the table, I see my two brothers staring at me. I'm sure both of them hate Seth at the moment. Even if we occasionally clash among ourselves, we are protective of one another.

I also notice that one of my grandfather's best friends, perhaps the only advisor supporting me at the moment, Ellington Bixby, shakes his head "no" because he has known me since I was a baby and knows all about our family's war history, just like my hatred for Seth.

I ignore him as always. As much as I like Ellington as if he were my own blood, my anger at the bastard Seymour is greater.

"Intrigues, Westbrook? I wouldn't call the multiple scandals in the tabloids, the parties, the inappropriate behavior that. That undermines the trust of our investors."

"Maybe it was an orchestrated attack to divert attention from the poor management of the financial sector, in which *you* act as director," I say.

"Poor management? Despite your reprehensible conduct, we are about to close a deal for *Tempus* with an Arab Emirate, a promising market we hadn't entered yet. The only 'but' is that the Sheikh of the place doesn't want his name associated with tabloids that mention the involvement of our company's CEO with exotic dancers."

The direct attack causes a heavy silence to spread across the room.

"My personal relationships have never interfered with the strategic decisions of the company. There are years' worth of data that prove what I'm saying. The problem is not my life outside of working hours, but rather an attempt at internal sabotage."

"So it wasn't you on that yacht, Westbrook?"

"That's none of anyone's business, especially since that is in the past."

"Are you going to become a celibate, my noble?"

I glance again at the three men who support me on the other side of the table.

It was Ellington who told me that the oldest of the advisors hammered it down, stating that the only way I could remain as CEO of *Tempus* would be by marrying and putting an end to my "libertinism."

He advised me to get a wife because he thought it would be the only thing capable of preventing Seth from climbing into my position within *Tempus*.

The idea of starting to spread the news that the wedding would be soon also came from my grandfather's friend. He told me that from the moment they learned about it, they calmed down.

However, time is passing, and since I haven't announced my "chosen one" yet, the Board has become restless again. And now, with this presentation from Seth, I see that I have no way out.

I stare at the bastard and know that what I'm about to admit will put a noose around my neck.

"No, far from it. I don't have the soul of a celibate. I'm going to get married. I've found the woman of my life, and soon I will present her to the world."

Seth's eyes widen for a fraction of a second, but soon he resumes his attack.

"Does your wife happen to know about stocks? Because only a miracle would correct that amount I pointed out that we lost and restore our profits."

I clasp my hands on the table.

"As I said at the beginning, my personal life is not on trial; it's the health of my company that is. But just so you know, my fiancée and I intend to marry quickly, and now, thinking about heirs in the future, more than ever, I want *Tempus* to thrive, since it is a legacy *from my great-grandfather* to his descendants*and their descendants*."

I emphasize the last sentence to remind these idiots who founded *Tempus* — my family.

Seconds later, I notice the expression of relief on the faces of the older men, and when I glance at my brothers, I know they are both thinking I've lost my mind.

We proceed with the miserable one showing even more graphs on the screen until finally, the meeting is adjourned.

"Thank you for your presentation, Director Seymour," one of the older advisors says. "Even in light of the evidence presented, however, I suggest that a potential change in the leadership of *Tempus* be examined more carefully."

He doesn't even flinch. Seth knows the advisors are traditional and want to keep the founder's grandson as CEO — me. But that, of course, is if I behave myself.

Bastards.

Seth gathers the papers that my assistant distributed with reports of the global stock decline, although I suspect that as soon as he leaves the room, he will toss it all in the trash. He must know it by heart. What he's trying to do, as always, and of course, is reciprocal, is to torment me until I punch his face in front of everyone, which would make my exit from the leadership of *Tempus* immediate.

No one wants a man who cannot control his own instincts to run a company that is currently worth over a billion dollars.

Now it's just me, Vernon, London, Ellington Bixby, and Seth left in the room.

He pretends to leave, but as he reaches the door, he turns back.

"I'm watching your every move, Westbrook. Remember to never forget to look over your shoulder."

"The opposite is true, Seymour. I know what you did, and you can be sure that it will come back to you."

He smiles.

"Any time, Westbrook."

"You can't let him get into your head like that, Dell," Ellington says when he disappears from our sight.

I massage the middle of my eyebrows with my thumb. It's the effect that Seth has on me every damn time we meet. The bastard always leaves me as tense as a tightened guitar string.

"What you just saw was my controlled version. In my mind, we were rolling on the floor, and I was ending the fight with both of his eyes in my hands."

Vernon laughs.

"If I didn't hate the Seymours so much, I'd say Seth is a fun opponent to deal with."

"I hope you weren't bluffing about your fiancée, Dell. Until now, the possibility of you getting married was just a 'maybe,' a rumor I spread myself to buy us time. Now that you've declared your intention out loud, they will be anxious for a union. And more than that, for the public presentation of your wife."

I stare at Ellington and decide not to tell him that there is no fiancée yet. Just a mere possibility. Although he treats me and my brothers as grandchildren, he is part of the board of *Tempus*.

He also has no idea that the so-called "fiancée" will be hired by the agency of a washed-up socialite.

Fantini Poulain was recommended to me by one of my lawyers for having helped one of his clients resolve a similar issue. I instructed Colton, my assistant, to turn her life upside down since then. Apparently, she has been in this business for decades and is so good at what she does in terms of discretion that her name rarely comes up.

There has never even been a case where the arranged marriage was discovered by the public.

"I will be getting married soon. Now, I need to go, gentlemen."

I quickly say goodbye to the three of them and decline my younger brother's invitation to go to a party that night. After what I just told the Board, I can't expose myself.

I go crazy thinking that I will have to make arrangements if I want casual sex from now on.

At least six months married, that's what Colton advised me, saying that the best would be a year. It's not such a long time, but for someone like me, who has never thought of getting tied down in a long-term relationship, it seems like hell.

My cell phone lights up with a call from the lawyer handling my fake wife situation.

"Good morning, Dr. Westbrook. I'm calling because it seems that Ms. Poulain has a viable candidate for... um... the position you wish to fill."

"Are you sure?"

"Yes. She is Russian, nineteen years old, and has no one except an older brother. I've already checked her, and the girl has nothing disreputable in her past, except for..."

"What?"

"She is a baker from a humble family, according to what Ms. Poulain put in the résumé she sent me earlier. She moved to Finland recently, but it seems that the café she owned exploded."

"Exploded?"

"Apparently, there is an abusive ex-boyfriend in Miss Volkova's life, and that is the reason she wants to leave Europe as quickly as possible. If I may offer my opinion, she is an excellent candidate since she has practically no family and, more than that, she doesn't want to be found because of the ex, so she won't expose herself, and she won't expose you either."

"Tell Fontaine that I want to see the woman. Schedule a meeting for today."

"It will be almost night in Helsinki. There is a seven-hour time difference."

"No problem. I'm in a hurry. The clock is ticking, and not in my favor."

Chapter 10

Evelina

"You must be crazy! For God's sake, Evelina, how can something like this work out?"

I asked Katya to come with me to the street because, although her boyfriend is an incredible guy, I don't know him well.

I also decided not to tell Katya everything about the possible marriage of convenience because Fantini reaffirmed that secrecy was paramount. If any information of this kind leaks to third parties, our deal will be canceled, and her offer will be withdrawn.

Besides possibly losing the chance to escape Europe, I concluded that the less my friend knows from now on, the better for her.

"I have no alternative, Katya."

"I know, believe me. I've been losing sleep thinking of a solution."

"I don't want you to feel this way because of me. You and Juhani deserve to live the love story you've waited so long for to happen. I've made a decision, and if you want my advice, I think you should go through with your plans and take that journey of discovery around the world. I can't imagine anything more romantic than a love backpacking trip."

Despite looking worried, she smiles.

"I really want to go on that trip. It will only be possible because Juhani inherited money from his uncle. But I also don't want to be a treacherous friend and leave you alone. Just think of myself."

"Please don't say that. Do what your heart is telling you, and I promise I'll be fine. It must be God who put that lady in my path to offer me a job in the United States."

I know Katya would be very scared if, even though I was authorized, I told her I accepted to apply to be a wife of convenience. So, I thought it would be best to preserve her peace of mind by letting her believe that I'm going to the United States as a mere employee, should that magnate accept me for the "position."

It's not entirely untrue. It's a marriage only on paper, and according to what Fantini explained to me during the end of our conversation in the café, it will be done by proxy.

Only then will I go to his country.

As we walk through the streets of Helsinki, I watch the leaves of the trees painted in shades between orange and brown.

I love autumn. It's my favorite season, and I wonder if cities in the United States look this beautiful too.

God, I have no idea where I'm going to live!

Fantini told me he would have to keep me hidden, appearing only when necessary. In fact, I wouldn't want to appear at all, if possible.

I kick some fallen leaves on the ground, my mind distracted by my uncertain future.

We walk in silence for several minutes, each of us caught up in our own thoughts until I realize we are at Esplanadi Park.

A gentle breeze blows, and now several leaves dance in the air, creating a kind of colorful ballet.

A few steps away, there's a group of excited children playing.

I remember my childhood.

When we're little, we want to grow up fast, having no idea how scary the adult world is.

"I've grown attached to you," she says as we choose a bench to sit on.

"And I to you, but we knew this arrangement couldn't last forever, dear. You and your man, even though you've known each other your whole lives, are now enjoying this friendship that has turned into love. You need space, privacy."

"Rationally, I know you're right, Evelina, but the thought of you being alone in the world makes me sad."

"I will never forget what you did for me, Katya. Our friendship won't end because we're temporarily apart, but I could never forgive myself if something happened to you because of me."

"Do you think they will keep hunting you?"

"Not forever, but for sure, if those guys are really from the mafia, they won't like that I outsmarted them, escaping before they could lay their hands on me."

I shudder with a chill of fear at the thought.

"I believe you're right. They won't be looking for you forever, but from everything I know about the mafia, they can't let people—whether allies or enemies—believe they can be easily deceived or lose the respect they hold. And in this world of crime, being disrespected means a death sentence. Speaking of which, I'm not trying to scare you, but I wouldn't want to be in your brother's shoes if the Bratva gets their hands on him."

"I believe Pyotr fled a long time ago, and I think he always had a plan B in case I didn't agree to lend him the money."

I was looking ahead, but when I turn to face her again, she watches me with what seems to be pity.

"What's wrong?"

"I don't know if you'll like what I'm about to say, but I'm going to say it anyway because I'm your friend, Evelina, and friends tell the truth above all else. Pyotr always knew you wouldn't be able to pay that debt. I believe all along, he thought of giving you as collateral."

I open my mouth to tell her she's crazy, that my brother would never do that to me. He's irresponsible when it comes to money, but we share the same blood.

And then I remember the men who came after me and the amount Pyotr owes. Katya is right. He had to know that I could never come up with half a million dollars, or even ten percent of that, to settle a debt with the Bratva.

I look at the leaf in my hand, thinking that once I leave Helsinki, I will have truly left my life behind.

Yes, I will be alone because my own flesh and blood treated me like an object. A thing to be traded.

"I didn't say that to hurt you," she says, taking my hand.

"I know."

"DO YOU WANT ME TO GO to your hotel now to have a meeting with my possible secret fiancé?"

"Oui. You have about an hour to get here. Take a taxi, and I will have the hotel valet pay for you."

"He... um... is he going to see me?"

"Yes, but the opposite will not be true. My client's identity will be preserved until you meet in New York. That is, if he accepts you, of course. I can't stop you from researching him online because, with the marriage, you'll know his name, but I reiterate that in this case, confidentiality is essential, Evelina."

My God, I feel like a piece of meat on display for the customer to touch and see if it's tender enough.

Except if he dreams of touching me, I'll kick him in the groin. The deal is "no physical contact."

I start sweating cold from how nervous I am.

What if the man doesn't respect the rules? What if he tries to take advantage of me?

No, I need to believe that Fantini is telling the truth and that all this man wants is a temporary wife to resolve whatever problem he's gotten into.

"I can almost hear the gears turning in your little head, Evelina. What's the problem? If you're thinking of backing out, now's the time to tell me. As I explained to you that day, I deal with very busy men, and there's no room for indecision. The offer is as I said. He will make you rich after the annulment of the marriage, but know that there will be a confidentiality clause in the contract. Make no mistake; if you breach it, you'll have to be reincarnated ten times to pay off all your debts because he will definitely sue you."

"It's not that I'm worried about. I know you don't know me, Fantini, but I'm serious about everything I decide to do. I don't intend to tell the world that I've become a wife of convenience. When it's all over, I'll actually disappear."

I've been thinking a lot about the future, and after my walk with Katya earlier, I concluded that the best thing to do is to stay in the United States after the divorce.

I can choose a small town and reopen my store if what Fantini said is true and the man I'm going to marry will make me rich.

"What troubles you then?"

"What if he's abusive? What if he doesn't respect the contract and tries to..."

"What? Non, chérie! No chance of that happening!"

"How can you be so sure? You said you don't even know who he is!"

"Yes, that's true, but only because he hasn't made a decision and chosen one of the candidates. Once that happens, he will have to show himself to me, at least. I'll know if he has a criminal record, if there have been incidents with ex-girlfriends, assaults, or even worse."

She doesn't explain what that "worse thing" is, but I can imagine and feel a chill of fear.

"I'm terrified."

"That's why I told you that if you want to back out, now's the time, but echoing your words, Evelina, you don't know me, but you can be sure I would never send a candidate into the hands of a scoundrel."

"And how would you know what he has or hasn't done? As you said, they are powerful men and can easily erase their tracks if they have skeletons in their closets."

"Yes, that's true, but I have ways of finding out. Believe it or not, in the high society underbelly, no secret stays hidden for long, and I give you my word that I would never let you go to that man if he has ever even thought about harming a woman, in any sense, Evelina. I really like the money I make from my arranged marriages, but not at the cost of my conscience."

"I didn't mean to offend you."

"You didn't offend me; you're right to be in doubt. Now tell me, was that the only thing worrying you?"

No, actually, I can't stop thinking that the Bratva is going to invade my friend's apartment at any moment and take me away by force.

"Yes, that was it. I'll trust your word."

"Then get ready, Evelina, and prepare for your new life. I would never be cruel enough to send you to an abusive man, knowing what you went through in Russia with your ex."

The remorse for having lied to her hits me hard, but if there's one thing I've learned about myself in these past few weeks, as my life has turned upside down, it's that I need to prioritize myself and ensure my survival, even if that means telling a lie or two.

Fantini is a pleasant and kind woman, but as much as I believe she's telling the truth, I can't forget that she's not my friend; she's a businesswoman who intermediates to get two people to close a contract and profits from it.

"Alright. I'll be with you shortly."

About forty-five minutes later, I get out in front of her hotel, and even a bit embarrassed for letting the valet pay for the taxi, as I arranged with Fantini, I hold my head high as I walk toward the fancy hotel.

After stating who I am at the reception, I'm directed to the elevator, and as it ascends, my heart is in my throat. In just a little while, I'll be exposing myself to the man who, if all goes well, I'm going to marry.

When the elevator doors open, all I pray to God is that I haven't made the worst decision of my life and gotten myself into an even bigger mess than I'm in now.

But what could be worse than having the Bratva hunting me?

Chapter 11

Dell

"She's not suitable," I say as the woman, Evelina Volkova, stands up from the armchair she was sitting in.

"Pardon, monsieur?" a very shocked Fantini Poulain says, as it takes me about five seconds to realize that the candidate for a wife of convenience is not right for me.

I got myself into this mess precisely because I like sex a bit more than the average man and have a special weakness for blondes with long legs. Exactly the type that the Russian is.

"Forgive me for speaking in French. I meant to say that I didn't understand your refusal. I didn't even have time to introduce you to Evelina."

The woman seems affronted, and at that moment, I know she's probably cursing me with the worst insults in her mind, but her refined education, along with the fee I'm paying her to find a candidate for me, will never allow her to open her mouth.

Unlike them, who see only a mirrored screen, similar to those in interrogation rooms, I can see the two of them perfectly, and while Fantini seems to be thinking about what went wrong for me to reject the girl so quickly, Evelina, who is a step behind, remains stoic, like a princess who has learned to behave in public and doesn't let her emotions show.

"I understood what you said, Fantini. I speak French, in addition to three other languages."

I know what most Europeans think of us Americans: that we are arrogant and don't care to learn another language. But what fault do we have if the world has succumbed to our native tongue?

However, I studied in a bilingual school and speak German, Spanish, and French fluently.

"She's not suitable. If she was the only candidate you had to present to me, you're dismissed."

I see the older woman's lips compress into a thin line that shows how much she's trying to control herself, but it's not her I'm interested in; it's the blonde I knew at first glance that if I marry her, I won't be able to keep my hands to myself.

I didn't even look at the woman's face, to be frank. I only let my gaze roam over the long legs clad in tight jeans. The ugly turtleneck sweater, which looks like wool but still can't hide the delicious-looking breasts and the golden hair.

That was enough for me to close a verdict of "not suitable."

All I don't need at this moment in my life is to consummate the marriage with a fake wife and make it real.

"I don't understand, sir. I trust my gift for uniting couples with mutual interests. From everything I know, Evelina is perfect."

"Exactly," I say, distracted by the blonde moving behind the woman.

"Once again, I'll say I don't understand."

"Don't worry, Fantini," my ex-future wife responds. "I wouldn't want to marry him even if he were the last man on Earth."

I believe this would normally be the moment when the wife negotiator would intervene because I don't think it's good to irritate a client, but as proof that Fantini's thinking aligns with Evelina's, she remains silent and just nods her head to the blonde.

"One moment, sir," she says, without turning to the dark screen and seeming more concerned about the candidate for a wife than about me. "I'm sorry, dear. I don't know what happened."

"Luck, that's what happened. He's an ass," she says, perhaps believing I can't hear her because she practically whispers. "When I was in the taxi on the way here, I asked God for a sign that I wasn't doing something wrong, and what brighter sign can there be than me hating the man at the first sentence that comes out of his mouth? Remember what you told me about some couples breaking the rules and consummating the marriage? That would never happen. In fact, it's more likely that I'll end up in jail at the end of the period I'm supposed to be married for killing my contractor. This man wouldn't lay a finger on me even if he came covered in jewels and diamonds."

I lean back in the high-backed leather chair in my penthouse office and look closely at the woman whose face I initially didn't bother to examine and now can't do so because she's in a shadowed part of the hotel room.

I conclude that despite the beauty, I was mistaken.

I found the ideal candidate.

Not because I don't still run the risk of wanting to take her to bed, but because at least when I have to coexist with her, I won't die of boredom. Evelina seems to have a fiery temperament, which could be fun.

Evelina

THE FEAR I FELT UPON arrival turned into anger.

It's unbelievable that in the thirty days when my life took a one-eighty turn for the worse, I felt more hatred than I ever did for the Russians.

Yes, I cursed them and wished they were wiped out by the rival mafia, the Brotherhood. I even memorized the name of the Pakhan of the Bratva's enemies, Yerik, because I wanted to ask him for a little favor: if possible, to blow up my enemies—who, luckily for me, happen to be his as well.

The fact is that not even those terrifying days I lived through made me feel as upset as I do now.

Looking at a computer screen without having the slightest idea who is on the other side is not pleasant. But having that screen conclude that you are "not suitable" without even saying a "good night" is infuriating.

"Forgive me for venting," I say to Fantini, who is not at fault.

"I'm so sorry again, Evelina. I will pay for a taxi for you, and if you're still interested, I'll find another candidate for a convenience husband."

She steps closer, I think to give me a kiss on the cheek, but before she completes the action, we hear the arrogant voice shatter the silence.

"You won't find another candidate for her. I've changed my mind. I want her."

Chapter 12

Dell

The two of them stop talking and look back as if expecting me to materialize in front of them at that moment, but Fantini's expression is still passive-aggressive.

I don't give a damn about what she thinks of me. The day I care about other people's opinions is the day I'll be dead. The only reason I'm accepting being subtly blackmailed by the Tempus Council is that my hatred for Seth is even greater than the anger I feel for allowing the directors of the company my great-grandfather founded to dictate my life.

"No, thank you," the blonde finally replies. "It was a mistake to come here."

A tense silence falls between us as I observe her. They both look at the dark screen, but while Fantini seems completely lost, Evelina has her chin held high, as if daring me.

"Step forward. I can't see you," I command.

"I'm not a mannequin in a showcase. Our marriage would be a farce. You don't need to look at me."

"You're afraid of me."

It's as if I pressed a "power on" button on the girl. The moment I say that, she moves closer to Fantini's laptop.

Her expression is even more defiant.

"It would take much more than a dark computer screen to scare me, sir."

Evelina

"LEAVE US, FANTINI," I hear him say to the agency owner.

I notice that Fantini glares at him as if she's reluctant to obey, but then I think she realizes the ridiculousness of the situation: the candidate for husband can't abduct me through his computer screen.

"Are you going to be okay?" she asks me.

"I will be, although I don't understand what he wants to talk to me about. Our conversation is over."

"Control your temper and think about the future, Evelina," she whispers before leaving the main room of the hotel suite and heading to the bedroom.

Now, it's just the two of us, and I have no choice but to turn to the screen.

I hate how my heart is racing, and I also detest that the voice of this irritating man gives me a sense of security that acts like a balm after all the fear I've been through since the Bratva invaded my café.

"What are you afraid of, then, Evelina?"

"What?"

"You said you needed more than a dark computer screen to scare you, but I can see you're afraid of something."

"I'm not. You don't know anything about me. Besides, I don't even need to talk to you. You rejected me without me being able to say a word."

"I initially rejected you because our marriage has to be a lie, and you are far too beautiful. I'm not known for handling temptations well."

I control myself not to move. I feel uneasy with his raw, unfiltered words.

He doesn't want me because he finds me too beautiful?

Don't be foolish, Evelina. Remember how rude he was.

"It doesn't matter if I'm beautiful or not; our conversation is over."

"On the contrary, it's just beginning."

"There's nothing you can offer me that would make me change my mind. I want to go to the United States, but not if it means having to live with you. I couldn't stand you."

I hear a laugh, which only frustrates me more. It's horrible not knowing who I'm talking to. From the voice, I would say he's not old. Maybe in his thirties. He's clearly someone used to giving orders, too.

"Are you sure there's nothing I can offer you that would make you change your mind?"

His voice drips with irony.

"Absolutely," I say angrily.

"Ten million dollars."

"What?"

"I'll pay you ten million dollars for one year of marriage. Of course, there will be special clauses in the contract. The main one being that if you ever mention my name during or after we're married, referring to our union as a marriage of convenience, you'll have to return that amount with interest."

He keeps talking, but to be honest, I can no longer pay attention to anything other than the amount he mentioned.

Ten million dollars, my God!

With that amount, I wouldn't even need to reopen a café. I could invest in a wedding cake business, which is what I truly love to do.

I would also have plenty of money to buy a beautiful house. What more could anyone want besides financial stability and health?

Well, it would be excellent if along with the offer came the guarantee that the entire Bratva would be exterminated, but I suppose you can't have it all, right?

"You can't give interviews without my authorization or go out alone without informing the security I will have looking after you. We'll need to attend some events together, of course. After all, that's what you're being hired for: to appear by my side when necessary. The key to this whole agreement, Evelina, and this is something you must memorize, is that for the time we are married, you owe me absolute obedience."

"Obedience?"

"Yes, like a good wife from the last century, you won't even be able to take a deeper breath without my permission."

I'm almost certain he's provoking me, and I decide not to fall into the trap.

"I have demands too, if I'm going to accept you as my husband. And I want each one of them in writing in the contract."

If I'm going to accept him? I'd have to be crazy to refuse such an offer.

"I'm listening, Evelina. Tell me what you want, and I'll see if I'm willing to agree."

Chapter 13

Dell

"You can't touch me," she begins, and instead of focusing on that, I watch the movement of her beautiful mouth.

Evelina's lips are full, almost as if they're swollen from being so plump.

She doesn't wear a drop of makeup, if I had to guess. However, I would bet that her skin has the texture of a delicate flower.

Her eyes are very blue, and her long lashes are dark like small curtains that prevent me from analyzing them completely because she looks at the screen, but focuses on a point below, I believe on the table where the laptop is.

Is she doing it on purpose? Does she not want me to see what she's thinking? And if so, for what reason does she try to hide from me?

It's not just because I was, according to her words, an ass. Within minutes of being in my presence, I understood that Evelina doesn't bow her head to anyone, and perhaps at this moment she doesn't consider me worthy of her full attention, not even through the computer screen.

"And what else?"

"When I said touch, I meant don't even attempt any sexual advances or physical aggression."

"I've never forced myself on a woman, Miss Volkova, and I've never raised my hand against one." Suddenly, a suspicion makes a ball of iron twist in my stomach. "Who did this to you?"

"I didn't say anyone ever attacked me."

I sigh, irritated.

"The first thing you need to learn about our relationship, even if it's a farce, is that you must never lie to me, Evelina."

Evelina

I SWALLOW HARD PRECISELY because I haven't done anything but lie to Fantini Poulain since she presented me with this crazy proposal for a marriage of convenience, but my intuition tells me that the strange man speaking to me is not someone easy to fool, so I decide to take an alternative path, continuing with the charade of the abusive boyfriend while partially telling the truth.

"You didn't ask for any information about me?"

"I know your age and that you're Russian."

"I can't believe a man like you seems to be would waste his time interviewing someone without knowing at least a little about them."

"I know your café exploded. Tell me about that."

I take a deep breath, praying to God again to make me a good actress.

"I had to run away from an ex-boyfriend. He didn't accept that I ended the relationship."

"Blowing up a business is much more than 'not accepting the end of a relationship.'
Yes, of course it is, you millionaire. They are in the mafia and can do whatever they want.
"I don't know what to say other than that's what happened."
"So you fled your country?"
"Yes. But I don't need protection."

Dell

I ALMOST LAUGH AT HOW much she wants to show her independence. Evelina is a small, delicate creature like a flower, although she also seems feisty.

She is beautiful, and even though I'm sure this will be a problem, it seems more appealing each time to have a fake wife who attracts me so much.

One year. I can only be with her for twelve months and then leave without looking back. And even if I give in to temptation and end up divorced instead of an annulment, my lawyers can prepare everything so that she doesn't receive a cent more than what was agreed upon.

"If she's my wife, I'll have her anyway. After we annul the marriage, she'll be on her own," I say, but I feel something disturbingly uncomfortable hit me at that moment.

The idea that this beautiful woman might be hurt—the woman who will be mine, even if only for a short time—leaves me unsettled.

"Why did you change your mind?"

"Because I need a wife, first and foremost."

"And that didn't stop you from rejecting me instantly."

"You were rejected for being too perfect, but that idea ended the moment you opened your mouth. I heard you call me an ass."

I can see a slight blush spreading across her face.

"I'm not rude, normally, but you irritated me with your arrogance. I thought our relationship, which didn't even start, was over, so I saw no reason to hide how I was feeling. In my defense, I didn't think you were listening."

"I was, and I don't give a damn what you think of me. You are a means to an end, Evelina. I don't like apathetic creatures, and your fiery spirit makes everything more interesting, as long as you don't do anything stupid while we're together."

"Like what, for example?"

"Running away from me. Failing to uphold your part of the agreement because I promise you that if it happens, I will hunt you down."

Evelina

I CLASP MY HANDS TOGETHER, not doubting for a second that he's telling the truth.

"Fantini spoke to my lawyers about your requests. I will make some adjustments to the contract so that your recent request is included as well, but with some reservations."

"Adjustments?"

"I will send you the contract by tomorrow at the latest, Miss Volkova. If you've made all the demands you wanted and accept the amount I offered..."

"And the Green Card."

"Yes. As I was saying, if you accept the amount I offered, plus the Green Card, and if you think you can fulfill your part, by tomorrow night our prenuptial contract will be ready, and we'll marry as quickly as possible."

"And what about where I'll live and other details?"

"I will ensure you are informed of everything. Fantini said she wants a lawyer who isn't part of the team assisting me to review the contract. Very well, I will take care of that."

My God, now I know there's no stopping this runaway train I've gotten on. I just hope it takes me to a better place than where I am at the moment.

Chapter 14

Evelina

Manhattan — New York

Almost six weeks later

Money moves the world. How many times have I heard my grandmother say that? Yet, I never imagined it would happen this quickly or that upon arriving in the United States, I would need to run away from the man who is now my husband.

I take a deep breath while I separate some ingredients my boss asked for.

As soon as I said *yes* in our conversation where I couldn't see his face, the man, whom I now know is named Dell Westbrook and who comes from one of the wealthiest families in the United States, literally made the wheels turn with his money and power.

The next day, I was settled into a hotel with instructions not to leave until further notice.

Between meetings with lawyers, signing the prenuptial and confidentiality agreements, the marriage by proxy, and getting my K-3 visa, which in theory should turn into a Green Card after I had been in the U.S. for a while, it took no more than fifteen days.

I felt like I was on a roller coaster, out of control in my life, scared and excited at the same time.

I researched my husband.

He is stunning, the kind of handsome that leaves a woman speechless and makes her turn her neck back when he walks by, and that's why I can't understand how someone with that appearance could need a wife of convenience. But one of the clauses in our prenuptial agreement is precisely never to question him about that.

The Westbrook family is respected and traditional, from what I've discovered.

The contract had twenty-five pages, and thank God I insisted on a lawyer because I would never have been able to analyze everything.

In the end, the legal operator told me everything was in order and that the agreement my future husband offered me was extremely generous.

Thus, the following week, I was married and on my way to the United States.

Relatively calmer and even a little happy.

I traveled first class, was treated like a princess, and there was even a driver waiting for me when I arrived.

Then, upon overhearing a conversation from this same man, who now I no longer know if he was a driver or a bodyguard, everything started to go wrong.

As I pull a packet of sugar from one of the highest shelves at the bakery where I'm working, I force my memory to recall the conversation that made my world take an unexpected turn once again.

"Can you give me a minute, ma'am?" the man spoke to me at the airport, and I noticed he had received a call on his cell phone.

"Sure," I replied, stepping back a few paces to give him privacy.

The man unlocked his phone and leaned against my only carry-on bag with all my belongings, looking very relaxed.

I waited patiently, but five minutes passed without him ending the phone call, so I was about to step away a bit more to check out a store window when I heard him say:

"Don't worry, boss, I've got the bitch. She won't go anywhere. I'll keep an eye on her, and if necessary, I'll personally train her to learn to obey."

I begin to tremble all over, telling myself that this is obviously a misunderstanding. Of course, he's not talking about me, until he continues:

"Should I keep her locked up, then? If you want my opinion, I think she could stay in a cage for a while. That way, she'll become tame."

My God, how could I have been so mistaken? Dell is a monster, maybe even a human trafficker in disguise!

"I'm sorry to have kept you waiting. Ready to go?" the man said, approaching me again, but I could barely hear him.

I tried to analyze my escape options because I knew that if I didn't manage to escape there at the airport, which was getting crowded and where there were several witnesses, I wouldn't have the slightest chance afterward.

"I would like to use the restroom first; is that possible?"

"Yes, of course, there's one right up ahead. Do you need your bag?" he asked.

In that moment, I almost said yes, but then I remembered it would be much harder to run carrying one.

Besides, I had five thousand dollars in cash inside my wallet, more than enough money to keep me going for a while.

"I don't need it. I won't be long."

What happened next can only be described as absolute madness.

I bought a scarf from an elderly woman for a hundred dollars and wrapped my hair in it. I also paid her fifty more to walk out of the airport with me, thereby blocking the view of Dell's accomplice, who would be looking for someone alone.

I jumped into the first taxi I found outside and, on the way, I asked the driver to take me to a cheap hotel, which, in terms of the island, is still ridiculously expensive.

However, as if God thought I was already going through too many trials, the next day I managed to find an apartment and a job at a bakery.

To change things up, I lied, saying I was in the country illegally.

The owner hires undocumented workers, paying them much less than registered employees, so of course, I jumped at the chance, as I am terrified that Dell will find me.

I have a plan: to leave Manhattan at the latest next week, and when I'm far away from my husband, I'll divorce him. After that, I'll try to move to a country where it's easier to get a permanent residency visa.

I will succeed. I escaped the Russian mafia. It won't be that hard to get away from an American businessman.

Chapter 15

Dell

"**N**o sign of her?" Vernon asks.
I shake my head no, a feeling of guilt like I've never experienced hitting me since my wife disappeared, making my temple throb.

"Evelina Volkova is everything but a wife of convenience. In fact, on the contrary. She's bringing you a *massive* inconvenience," London says.

"It's no joke. She doesn't know anything in the United States, is beautiful, and too young. As far as I know, she could have been kidnapped. She's just a girl," I say.

"And she's not Evelina Volkova anymore, brother. She's Evelina Westbrook now, which makes her ours to protect," Vernon corrects him.

Evelina Westbrook. My missing wife.

It doesn't matter that we are only married on paper and that this is nothing but a sham. I have to find her, or I won't have peace in my life imagining what happened to her.

"I should have gone to pick her up at the airport myself," I voice what I've been thinking since she disappeared.

"You couldn't have predicted, Dell. Who gets kidnapped in an airport in the middle of Manhattan?"

"She had an abusive boyfriend."

"And you think he followed her to the United States? Why didn't he grab her in Finland, where she was unprotected?"

"She wasn't unprotected there. I had her installed in a hotel and kept security watching over her," I say, feeling bad because to be honest, the reason I sent men to guard her was not for her benefit but for mine. I didn't want to risk her running away or, worse, deciding to break the agreement by telling the world about our convenience marriage.

It never crossed my mind to ensure that her ex-boyfriend wouldn't track her down because, like the arrogant person I am, I thought that by becoming mine, just like all family members, that would make her untouchable.

"Maybe we should put someone to look for her in other states as well," London says.

"I have a detective in each of the damned states of our country looking for her, and so far, they haven't found anything. They're also communicating with each other; if there were any news, I would know."

"She can't have disappeared into thin air," Vernon says.

"Maybe you should look at the statistics," I respond. "I did some research. About seven hundred women on average go missing every day in our country."

"Holy shit! But not all of them disappeared involuntarily, I presume."

"Yes, many just want to change their lives, but that's not the case with Evelina. She was looking for a chance to start over. Why would she give up a marriage of just twelve months, where she would walk away with ten million dollars and a Green Card?"

"Yeah, that really doesn't make sense," my middle brother says. "And what about her cell phone?"

"Off. I gave her one so we could communicate, which means if Evelina had it, she would have talked to me by now."

"And the agency owner, doesn't she know anything?"

"No. Evelina hasn't contacted her again."

"And what about the credit cards you made for her?"

"None of them have been used."

"Damn! Someone must have seen her leaving the airport or at least being taken if she was indeed kidnapped. There are cameras everywhere."

"I already have people checking that for me. An entire team analyzing the footage. I will find her."

They say nothing, and I know what they're thinking.

Evelina is at the age when young women are taken for human trafficking. The statistics are a real horror movie.

"Given the current situation, the issue with Seth is even losing its importance," Vernon says.

"I'm operating on both fronts. I will bring my wife home because I need to appear in public with her, even though everyone already knows I got married," I say, as if that were the only reason and not because I've been in a state of worry, which makes me want to find her so badly. "At the same time, I'm setting a trap for that bastard Seymour."

"Are you sure he's the one who paid the exotic dancer, then?"

"Yes, the woman was paid. She insisted that we stay outside the yacht. Besides, I can't contact her on her cell phone."

"And since when do you keep the phone numbers of women you go out with?"

"I don't, but I sent people to the club where I met her. She disappeared. No one even knows if she moved, and the old phone goes straight to voicemail."

"I swear I'm trying not to make jokes about your women running away from you," Vernon says.

"The dancer was hired. She disappeared because she must have filled her pockets and knew that when I found out the truth, I would go after her to find out who paid her. But she's not to blame for anything. It was a means that Seth used to achieve an end. My reckoning will be with him."

"And what do you plan to do?"

"I don't take revenge in proportion to what was done to me. I don't return the favor in kind. He will regret hiring that woman."

"As long as it's nothing that kills or permanently injures him, I'm on board."

"I'm not a criminal. I hate Seymour, but I wouldn't kill him. I prefer to torment him in life."

"And you can bet the opposite is also true."

I nod in agreement.

"I'm not worried about Seth. We've despised each other long before we learned to speak. My focus now is on Evelina. I need to find her."

"Changing the subject, are you going to Eric's birthday party next week?" London asks.

"The second birthday party, you mean. I don't know why the hell Jack Prescot insisted on throwing another one, now at his own apartment when we already celebrated with Eric's family. He told me he's planning a surprise."

"Which means it's some big shit to annoy the birthday boy."

"Yeah, and I'm not the least bit excited to witness it. What could it be? A stripper? Aren't we too old for that kind of nonsense?"

"Especially after the last one you had on the yacht ended up creating a situation that led you to the altar, figuratively speaking. Now you're a married man."

I run my hands over my face.

"I didn't plan things this way. It was supposed to be clean and simple. Evelina is my contracted wife. That's it. Now it's turned into an obsession to bring her to me safely. I need to find out what they've done to her."

"We will find her, Dell. If this had happened twenty years ago, I wouldn't be so sure, but nowadays, you can't just disappear without leaving traces."

Chapter 16

Evelina

"With all due respect, sir, but you're getting on my nerves."
"Calm down, girl. I'm not hitting on you."
"Well, because today my day is a tragedy. I hate this island. No offense."
"I wasn't born here. What's the problem? Share."
The shop is empty, so I could vent to the customer, I suppose. The man looks like a millionaire, though I doubt he's interested in the drama that has become my life.

Fled from Russia to avoid falling into the hands of the Bratva;

Married to a stranger who is a pervert who wanted to lock me in a cage;

And last but not least, robbed by a dishonest landlord.

My existence couldn't get worse, unless, of course, my brother's creditors came after me here.

"No, thank you. Now, I don't want to be rude, but do you want anything else? Because the coffee you're drinking must be cold since you've been staring at me for almost ten minutes."

"I have a proposal for you."

When he finishes speaking, I can't close my mouth in shock.

"Nobody pays three thousand dollars for that."

"The reason I want to hire you is that you're not American, you're beautiful, and you hate Manhattan, which means you'll be leaving soon."

"And all I have to do is pop out of a cake wearing lingerie and pretend I'm your friend's present? He's not going to touch me?"

He throws his head back, laughing.

"Believe me, he won't. In fact, if you're scared, you can bring your boyfriend. He just can't enter the room with you; other than that, if it makes you feel safer, bring him along."

"I will bring him. You can bet on that. And he's quite big. Huge, actually."

The man laughs.

"You're a delight with that accent, princess face, and MMA fighter pose."

"I'm taken."

Even though I've run away from my fake husband, he's still my husband. Until this crazy story is over, I won't look at another man.

"Don't worry," he reads my name on the badge, "Evelina. All I want from you is to help me pull a prank on a jerk."

Days later

"YOU CAN'T PUSH THE cake cart too fast, or I risk falling in the middle of the room," I warn for the thousandth time to the helper I hired for ten dollars. "This is supposed to be a sexy surprise, not me sprawled on the floor, covered in whipped cream."

The guy winks at me.

"That would be pretty sexy, in my opinion."

"Oh really? If that happens, I won't receive the rest of my payment, and you'll be in a bind too."

"Hey, that's not what we agreed on. I'll help you because I'm a man of my word, but ten dollars doesn't even buy a snack, and thinking it over, I want to be paid upfront."

"That's not happening, buddy. What if you run off with the money?"

"You're offending me."

"Look, you could've fooled me when I arrived in your country, but I've been taken advantage of before, so don't try that trick with me."

"Ten dollars in hand, or you don't go in there."

"Fine, I'll pay you now, but you have to promise to stay until the end. I need someone to push me back afterward."

"Push you back? You're not getting out of the cake?"

"I'm hoping not."

"I don't get it. Isn't the idea for you to show your bun..." he pauses "perform in lingerie?"

"I hope I won't have to do anything but wave and smile."

He laughs.

"Sweetheart, this isn't a Miss World contest where you just wave. I'll bet my bike there are a ton of perverts in there, and when you show up with that doll face of yours, the guys are going to go crazy. I don't know why you accepted this job. I consider myself a good judge of people, and I don't think parading in lingerie suits you."

"It's a long story to explain. So, are you going to help me or not?"

"We're not friends; this is a job. Hand over the cash, and I'll do my part."

"Wow, you almost fooled me by acting all 'nice.'"

"I'm not."

He keeps his hand outstretched, and I see no alternative but to hand over the money. Only God knows how ten dollars will hurt me in my escape.

"I'm going to change. Don't go anywhere."

I glance at the cook and a man who looks like a bodyguard who have been watching our interaction the whole time. There are also several waiters coming in and out of the kitchen.

"Don't let him escape," I ask the staff because nothing guarantees that now that he has ten dollars in his pocket, he won't leave me high and dry. "I need to get paid for my performance as the cake girl, and without it, it will be a fiasco."

"You realize how much you depend on me?" the smartass asks.

"I never said I didn't need you, and that's why I paid you a good amount."

"*Good amount?* This is Manhattan, baby. Ten dollars is a very insignificant tip."

"Don't push your luck, and don't test my patience."

"Don't worry, miss, he won't go anywhere," the big guy says.

"I'll play my part, but if I wanted to leave, you couldn't keep me. That would be unlawful imprisonment."

I roll my eyes.

"I'll be back in five minutes."

I head to the bathroom that one of the waitresses points me to because that's where the "uniform" I'll have to wear is, according to my contractor's instructions.

On the way, I pray that no smartass decides to film my performance because if I show up in the newspapers, I'll lose my job at the candy shop. And worse, Dell might find me. But soon, I conclude that it's almost impossible for that to happen.

As my "helper" pointed out, most of the guys at this party are probably married and are just here for fun.

Well, the one who hired me swore he just wanted to play a prank on his friend.

I don't take long to change, but when I look in the mirror, I feel like running away. The black and pink lingerie set with garters is tiny, and I thank God that at least he left a mask to cover a little around my eyes. You can still tell it's me, of course, but I feel more protected this way.

No, I can't do this, I'm sure, as I turn around and see that the panties are way too small.

"Three thousand dollars for a few minutes, Evelina," I repeat out loud. "Your one-way ticket out of this millionaire island."

If there's one thing I've learned in Manhattan, it's that there's no way to save money here.

What if it doesn't work out? What if the crazy guy outside drops the cake with me inside? Even though it's a foam cake, it's covered in real icing.

My God, if everything turns into a fiasco and my bosses find out that I accepted this invitation to be the "cake surprise," I'm done for.

I leave the bathroom before I change my mind, both hands covering my backside. But it doesn't help much because my breasts are almost exposed in the lingerie.

"I'm ready. Can someone lend me a ladder?"

I try to sound natural, as if the entire kitchen hadn't stopped to watch me.

"I don't think you'll manage. Come here; I'll help you," the guy with a bodyguard look says.

Two minutes later, I'm all set inside the fake cake that was already here when I arrived.

When I told the staff what I came to do at the party, they looked at me as if I had just come out of a lunatic asylum.

I was wearing jeans and a t-shirt but with heavy makeup that didn't match my look at all. I looked like a mix between a stripper and a college student.

Before closing the cake lid, I say to my "contractor":

"Don't mess this up."

"Don't worry, boss," he mocks.

Chapter 17

Dell

"I don't like it when you all look too happy. Or calm. You're grumpy bastards, and when I see you with those smirks, I know you're up to something," Eric Lowell, a good friend of mine from high school and the birthday boy, says. "Besides, why would I need a second party when we already had one with my family? I don't even like birthday celebrations, to begin with."

I didn't want to come either.

At the moment, I have an immense amount of shit to deal with, with the Tempus Council pushing me to publicly introduce my wife.

Most of the time, I go crazy wondering if something has happened to my missing Russian wife, but I can't deny that after weeks of hell, this is the first time I've been able to relax a little.

There's a small group of about fifteen friends here. Or better to say, party partners. The only real friend I have at the event is Eric.

Over his shoulder, while I take a sip of my whiskey, I glance at Jack Prescot, who is clearly enjoying himself just with the anticipation of what will happen shortly.

We are in his apartment.

Before a very suspicious Eric can insist or pressure us further for answers, however, one of the waiters from the small party comes in and says something in a very low tone to Jack, who then gestures for me.

"Eric, we're about to cut the cake," Jack announces, not bothering to hide a laugh.

Once, Eric told us that his grandfather was surprised by a prank from friends when he was younger, with a stripper coming out of a cake at his bachelor party. Eric would repeat this story to us, saying how his grandfather, an extremely traditional man, was embarrassed and would hate for something like that to happen to him as well.

Jack, of course, could never pass up the chance to torment him, and since the marriage Eric will have to make soon will also be one of convenience and not a happy occasion, we could hire a "cake girl" for his bachelor party; the alternative was to bring the woman in celebration of his birthday instead.

Although his life is at a crossroads similar to mine, and he's looking for a wife of convenience, unlike me who just needs to find out where Evelina has gone, Eric has just a couple of months now to fulfill that requirement and thus take over the presidency of his family's company.

"What the hell is going on here? I don't even like sweets," Eric says, and now I notice he's become very suspicious.

"*This*, you're going to love," Jack mocks.

None of us doubt that he will hate every second of the experience, and that's precisely what makes everything more fun.

I see a guy, around twenty years old, but looking like he just graduated from high school if you take his long hair into account, coming in pushing a cake the height of an average woman. It's obvious that it's not a real cake, although it's clear the frosting is creamy.

I shake my head and raise an eyebrow at Jack, wanting to convey that he has gone overboard. The cake looks more like one of those wedding cakes. It doesn't suit an executive at all.

Suddenly, a sensual song begins.

It's fucking weird to have a bunch of grown men gathered with no women around and music set to screw.

The guy pushing the cake walks away, and I hear Jack shout: "Now!".

The "lid" of the cake lifts, and the first thing I see are delicate arms coming out of the opening. Then, a platinum blonde mane appears, followed by a face that looks like a painting it's so perfect. Not even the small mask she wears can prevent us from confirming she belongs to a beautiful woman. Although from a distance I can't define the color of her eyes, I know they are light.

"What the hell..." Eric begins, but is interrupted by Jack's order: "Get out of there!"

"I can't. I'll need help," a voice with a strong accent replies in English, and in the back of my mind, an alarm goes off, even though I still can't understand why.

I watch as Jack pulls the woman from inside the cake.

Until then, everyone was chatting, relaxed, as typically happens at this kind of event, but as soon as he deposits a gorgeous goddess dressed in black and pink lingerie with garters and high heels just a few steps away from me, a sudden silence falls over the room; I'm sure it's because they are all fascinated by the exuberant creature.

My brain short-circuits as I connect the dots.

No, it can't be.

I let my eyes roam over her sensual curves, and soon find myself focused on her face.

"Smile and be sexy, baby!" Jack commands, and I watch her raise one arm, her other hand resting on her hips, trying to strike a sensual pose, even though she looks intimidated.

"Do a little spin..." he commands again, and my blood boils, even though part of me says I'm going crazy and that it can't be her.

"No. I didn't agree to show my ass to your friends. I've done my part, and now I want my payment. Oh, and by the way, happy birthday, Eric."

I take a step forward.

"Say your name," I command, as a suspicion begins to turn into certainty within me, even though I can't believe it's true.

She wasn't looking in my direction yet. At my command, however, she positions herself so that I'm completely in her line of sight, her chin raised in a challenging pose.

"Interested, Dell?" Jack asks. "Sorry, but Evelina is taken."

My ears buzz, rage spreading through my blood.

I've spent the last few weeks searching for her, convinced that something could have happened to her, and here she is, my wife, showing herself to these jerks.

Wife of convenience or not, she is mine.

"Evelina!"

"Dell?"

The names come out at the same time.

"Is *that* your Evelina?" Eric asks because only he and my brothers know the name of my mysterious wife.

I ignore him. I feel like an animal. Territorial, jealous, furious.

I leave the whiskey glass on a small table and move toward her, feeling the fury spread through my blood.

"You're coming with me!"

"What? I'm not going!"

She takes a step back just as Jack steps into my path, blocking her. Maybe he feels responsible for her because he's the one who hired her.

"Do you two know each other?" he asks.

"Get out of my way, damn it. She's my wife."

Following my declaration, everyone freezes in silence, and I take the opportunity to go around Jack. Before she has a chance to take another breath, I throw Evelina over my shoulder and start walking out of the room.

She kicks and punches my back. I'm far enough away from curious eyes and ears now.

"Let me go!"

"No way, you crazy girl! I've spent the last few weeks waiting for the police to call me to identify your body alongside the coroner, and I still haven't decided if I'm relieved that you're not dead or happy to finally have my hands on you. We have a deal. I did my part, and you can bet that beautiful ass of yours will do yours too."

Chapter 18

Evelina

He ignores all my pleas to put me down, and I decide to save my energy and stop squirming while I'm carried like a sack of potatoes, swearing to myself that as soon as Dell sets me down, I will run away.

It seems my husband can read minds, however, because he doesn't let me go until I'm in the back of a huge car.

I curl up as far away from him as possible.

"You'll have to kill me first! I'm never going to let you lock me in a cage!" I say in a panic as I watch him take off his blazer.

For a moment of madness, I think he's going to pull out handcuffs from inside the blazer to restrain me, or maybe even a gun, but he just offers it to me so I can wear it, and a thought flashes through my mind at lightning speed: *would a woman abuser do that?*

"Lock you in a cage? What the hell are you talking about?"

"I heard your driver, or whoever the man was who picked me up at the airport, saying *'don't worry, boss, I've got the bitch. She's not going anywhere. I'll keep an eye on her, and if necessary, I'll personally train her to obey.'* I pause as a chill of terror runs through me. "He also asked if he should keep me locked up and that, in his opinion, I should stay in a cage for a while, because only then would I become tame!"

Dell

AT FIRST, I STARE AT her, convinced that I made a huge mistake by entering into a proxy marriage with the Russian because it's clear the woman is completely insane.

Then I observe her posture. Even half-naked and clearly uncomfortable with that fact, Evelina doesn't accept the blazer I offer her to help her feel less exposed.

She is afraid, and this situation is unprecedented in my life. I usually become someone hated by women as soon as the relationship ends, but I have never experienced an episode where one of them felt afraid of me.

"Take the blazer, Evelina. I've never taken advantage of a woman in my life, and I don't intend to start now. I can see you're uncomfortable being almost naked in front of me. Later, you'll explain to me why the hell my wife accepted to participate in that circus up there, but for now, cover up and tell me what you're talking about."

She still hesitates before finally putting on my blazer, which is enormous on her small frame, but when she does, she buttons it up completely.

"Now, repeat what you just said."

"The man who came to pick me up said that *'he already had the bitch and would lock her in a cage.'*"

"And you thought he was talking about you?"

For the first time, she looks flustered.

"I..."

I take my phone from my pocket, trying to control my anger. I unlock it and offer it to her.

"Take it," I command when she doesn't move.

She finally decides to act, and when she looks at the screen, she seems surprised.

"What does this mean?"

"This is the bitch that my *ex-driver* wanted to put in a cage. She belongs to my eighty-seven-year-old great-aunt who ran away from home, causing my aunt to need to be hospitalized due to worry. And before I forget, the driver was fired. I'm not in favor of animal cruelty. When he told me he wanted to lock the puppy in a cage, he was shown the door."

She holds the phone with both hands and doesn't look at me.

"The bitch..."

"It wasn't you. I would kill someone who referred to my wife, fake or not, in that way, Evelina."

Evelina

I RECONSIDER THE ENTIRE conversation I heard at the airport, and of course, what he's saying makes sense.

Jesus, did I create a huge mess with my own life?

By running away from him, I broke my part of the deal, was robbed by my landlord, and spent almost a month hiding, scared. And all of this for nothing?

I lift my eyes to him, feeling like an insect.

If he's being sincere, and my intuition tells me he is, Dell hasn't done anything but be honest with me, and I rewarded him by disappearing from his life.

I recall his words when he threw me over his shoulder.

"I've spent the last few weeks waiting for the police to call me to identify your body alongside the coroner, and I still haven't decided if I'm relieved that you're not dead or happy to finally have my hands on you. We have a deal. I did my part, and you can bet that beautiful ass of yours will do yours too."

Yes, we have a deal, and I was the one who broke it, and I even pocketed five thousand dollars from my husband.

My God, what if he decides to accuse me of theft?

"Is it a bit late for me to apologize?" I ask humbly. "I can also work for you and return the money you gave me for the trip. I don't have it anymore. I was robbed by my landlord and..."

He turns to the window as if he can't bear to look at me.

"Robbed by your landlord?"

"I got a job at a bakery and kept my money at home." I look at my hands because even though Dell isn't looking at me, I'm dead embarrassed. "I didn't use a credit card so you couldn't track me. I kept everything... um... under the mattress. One day I came home and my money was gone. I couldn't call the police, so basically, I'm living off what I earn weekly."

I see him stomp his foot on the ground, as if he's very irritated.

And between us, it's a big damn foot, just like the rest of him. In the photos I saw of him online, Dell didn't look so big. He's much more handsome in person, too.

I observe his profile. He looks like a prince. A very angry one who must now want me miles away, but still, a prince.

"As I said, I apologize for the trouble I caused, and I can also pay you back what I owe by working for you."

"Trouble?" You didn't just cause me a mere inconvenience, Evelina. We made a deal; one where you were supposed to pose as a wife. Instead, you ran away from me, made me hunt for you, putting detectives all over the country looking for you. You showed yourself to a bunch of assholes who, by now, might have filmed you and put it on the internet. I don't care about an apology; it doesn't mean anything. You have no idea what you've done to yourself."

"What does that mean?"

"From now on, I won't let you out of my sight. I don't trust you."

Chapter 19

Evelina

He doesn't say anything else until, when I calculate that half an hour has passed, the car stops.

During the ride, I heard him speaking on the phone with Eric, asking him to make sure none of the guests filmed me.

Thank God! At least I won't have my body exposed on the internet.

I'm no longer afraid of Dell. No one needs to prove to me that I was wrong about him for me to be sure of that. The man screams honesty and honor. Still, I don't like being carted around like a doll with no will of my own.

I look around where the driver has parked.

It's the door of a fancy building that looks more like a luxury hotel, the kind you see in movies with billionaires in Manhattan.

I'm living my own cliché, except this isn't a love story, and the CEO in question doesn't seem inclined to seduce me; rather, he looks eager to strangle me.

Dell gets out of the car, even though the driver has gotten out to open the door for him. I don't know if the man usually does this for his boss, but my husband seems completely independent, the kind of guy who doesn't ask for help from anyone.

I prepare to get out too, but of course, I forget to unbuckle the seatbelt and let out a squeak when, trying to stand, the strap pulls me back into the seat.

In two seconds, maybe less than that, Dell is back. He leans into the car too quickly, I think to help me, and our faces are inches apart, almost touching. For a moment, I forget who we are or why I'm here.

All I see is a handsome man with his eyes fixed on mine. His masculine mouth almost touching mine.

The mouth of my husband.

I swallow hard as the urge to touch Dell Westbrook's lips becomes so intense that I have to keep my hands clasped together to resist temptation.

"What happened?" his voice sounds like a growl, something guttural and primitive, and I feel my stomach tighten with a desire for something I don't even know.

"I forgot to unbuckle the seatbelt," I say, embarrassed, but it soon irritates me that he doesn't seem affected while I feel my whole body trembling.

Instead of saying anything, Dell frees me from my prison, but contrary to his tense expression, he releases me with a gentleness and care I thought impossible for such a large man.

Then, without me having the slightest idea of what his intention was, he grabs me by the waist and steps out of the vehicle with me as if I were light as a feather.

He doesn't set me directly on the ground. He leans me against the car very slowly, and our bodies brush against each other.

I feel sensations I don't recognize washing over me, especially when, instead of pulling away, he lowers his face, his warm breath mixing with mine.

"Where have you brought me?" I ask, trying to hide how shaken I am by his closeness. "I didn't even get my things from Jack's apartment."

His mood seems to worsen again.

"About that, don't worry. My driver will pick up your belongings and bring them to you. I also want the address of where you were living. I'll send someone to collect everything that's yours and bring it here."

This finally breaks the trance I was in.

"Bring it here?"

"You'll be living with me now. I don't trust you anymore."

"What? Are you crazy? I have to break the contract with my landlord!"

"The same one who robbed you?" he mocks.

"It doesn't matter. I can't just run away."

"You have scruples about running away from a stranger, but not from your husband?"

"We both know this marriage is as real as a three-dollar bill. I can't just move in here. I have a job and..."

I see him step back and take the phone from his pocket.

"What are you doing?"

"Contacting my lawyer. You're not what I need. — He lowers his tone. — I want a temporary wife because I need one, and you've been nothing but a problem."

"Are you going to blame me for running away? I thought you were a monster! That's the only reason I've been hiding all this time, Dell."

"Maybe you should ask before judging people."

"I..."

He gestures with his hand, as if to tell me to spare him the argument because it won't matter, and that irritates me.

I know we come from different worlds, and besides that, Dell doesn't seem like the type to be afraid of anything or anyone. I, however, am a survivor.

"What's going to happen? Why did you bring me here?"

"Because I thought we still had a deal, but I've changed my mind. You're not suitable for me, Evelina. So you're sleeping here tonight, and then I'll put you in a hotel so you won't have to stay in a place where some asshole can break into your room to rob you."

How stupid am I for the fact that my fake husband just rejected me affecting me so much?

"Are you going to ask for the annulment of the marriage?"

He ignores my question as he continues:

"Did you think that instead of breaking in to rob you, he could have invaded the place while you were sleeping and done something worse?"

My shivers return, and now it's no longer because of the physical attraction he evokes in me; it's out of fear.

A whole movie plays in my mind.

The mafia invading my bakery. Me having to flee Moscow. Them blowing up the establishment and then my coming to New York to marry a stranger.

I raise my eyes to Dell, and his face looks like sculpted marble, so angry.

Suddenly, everything becomes too much for me, and the city closes in around me as if invisible walls are squeezing me.

I feel short of breath.

What happened to my life? All I wanted was to have a thriving café and make beautiful wedding cakes. Yet now I'm about to be sent back to my country because the temporary visa will expire if Dell decides to annul the marriage.

I feel as if a hand with sticky, frightening fingers—the hand of those men in Moscow—is closing around my throat, and I remember the words of the men who were in my café.

"She'll be the boss's new toy until he gets tired of her."

"No!" I moan and push Dell's chest, wanting him to step away from me.

I need to escape to another country. I can't go back to Russia.

He doesn't move, and I take a step to the side, but the street begins to spin.

"I can't go back there. They'll catch me."

"Run" an inner voice screams as I feel my eyes closing.

"Evelina, who's going to catch you?"

"Leave me here in the United States. I won't cause any problems. I'll sign the annulment, but don't send me back to Russia."

My legs feel like they're losing strength, but before I can fall, strong arms wrap around me.

"Talk to me, Evelina."

"I'm tired of running, Dell. Let me stay."

It's the last thing I remember saying before the night swallows me and darkness spreads inside me.

Chapter 20

Dell

"Evelina!"

"Sir, do you need help?" the driver asks.

"Call a doctor. She fainted."

Evelina is completely out cold as I carry her into my building.

Without even looking in the direction of the doorman, I head to the private elevator that will take me to the top floors, to my triplex apartment.

I look at the wife who was supposed to be just a contract, an employee, but instead, she brought a storm into my life.

Vulnerable in my arms, Evelina looks like a sleeping princess, and all the way to the apartment, I study her beautiful, albeit very pale, face.

She has a strong temperament, but the appearance of a fairy. Small, delicate, and lovely.

"I can't go back there. They'll catch me. Leave me here. I won't cause any problems. I'll sign the annulment, but don't send me back to Russia. I'm tired of running, Dell. Let me stay."

They?

I remember the story of that son of a bitch, the abusive ex-boyfriend, and just thinking that someone could hurt her drives me crazy. Yet, she spoke in plural. They. Who the hell are they? I won't stop until I find out.

Would it be so complicated to keep her? Right now, despite her initial flight, we are what the other needs.

I could protect her, and she could help me calm the Tempus Council.

However, the questions are unnecessary because I know myself and I know that I won't leave her unprotected. From the moment I gave my name to her, Evelina is mine to take care of. No one will touch her.

Not even me?

The question has been hammering in my brain since the moment I saw her in Jack's room.

I've made peace with the fact that I'm a territorial guy. My relationships don't last, but I always have one woman at a time and demand the same. However, what I felt when I saw Evelina half-naked in that room full of assholes was visceral and primitive.

Possessiveness, desire, because it doesn't matter that I've never touched her or if I even have the right to touch her; all I saw was my woman being coveted by others.

Fuck! I must be crazy.

"Hummmm..."

"Shhh... You fainted. I called for a doctor."

"Are you going to let me stay?" she asks, still with her eyes closed.

"We'll talk about that later, Evelina, but hell yes, I'm not going to send you away from my sight."

She had started to stiffen in my arms, but soon relaxes again, resting her face on my chest.

"I'm not crazy or bad, Dell. I didn't mean to break our deal, but I'm a survivor. I have no one and needed to protect myself."

I enter the apartment carrying her and head straight for my bedroom, but as I walk, her words hit me unexpectedly.

It's not that I feel pity. I feel protective toward her.

Yes, if I'm her protector, that will be safe for her. No sex. I will treat Evelina like the girl she is and who doesn't belong in my world, and at the end of our time together, she will leave rich and whole-hearted.

I can do this. Contrary to what I thought when I saw her through the video in Finland, I won't take her to bed.

"Dell?"

I didn't realize that I had laid her down in my suite or that Evelina was staring at me, so lost was I in the purpose of not giving in to the blonde temptation carrying my last name.

In fact, I'm leaning over her, my face just inches from hers.

I force myself to straighten up, take a step back, which only worsens the problem because Evelina is only in lingerie and high heels, and the blazer I lent her is open, allowing me to see every delicious curve of her.

"You'll be fine. I'm not sending you back to Russia."

"Dell, why do you seem a bit crazy?"

"Looks like you've recovered from fainting."

She turns red and sits up on the bed.

"Yeah, I haven't eaten anything all day, and I think that along with the fact that I was going to have to expose myself to..."

"No."

"No what?"

"Don't say that because reminding me of you coming out of that cake almost naked makes me..."

"What?"

"Angry. I feel protective of you. You're just a girl, so I got angry seeing you so exposed in front of strangers."

"If it was in front of you, it wouldn't be a problem, then? I'm your wife." She shrugs. "At least in the eyes of the law."

"Nothing is going to happen between us."

"I didn't say it would."

"Because it would only complicate things."

"And I don't like flirtatious women. I saw your pictures in the newspapers. You go out with a bunch of 'girlfriends'. But we can be friends, though."

"I don't have friends."

"I've never been friends with a guy either, so I guess this will be our first time."

"You'll live here, but we won't be a real couple."

She looks around, seemingly just realizing she's in my room.

"I didn't think I'd actually be in your suite."

"No. I meant you won't be staying in my space in this apartment. There's a third floor I don't use. It's practically an independent apartment. You'll live there. And when you want to leave the house, you'll also have bodyguards at your disposal."

"Thank you."

The calm and polite agreement doesn't suit her. From everything I've learned about Evelina so far, she's a fighter.

"You don't have to thank me. I didn't bring you to the United States to leave you unprotected."

She nods her head without looking at me.

"Could you lend me something to wear? Sweatpants and a t-shirt would be great. I promise to return it tomorrow when my stuff arrives. I suppose you'll bring it by tomorrow, right? I need to give you my address."

Before I can respond to her rapid-fire sentences, as if she's nervous, one of my bodyguards appears in the bedroom doorway.

"Sorry, Mr. Westbrook, but the doctor will arrive in thirty minutes."

"Thank you. Have someone pick up my wife's belongings from Jack's house."

I see the man's eyes widen; he quickly looks away to focus on Evelina and then back at me.

I have no doubt why he reacted that way. It was the "my wife" that I casually let slip.

"Yes, sir."

He leaves the suite right after.

"I need your address, as you pointed out. Tomorrow I'll send someone to pick up your things."

"Can I take a shower before the doctor arrives?"

She stands up, and thank God, my blazer goes down to her knees, covering her almost completely.

Evelina is too beautiful. I can't take my eyes off her.

"I'll lend you a boxer and a t-shirt."

"Thank you."

I enter the closet, grab one of my dozens of black t-shirts, and then the boxer, although I doubt it will fit because...

No, I'm not going to think about my wife's pussy filling my boxer. That's too perverted even for me.

I return to the room and hand her what she asked for. Evelina starts walking toward the door.

"Where are you going? The bathroom is that way," I say, gesturing behind me.

"You said you don't want me in your apartment space. I just added two and two. Can you show me the floor you said I would be staying on?"

"Use my bathroom. We're wasting time. The doctor will be here soon."

"Thank you."

"Why are you being so formal?"

"Because I feel intimidated by you."

"I won't harm you."

"Now I believe you. But I didn't mean I feel scared; it's about all this... *wealth*. It's not part of my world. You know that hotel you sent me to in Finland? I didn't even know how to adjust the shower! I've never seen one controlled by buttons." She turns red. "I had to call a maid to help me. What I'm trying to say is that I'm poor and grew up in poverty. I didn't receive a refined education. I never even thought about going to college because we didn't have the money for that. I know how to make wedding cakes."

"What are you trying to say?"

"I don't pick up on subtle messages well, Dell. I'm the type who speaks my mind, and I believe it would be easier if everyone were like that. So don't tell me you want me to leave your apartment space and then send me to take a shower in your bathroom. I'd prefer to keep the lines clear between us."

Chapter 21

Evelina

The doctor just left, and even though I think calling him was an overreaction on Dell's part since I knew exactly what happened—I hadn't eaten all day because I was so nervous about the "performance" I would have to execute at Jack's house—I appreciated having this break between my "husband" and me.

Now, however, I don't have many options but to leave his room, where I was "examined."

I sigh, thinking that I'll have to message Fantini, explaining that I'm with Dell. When I ran away, I didn't contact her. As far as I knew, she could be a "partner" of my husband.

Jesus, how embarrassing. I judged everyone.

The only person I spoke to through my new phone was Katya, and even that was sporadically. She is doing well and is happy, and I didn't have the heart to tell her that my life had turned into an action movie where it felt like I was always on the run.

I braid my hair "to the side" with an elastic I grab from my bag. As soon as the doctor left, one of Dell's employees arrived with everything I had left at Jack's house—clothes, shoes, documents, and what remained of my savings.

I wanted to kill the landlord when I found out I was robbed. Since arriving in the United States, I've been saving as much as I could because I planned to leave, and I panicked when I noticed all my money was gone.

My God, remembering what Dell said, I ran a real risk. The man could have entered the apartment while I slept, wanting to steal much more than just money.

I gather the lingerie I wore for my "girl-in-the-cake" show and put everything inside the bag.

I put on my jeans and sneakers but keep on his boxer shorts and the huge t-shirt he lent me.

Although I should leave the room since the employee told me Dell would be waiting for me, I walk over to the window, pull back the curtain, and look out at the night. It's late, eleven-thirty, but I'm not even close to feeling sleepy.

My body is restless, but contradictorily, for the first time in a long time, I don't feel fear or worry about looking over my shoulder to see if anyone is following me. From everything I learned with Dell, I'll be safe by his side.

I don't like needing someone, especially a man with a deadline to exit my life, but at the moment, I see no way out.

"Evelina."

I look back, startled because I didn't realize I was being watched.

I notice he's also showered. His hair is wet and messy, probably because he couldn't comb it. He must have used one of the guest suites.

I let my eyes roam over his body because I can't help myself.

Dell is wearing only sweatpants, shirtless, and I force myself to look at his face because the muscles of the man... let's just say it should be illegal to have a six-pack like that on display.

"Come eat, Evelina."

I swear on everything sacred that my body tingles all over when I hear him call me "Evelina." It's like my name slides off his tongue like chocolate.

And I love chocolate.

"I can prepare something."

He shrugs.

"I don't know how to cook, but according to my great-aunt, I make the best sandwich in the world."

I smile, managing to relax a little.

"The owner of the runaway puppy?"

He doesn't smile back. He just nods and watches me intently.

I feel awkward.

"Thank you for taking the trouble to make something. It's late."

"I haven't eaten either. Come on."

I hold my bag against my body and walk toward the door. Dell doesn't move, which forces me to stop because his huge body fills the entrance.

"I need to pass."

Nothing yet. When I think we're going to stand here forever, his hand touches my chin.

"I want you, Evelina, and I know you're attracted to me too, but if anything happens between us, it won't change the fact that in a few months, you'll be leaving my life. I know you've been hurt in the past by that bastard and I don't want to take advantage of you."

I hate that he sees me as a fragile creature. As someone he'll keep and then discard, leaving me broken by abandonment.

What would Dell say if I told him that since I was sixteen I've been supporting my home because my grandmother was too sick to even get out of bed, and my brother only showed up to ask for money?

I don't pull away from his touch, even though I know letting him touch me is dangerous since I like the feeling of his skin against mine. However, I won't allow him to realize how much he affects me.

In fact, if I were a great liar, I would tell him that I'm not even attracted to him, but I have a feeling that no one can fool this man, so I opt for an alternative route.

"As you said, we have a deal. I think if each of us fulfills our part, everything will be fine, Dell. And, of course, that means I'll stay, for as long as necessary, where I'm supposed to be. Appearing when needed."

"And then?"

His hand falls to his side, and I follow the movement, which is now clenched into a fist.

"I'll follow the plan I made before you found me. If I can get the Green Card and continue in the United States, I'll move to a small town and set up my business. Of course, I don't know anything about starting a company here, but I learn quickly, and I know it will work out."

"I'm not going to leave you to fend for yourself."

"What?"

My lonely heart races, even though I can't understand the meaning of those words.

"After our marriage ends, I'll help you get what you want, to set up your business."

I give him a weak smile.

"You're a fool, Evelina. Did you think a magnate would offer to be your friend?"

"Thank you."

"I'm starting to realize that you use that word when you want to push me away."

"I don't understand."

"You do. When I say what you don't want to hear. Believe me, I'm trying to protect you, Evelina. Our relationship is nothing like what I've experienced before. I've had many girlfriends, but I've never had to live with them for more than a couple of months. The minimum time I need you to stay with me is six months. I don't stick with the same woman for long. What will happen if, after we fuck for the first time, I don't want you anymore?"

I wasn't expecting that. Neither the rawness of his words nor the "preemptive rejection."

How arrogant does a man need to be to think not only that I would fall in love if he took me to bed but also that I wouldn't be able to satisfy him for long?

I step back a little because he's very tall, and I want to face him when I say what I intend:

"I suppose that in a remote hypothetical situation where we had sex, there would be a fifty percent chance that one of us would end up addicted to the other, but I'm not taking that risk. I'm very demanding in bed. It's not *just anyone* who satisfies me."

Chapter 22

Dell

I don't know what makes me cross our boundaries. Whether it's because I like to come out on top in any shit that has my name involved. If it's the fact that thinking of her with another man, giving her the pleasure I want her to taste, makes me jealous. Or if it's just because I'm an arrogant jerk who didn't expect someone so young and sweet to give me this kind of response.

The fact is that in a fraction of a second, I break the rules I set for myself regarding my wife and without her being able to complete her next breath, I have her in my arms.

One of my hands is on her ass, pulling her to me, the other holding her neck. At that moment, I don't think about how kissing her could complicate things between us because I want that mouth.

To my surprise, despite her combative words, Evelina doesn't push me away or try to flee; she digs her nails into my biceps and gives me her lips, which are like warm honey.

The moment my tongue penetrates her delicious mouth, I know I've just set a trap for myself because kissing her is addictive.

Evelina moans and rubs against my body. She lightly bites me, digs her fingers into my flesh, and whimpers my name.

I pick her up and carry her to the bed. I spread her thighs, fit myself between them, and with my hands pinning hers against the mattress, I deepen the kiss and rub my hard cock against her sex.

She rises from the mattress and offers herself, which drives me wild.

"You said..." she starts, murmuring in the midst of the kiss.

"I know what I said. Be quiet, wife. Don't remind me why we can't be together. Do what you feel like."

It's like flipping a switch on her. Evelina locks her thighs around my back and opens her mouth wider. She brings her tongue to dance with mine and becomes fire in my hands.

The wildness makes me even more turned on, if that's even possible, and I spin us on the bed, leaving her on top of me. Now, holding her body with my arm across her back, I position her perfectly over my cock; I grip her ass to encourage her to rub against me better.

"Delicious. I want you, Russian."

"We can't."

Despite the denial, she doesn't stop kissing me. On the contrary, she seems to be just as turned on.

I grip her waist under the shirt, but what I can touch of her skin doesn't feel like enough.

"I need you naked. I'm dying to taste your breasts. I'm going to suck you dry."

I'm about to pull off her shirt completely when a loud buzzing from my phone cuts through. I ignore it, but Evelina does not. She breaks free and stands up like lightning.

"No!" she repeats what she said a moment ago, her face still flushed with desire. "I won't be just another name on your rejected list. I don't want to be with you, Dell."

I get out of bed too.

"You're a liar. You might be scared, especially now that you know how we are together, because the chemistry between us is undeniable, but to say that you don't want me? I'm not a boy, Evelina."

"What I meant is that I don't want to be one of your abandoned women. Don't confuse the fact that I come from humble beginnings with being stupid, Dell. I won't let myself be used by you or any man. A few minutes of pleasure aren't enough to make me accept casual sex."

My crazy, possessive mind is hammering the question: what would it take to make her accept sex? A guy who wants her for more than just a few days?

Because as beautiful as she is, there will be a line of candidates crossing the country.

Jealousy spreads within me, and I don't like the feeling.

"It wouldn't be a few minutes, baby, but hours or whole days. You'd never be able to fuck without thinking of me again."

She looks affronted.

"I don't want to, thank you. Please, can you tell me which room I should sleep in, or is there only one on the third floor?"

I wait a few seconds to make sure she's not bluffing. I've never been rejected by a woman before even putting my hands on her. After kissing her, then? It was a guaranteed conquest.

"Dell, can you show me where I'll sleep?" she asks again, slowly, as if she thinks I'm having trouble understanding her.

"You can't sleep yet. I haven't fed you."

She lets her gaze slide over my body, unabashedly focusing on the part that draws her attention the most: a *part* that at this moment makes my sweatpants pitch a tent.

"I don't think..."

"I'm not going to attack you, Evelina. My cock is hard because I'm turned on by you. Soon, it'll go back to normal, just like the center of your thighs."

"You're a jerk, Dell. You don't say things like that to a lady."

"What? Feeling turned on is biological. Forgive me if I have to measure my words with you, my *virgin wife*."

"Virgin? Wow, that's rich. I'm very experienced. I don't even remember the number of guys I've slept with."

"You're full of it."

"What?"

"Tell *me how many guys you've slept with.*

"Me, no."

"You can't even say it, you know why? You're just a little girl compared to me, Evelina. Don't play that femme fatale game with me. I've had tons of sex in my life since I was fifteen."

"I didn't mean to play the femme fatale; it just irritates me. You're an arrogant man who told me I'd fall at your feet in a blink of an eye and suffer when you left me. Then you changed your mind and wanted to have sex with me, but based on your own advice that you would 'get bored' with me, knowing we'll have to coexist for a while, I'm going to give myself the right to say *'no, thank you for the generous offer, my dear husband, but I'm not disposable.'*

She leaves the room, though she has no idea where the stairs are that will take her to the third floor. In a crazy way, her bad temper only makes me hotter.

"Evelina." I grab her by the arm, already in the hallway.

"I'm not going to eat."

"Don't be stubborn."

She doesn't turn to face me.

"I shouldn't even be here, Dell. We're a work contract. Boss and employee don't kiss."

"You're not my employee."

"I am, yes." Her voice calms, and she finally dignifies to look me in the eye. "I don't want to make these months hell for both of us. You helped me by bringing me to your country. I will fulfill my part, but I was mistaken when I asked us to be friends. Besides our very different backgrounds, we hate each other."

"No, we're attracted to each other. If we hated each other, it would be easier." I pause because I've never apologized in my life, but I know I crossed a line with her and want to fix that. "I'm not a jerk, and I shouldn't have spoken to you that way."

Surprisingly, a corner of her mouth lifts.

"You shouldn't have. Didn't your parents teach you that you should honor your wife? All that nonsense about *loving and respecting until death do us part*, what happens to that?"

"I was raised only by my father, so I don't know much about that part of how to behave in a marriage."

"Oh! What happened to your mother?" She puts her fingers over her lips. "I'm sorry if I was indiscreet."

"You were, but I don't mind. My mother died during childbirth with Vernon. We have a one-year difference between us, so I hardly remember her."

She approaches me and catches me off guard by pressing her body against mine.

"I'm really sorry, Dell. I shouldn't have played with that."

"Don't be sweet. I prefer you aggressive."

She has both hands on my waist, holding only the skin, but not hugging.

"Why?"

"I don't know, I guess because I don't handle delicate creatures well. You look like a fairy."

"In appearance, maybe, but believe me. There's not a fragile bone in me. Now, take me to eat before we fight again." She pulls away and starts walking again, still unaware of where she's going. "Oh, and you're forgiven, but don't kiss me again. I didn't like it."

I pull her back, making her back press against my chest, and whisper in her ear:

"*Liar.*

Chapter 23

Evelina

"How can I help you?" I ask, trying not to look at his broad back.

Dell is sin in human form, and it's easy to understand why he's had so many girlfriends throughout his life.

I think having a powerful last name might be attractive to some girls, but I bet that even if he had nothing but looks, women would still be throwing themselves at his feet.

"I have everything under control. What do you want to drink?"

"In your country, I can only drink juice."

He looks back, and a "v" forms between his eyebrows as if he just realized I'm not yet twenty-one.

"Evelina..."

Just by his tone, I kind of predict what he's going to say.

"You didn't take advantage of me. I could have stopped you before, but I wanted to know what it was like to be kissed by you. It was just a kiss, so you don't need to worry about being an old man and me being a young girl, Mr. Westbrook. Or should I call you... what's the name that girls who are supported by older boyfriends use? — I pretend to think. — Ah, yes. *Sugar daddy.*"

He sets the plates with sandwiches in front of me and leans in with both hands resting on the counter, making every beautiful muscle in his shoulders, triceps, and biceps pop before my eyes.

Dell gives a slow smile and becomes even more irresistible.

"Don't make me like you, or you'll be in trouble, wife. I might become obsessed or addicted to how easily you make me smile."

"Don't you usually smile?"

"I don't have many reasons to." He says, and I feel guilty because his expression falls.

I decide to return to the topic that made him gift me with that seductive lip movement. Inexplicably, seeing him sad makes me upset.

Is there any sense in this? No, because today is the first time we've met in person, so why do I care about making him smile or not?

My God, this evening feels like an emotional rollercoaster.

"To become obsessed with someone, you need to spend time with them. That won't happen between us."

"It's a Westbrook family trait to be obsessed. Just say something is forbidden, and we become determined to conquer it."

"With me, it won't happen. We don't match at all."

"We match on the main thing."

He looks at my mouth, and I feel a shiver down my spine.

"I'm starving. You said you'd feed me. It's almost midnight."

He still takes a few seconds to stare at me, but finally goes to the fridge, grabs juice for me, and a beer for himself.

He sits next to me, but he's so big that our thighs touch.

We eat in silence, but every cell in my body feels his presence.

"Aren't you going to finish your sandwich?" he asks when I get distracted some time later.

I cut a little piece and put it in my mouth. I feel his gaze on me, and when I turn to him, Dell is focused on me.

"Your great-aunt is right. It's the best sandwich I've ever eaten, but it's too big. I can't finish it." I push the plate away. "If I ever give up being a mogul, I might even consider hiring you for my staff at the new café I'm going to open."

Dell smiles, takes my sandwich without ceremony, and takes a bite.

"Café staff? I thought you only liked making cakes."

"I prefer making cakes, but I owned a café in Moscow. You must have forgotten. And who knows, opening one in your country might work out?"

"I haven't forgotten anything about you. Tell me about your life in Russia."

The temptation is great. Dell is solid, and it's not just because of his nearly two-meter physique, muscles, and the square jaw that even the beard can't hide. He seems like the type you can trust.

Except with your own heart.

What do you think you're doing, Evelina? Don't get attached to him.

"I have a brother who likes to owe money to the wrong people, and right now, I'm very angry at him. My parents died when we were little. I was raised by my grandparents. Or rather, by my grandmother. She taught me how to make cakes. I've kept the house going by continuing her work since I was sixteen."

He pushes the plate away and turns fully toward me. His face is serious.

"And your grandfather?"

"He was already dead by then. But it wouldn't have mattered if he were alive. He was never home. For almost my whole life, it was just the two of us. My brother came and went as he needed money."

"There's no one else?"

He tries to take my hand, but I won't make the mistake of seeing Dell as someone I can count on, even just to vent, so I stand up and take the plates to the sink. I barely lift my hand to turn on the faucet when I feel his arms on either side of me, resting on the counter.

"I asked you a question."

"To which you probably already know the answer. I manage well. I don't need people around me taking care of me."

He doesn't move, and neither do I flee.

"It's never going to work having you so close. I'll end up taking you to bed."

I let out a squeak when he lifts me, sitting me on the counter, fitting himself between my legs.

"I think we already settled that. You're not taking me to bed. And to avoid temptation, I won't stay so close, nor will I come down from the third floor. You said it's an independent apartment, so I'll cook up there. By the way, could you give me an agenda of what we'll have to do together?"

"Why?"

"So I can organize myself."

"Once a week," he says. "That will be enough."

"Fine."

His expression closes.

"No."

"No what?"

"I've changed my mind. It's insufficient. Three dinners a week."

"Okay, boss. We'll need to know a bit more about each other too, just in case I get asked questions. I have no idea why you needed to get married, but it seems to me it was because you're in trouble or need to convince someone you're a serious man. The person you need to pretend to be will find it strange if I don't know anything about you."

"I don't give a damn what they think of me. I got married to fulfill a promise I made to my father before he died."

"Oh! — Jesus, this man is a danger. He can be an ogre one moment and sweet the next. I can see from his face how sad he became when talking about his father. — You loved him."

"Yes, I loved him very much."

"I'm sorry for your loss, but do you have any idea how blessed you are, Dell? Most people don't appreciate having a family to celebrate special dates, holiday parties, anniversaries..."

Jesus, I don't want to be a victim.

"What were you going to say?"

"Nothing. I'm sleepy. Thanks for the food. And for the doctor." I smile. "And for lending me the boxer and this T-shirt. And for letting me stay with you after the scene I made running away. Oh, and also for saving me from your perverted friends. Maybe by ninety I'll be able to pay off all these debts."

I push him away, jump off the counter, and run out because the joke I tried to make to break the tension between us didn't work. He didn't smile, and my heart keeps racing. The physical attraction I feel is uncontrollable. The man just has to breathe to make me tremble.

I return to his room and gather the things I left earlier, but when I turn to leave, he's once again in the doorway.

"I'm going to take you to the third floor," he says, but his posture seems to show that he doesn't want me to leave.

He places his hand on the small of my back when I approach, and it feels like getting burned with hot iron in that area. I'm on fire for him.

"Here," he says after we climb the stairs, showing me the room. "It's more than a suite. Like I said, an independent apartment."

"Thanks. I'll need my things tomorrow."

"Do you still have your phone?"

"Yes." I show him the bag I'm holding.

"Message me shortly with your home address. I'll have my driver pick it up."

"He'll need the keys."

"Your landlord must have an extra or he wouldn't have robbed you, Evelina."

"And you think he's going to hand my things to his employee without causing a scene?" Dell says nothing, and I understand his silence: no one stands in the way between him and what he wants. "Fine. Good night, husband. I won't apologize again for the scene I made running away from you. It's pathetic to keep saying sorry."

"I agree, but why do you think that?"

"I think it's the same as saying you love someone all the time. You end up devaluing the feeling. In my case, I believe that more than asking you for forgiveness, I can be a good, well-behaved wife, the woman of your dreams for the next few months."

I spill all this on him in seconds, and only when I finish do I realize the monumental nonsense I just spoke.

"I'd better go. Every time I open my mouth, I embarrass myself."

"Message me your address, Evelina."

"Yes, sir."

This time, when I run out, I slam the bedroom door in his face.

The desire not to say goodbye, to stay up all night with him is too great, and I can't risk ruining everything by letting him treat me like his new toy for a week because after that, the rest of the months we'll spend together will be humiliating.

Chapter 24

Dell

Five minutes after I resend Evelina's message to my driver, giving him the address of where she lives, I still look at the screen of my phone.

I should turn it off, wait for daybreak, and send her to one of my apartments, not keep her on the third floor, but the question she raised, about what people will think of a marriage where the spouses don't cohabit, still lingers in my mind.

Is that all? Or is it because you were caught off guard feeling a bond that goes far beyond lust with the woman who should have just been another one of your employees?

"You're not going back there." I type to her.

I knew exactly what I was doing when I sent that and also that if she hadn't fallen asleep yet, Evelina would respond.

"I'm not your property. I won't go back there because I don't want to. I thought about what you said, about how the landlord could have invaded my room. I just need to give my boss my notice, and I'll do it over the phone. Do you need me tomorrow or next weekend?"

Reason tells me to say no to both questions, but I excuse myself by saying they need to see us together.

"I'll be traveling for work tomorrow, but next weekend, I will need you. We've delayed our public appearances long enough. I'm taking you out for lunch and then to meet my great-aunt Wilma."

My phone rings.

"Your great-aunt? But I thought our relationship..."

"Let me clarify something about us, Westbrook, Evelina: we know everything about each other's lives. My brothers, of course, are aware of our 'arrangement,' just like my aunt Wilma."

"I'm not saying I don't want to meet them; it just seems a bit confusing that you want to keep me on the third floor like Rapunzel trapped in her own tower, and at the same time, that I should be introduced to your great-aunt."

Yes, that was exactly what I intended to do, keep her away from my family, until I realized how lonely you are, wife.

"Why make a big deal out of it? Do you have any plans for next weekend?"

She takes a few seconds longer than necessary to respond, and a jealous monster I didn't even know existed inside me is activated.

"You can't be with someone else while we're married."

"I wasn't planning on seeing anyone, but since you brought it up, how is our life going to be in that department?"

"In what sense?" I feign ignorance about the question when, in fact, I know perfectly well what she's talking about.

Evelina tries to clarify how our sex life will be since to the world, we'll be married.

When my brothers talked about this, I had no doubts about what would happen: I would keep her in a house and let her satisfy herself with some partner just like I would, but now I know it's not going to work.

"I want to know if we're going to be celibate for a year." She pauses and laughs. "Forget it, what a stupid thing to say. I doubt you can stay celibate for a day."

"And you?"

"I'm not driven by sex."

"What are you driven by then?"

"By a life that's not empty. As soon as our agreement ends, I want to fill every piece of my existence with moments."

"Happy moments? That's utopia. No one is happy all the time."

"No, with my moments. I haven't had a chance to live yet. I loved my grandmother, but I could never be myself. I lived to help her, then to save my brother from trouble these last few months since she passed away. Now, I will fulfill the role of a billionaire's wife for a reason I can't even guess. So, I'm looking forward to the moment when I'll be just Evelina, a twenty-year-old woman eager to live."

I've never liked talking on the phone, but hearing her voice, her plans, calms my "kick the door down" nature.

"Twenty?"

"A figure of speech" she replies quickly.

"You won't be a prisoner while you're with me. You'll have everything money can buy. Next week, I'll arrange for a personal shopper to help you set up a full wardrobe. Think of something, Evelina, and you'll have it at your feet."

"Is that how you live?"

"What?"

"No, I was just thinking: it must be a bit boring to have everything you want. Oops, wait, but you can't have everything you want because you want me, and you won't get me."

"I could if I insisted, but I don't want to hurt you."

This time, she doesn't try to act tough.

"Thank you for that, Dell. You're right. I have no experience, and there would be a great chance of leaving my heart in pieces when I have to leave. Good night."

She hangs up without waiting for my response, and I keep looking at the phone, thinking about her words.

There's something about Evelina that makes me want to protect her and at the same time, tame her.

Contradictory and inappropriate desires, but uncontrollable ones, too.

I close my eyes, and at that moment, her face while I kissed her pops into my mind. The way she responded... fuck, she's a delight.

My delicious forbidden wife.

"I DIDN'T THINK IT WOULD be so easy for your employees to get my things," she says on the morning of the following weekend as I drive to my great-aunt's house.

"What?" I ask, a bit lost, because Evelina is wearing a dress that, when standing, reaches her knees, but sitting next to me in the car, rides up her thighs, making me want to rip it off her body. My wife's skin is soft and delectable. I've dreamt of its texture all week while I was away from New York.

"I was referring to my clothes. I didn't expect the landlord to make it easy for your employee."

Waking up the day after she arrived at my house, I know she found a small suitcase with all her belongings at her door, because my employee arrived at dawn, which tells me the bastard landlord must have been quite startled by him.

"It helped to convince him that we accused him of theft. My employee threatened to put him in jail."

"My God, I don't even know this guy and I'm already a fan of his!"

"She's a married woman," I reply with jealousy because if there's one thing that's certain in this life, it's that Evelina isn't my fan.

"I know, my dear husband. It was a joke. Why are you so grumpy?"

"I don't know what you're talking about."

I notice, from my peripheral vision, that she continues to look ahead in silence, but when I turn to see her better, a corner of her mouth is raised.

I intended to have lunch with her earlier, but as soon as I informed Wilma that I finally had my convenient wife in hand, since she knew about Evelina's disappearance, my great-aunt asked me to bring her over immediately to meet her.

"What is she like?"

"Good, generous."

"I imagine she must be good, because if she knows we're a sham, why would she want to meet me?"

"Maybe she misses female company. She raised us, helping my father with the four of us the best she could."

"The four of us? I only found pictures of two of your brothers online."

"There was a fourth, a year younger than me. He died in adolescence."

"My God, Dell, I'm so sorry. It seems like every time I open my mouth, I'm being indiscreet."

"You couldn't have known."

I remain silent for the rest of the drive because thinking about Lee, even after so many years, still feels like a knife piercing my heart.

Chapter 25

Evelina

"Call me Wilma, my dear," Dell's great-aunt asks, not for the first time, after the servants come to clear the lunch dishes at her mansion.

And when I say "mansion," that's exactly what I mean.

The house would be immense for a family with half a dozen children, so I can't help but wonder how a woman of nearly ninety lives alone in a place like this.

She is the perfect opposite of Dell.

Sweet, friendly, not intimidating at all.

She doesn't have classical beauty, but there is so much liveliness in her face and such an easy smile that it makes her beautiful.

"Thank you, Wilma. I'm relieved I don't have to lie to you."

Dell has been watching our conversation during lunch, although he only responded when his aunt directly asked him something.

I'm not sure if he acts this way because he's upset or if he wants us to feel more at ease.

Wilma, however, seems to be used to his moods, because even though her nephew's expression is closed, she doesn't show it.

You don't need to be very perceptive to see how much he loves the elderly woman, and the feeling is mutual.

"She doesn't have a ring!" the lady suddenly exclaims, looking horrified.

"What?" For the first time, my husband of convenience sounds flustered.

"How do you expect those crafty foxes at the Tempus Council to believe you're married if..." She pauses. "Oh! I think I've said too much."

I notice the exchange of glances between the two and realize I've just received a clue about why my handsome magnate needed to get married. Putting the pieces together, I know it has something to do with a promise he made to his father, but it's also related to this Tempus thing, whatever that is, and...

"My God! You own that watch brand that kings and queens use?"

I'm not pretending to be shocked; I'm genuinely taken aback. I knew he had money, but this Tempus company is for the elite of the elite.

I feel very embarrassed when a heavy silence falls over the table.

"Yes, it was founded by his great-grandfather, but it's just a small business compared to my boys' companies. You didn't know?"

I glance at Dell, and it seems his mood has worsened significantly with his aunt's indiscreet revelation.

"I didn't know, but with all due respect, it wasn't a topic that would interest me. I really just enjoy baking. Nothing related to working in an office, or a factory, as I suppose is the case with the watch brand, would catch my attention."

I don't look at either of them when I say this. I know Wilma spoke the truth, unintentionally, about the marriage arrangement, but Dell's reaction has left me upset.

What does he think?

Does he believe that now that I've discovered how rich he is, I will want more?

"You're upset about something," Wilma says when she sees me push the dessert aside after barely touching it.

"No, it's just that I ate too much at lunch. I think I got a little carried away," I tell a little white lie because she's too sweet for me to want to upset her over the miserable man I married.

"I was indiscreet, so I apologize to you both," she says. "But that doesn't change the fact that I'm right. They will never believe you're married if you both don't wear rings."

"I don't think that..."

"My aunt is right, Evelina. It was my mistake. I'll fix this. Excuse me."

He stands up from the table, and I look at the elderly woman, not understanding anything.

"Don't mind Dell's angry face, dear. He gets a bit grumpy when things don't go his way," Wilma says.

"If it helps to know, I don't think it was you mentioning the ring that upset him. Besides the fact that I'm a runaway wife," I didn't tell her about leaving lingerie from inside a cake at one of my husband's friend's house, and since Dell didn't touch on the subject either, I'll pretend it didn't happen "I believe it was something I asked about on the way here that made him angry."

"About his grandparents?"

Oh, it seems this family is full of secrets.

"No, about the fourth brother. I researched Dell online and only found mention of three Westbrook brothers, so when he told me you took care of his father and 'us four,' referring to himself and the brothers, I commented that I had only heard of three. That's when he revealed that the fourth died in his teens."

I see her eyes fill with tears.

"Actually, he was almost a teen. Lee was practically still a child. He had barely turned twelve."

"Oh! Can I ask what happened?"

"I'll tell you, Evelina, but then I must ask you never to bring this up with any of my boys. It doesn't matter that almost two decades have passed. They haven't recovered from the loss yet. Lee committed suicide with a gun. London found him."

"My Jesus!"

I was not expecting this revelation at all.

"It's a forbidden subject, Evelina. Never forget that."

I want to ask more about it, but at that moment, two giants who look a lot like Dell enter the dining room, and even if I hadn't seen their photos in the newspapers, I would know they are Vernon and London Westbrook.

Chapter 26

Evelina

"Well, if it isn't the runaway wife!" one of them says, but despite the words dripping with irony, he is smiling at me.

My God, has Dell already told his brothers that he found me since last week? Yes, of course he has. That's why they must have come.

The other stands two steps behind the sarcastic one, and unlike his brother, who looks ready to strut in a fashion catalog, the image of a rich man in casual clothes, the one in back wears a leather jacket and has a motorcycle helmet in hand.

"My name is Evelina Volko..."

"No, princess. Your name is Evelina *Westbrook*, and you'd better remember that next time you think about running away," the one in the leather jacket says.

I feel my cheeks burning because there's nothing I can do to defend myself, especially since I did escape from Dell.

Besides, I won't try to explain that I disappeared because I thought the driver was calling me a bitch and wanted to lock me in a cage.

"Boys, behave yourselves. Evelina is your sister-in-law."

"We know that. Now, does she know her role?"

"London!" Wilma scolds him, who raises both hands as if apologizing, though the words don't leave his mouth. "You two behave. Evelina is not just Dell's wife, which would be enough for you to respect her. She is my guest too."

They both kiss her, and the old lady melts with love for my "brothers-in-law."

After the tempestuous arrival, Wilma leads us to a smaller room where the maid will serve coffee, according to what she said, but neither of Dell's brothers sits down.

"Where were you?" the surliest one, who also happens to be the one in the jacket, asks.

London, based on the scolding he received from his aunt.

The other, Vernon, smiles mockingly, raising an eyebrow at me.

"Tell us all how my brother found you, sister-in-law."

His gaze assures me that he knows, and I want to kill Dell for that. I decide to lay it all out.

"Last week, I came out of a birthday cake for Dell's friend, Eric, in lingerie and high heels. Jack Prescot hired me. Dell was there. He dragged me out of the party over his shoulder. As for the reason I ran away from my husband when I arrived in your country, it was because I overheard a conversation from the driver... I mean, Dell's former driver, saying he was going to *put the bitch in a cage to learn to be tame.* I thought he was talking about me."

It's as if a higher entity imposes an obligatory silence. For a moment, I think if a piece of paper fell to the ground, we would hear it because the feeling is as if everyone is holding their breath. Then Wilma starts laughing and clapping.

"Jesus, at my age, I never thought anything could make me laugh this much!" she says, placing a hand on her stomach, and even the mocking Vernon and the grumpy London have their lips turned up slightly.

The Westbrook matriarch is the first to speak.

"Dear, what a big misunderstanding. I'm not going to say Dell is perfect, but I can assure you with a hundred percent certainty that any of my three boys would rip someone's head off if they even treated one of their girlfriends like that. Now imagine a wife! That horrible man was fired. He had no patience with my Dasy."

"Dell told me about it," Vernon says, "but it's much more fun to hear it from you. What the hell were you thinking, Evelina? For all I know, you don't know anything about our country. You could have fallen into the hands of dangerous people!"

Yes, I could have, but I will never admit that.

"She did what she thought necessary to stay safe," London says, and while his words can't be considered a "defense," he at least seems to understand my situation in escaping from his brother.

"Dude... *ramba*," Vernon corrects himself quickly after nearly saying a swear word in front of the aunt who looks at him reproachfully. "I'd give anything to see the look on my older brother's face when he saw the 'surprise' Jack prepared for Eric."

"Vernon, that's not funny. Or maybe it is a little, but never forget that Evelina is your sister-in-law, temporary or not, and Dell won't like it if you make jokes about her blunders."

I'm as awkward as when I revealed to Dell the reason for my escape, so I decide to change the focus of the conversation.

"Dasy is your little dog?"

"Yes, she is. She didn't come down to see you today because like me, she's already very old. She sleeps most of the day."

"I'm glad he's no longer taking care of her. The man seemed to dislike animals."

"Have you had dogs?"

"Yes, we had one. My grandmother loved her. She lived almost until the beginning of my teenage years. After that, due to circumstances in life, we couldn't have another, but it's on my list of dreams to get a companion. I'm sure that with a little dog, no one ever feels alone."

I notice once again that I said something wrong when Wilma looks at me with pity.

My God, will I never learn how to behave around the Westbrooks? I don't want to make myself a pitiful creature. The way I feel, lonely or not, is not their problem.

"Dell, your wife was just telling us about her escape," Wilma says, as if trying to lighten my mood, but I feel even more embarrassed when I realize he has returned and may have overheard what I said.

"Evelina was scared, and it's my fault for not picking her up at the airport personally." I look back, startled, and my heart races at him coming to my defense, but my husband ruins it all when he adds, "It was my duty to keep her safe."

Duty.

He's just upset that he didn't cross a task off his checklist, silly girl. Don't be foolish enough to see anything beyond what exists in his intentions.

"Oh, you brought her a jewel!" Wilma exclaims, seeming oblivious to how I feel.

He says nothing. He comes closer to me and takes my hand to help me rise from the sofa.

"Choose any ring you want."

Dell opens a box containing several pieces, and I soon see that some would never fit me, as they are large.

"It was my grandmother's favorite ring," he says when I pick up a pear-shaped solitaire.

"Oh, are you sure?"

"Yes."

"I'll take care of it and return it in one piece."

He doesn't say anything. He places the jewel on my finger, and it feels like it was made just for me.

"I'll adjust the rings that belonged to my parents so that we can both wear them. They'll be ready by the day after tomorrow."

I almost say it's an exaggeration, that it makes no sense for us to wear pieces that were created for two people in love, but I don't want to cause more confusion than I've already made.

"Alright."

"I think we should open a champagne to celebrate," Wilma suggests, and at that moment, I'm sure she's forcing a cheerful tone for my benefit, noticing that I'm feeling awkward. "I'm sure this will be the only time I'll see one of you three put a ring on a girl's hand."

I can't hold back a laugh as I glance at my faux brothers-in-law, avoiding eye contact with Dell, though.

"Yes, maybe you're right. It's a good reason to celebrate. And I've never had champagne in my life. I'm excited to try it."

Chapter 27

Dell

"The rings from our parents? Grandma's engagement ring? What are you getting at, Dell?" Vernon asks as we talk in my aunt's library.

I'm only partially paying attention to them. My mind is stuck on what Evelina said when I entered the room.

"Yes, we had one. My grandmother loved her. She lived until the beginning of my adolescence. Then, due to life circumstances, we couldn't have another, but it's on my list of dreams to have a companion. I'm sure that with a puppy, no one ever feels alone."

It's incredible that someone so lonely and young can be so strong. Feelings I never expected to go beyond physical attraction to her beauty are slowly solidifying within me.

Admiration. Affection. Respect.

And something else I can't identify.

"Are you planning to get married?" I ask, teasingly, forcing myself back to reality.

"Not in this lifetime."

I know neither he nor London has any intention of starting a family, so the question was merely to get him off my back, because the truth is I don't even know why I'm having my parents' wedding bands adjusted for us to wear.

"Did you make sure no one filmed her performance?" London asks.

"Yes. I spoke to Eric to check, just to be sure, although they won't be able to help but comment if that's the case."

"Why the hell did she do that?" Vernon asks.

"Run away?"

"No, come out of a cake."

"She needed money. She was robbed by her landlord."

"Son of a bitch!"

"Yeah, but I took care of it."

"You could say what happened at Jack's house was some kind of sexual game between you and your wife," Vernon suggests.

"I don't give a damn what they think of me. I just didn't want to embarrass her. I know I'd die of shame if photos of her in lingerie ended up in the papers."

I take a sip of the whiskey I'm holding, and after several seconds pass without them saying anything, I look back at them.

"What?"

"You started living with her a week ago, less if we consider you were out of New York for seven days, and you're already attached."

"I can't help it. Evelina, besides being beautiful, is..."

"What?"

"Different from the women I've been with."

"Just be careful not to confuse things between you two," London says. "Sending her away with a broken heart, knowing how lonely she is, isn't a fair game, Dell."

Evelina

"I'M SORRY THAT MY BOYS are so difficult to deal with, my dear. I've asked myself many times where I went wrong with the three of them, but looking back, remembering their father, I'm sure it wasn't my fault. My nephew was just like those three heirs."

"I don't mind. In a twisted way, the three of them are sweet."

She chuckles.

"That's a term I've never heard anyone use to refer to my great-nephews."

"I understood that London and Vernon were worried about their brother because of the scene I made by running away. I swear to you that I didn't take it personally. I was protective of my older brother too, even when he became worth less than the food he ate."

"If you want to talk about it..."

"There's not much to say. Just that it was because of Pyotr that I fled Russia."

"I thought it was because of an abusive ex-boyfriend," she reveals, leaving no doubt that the Westbrooks keep everything clear among themselves.

"It was, but they were related."

"Don't you ever plan to return to your country?"

"If everything goes well here, no."

She stretches her thin hand and holds mine.

"I think sometimes God, or fate, carves twisted paths to ultimately do the right thing."

"I don't understand."

"Dell didn't plan for you. In fact, I think he would never let a woman get this close by choice, but in the end, maybe you're exactly what he needed."

"We're temporary, and I can assure you that in the few hours we spent together last weekend, we argued several times."

"As I said, you are the answer I asked the heavens for my nephew. The others need an Evelina in their lives, too."

"Am I being too indiscreet if I ask why he needed to get married? I already understood that it has to do with the family business, but also that it relates to a promise Dell made to his father."

"Did he tell you about that?"

"Yes. Vaguely, but he mentioned it."

"It's a complicated story, my dear, but suffice it to say it involves a war between two families that has been going on for decades."

She sounds sad when she says this, and I decide not to press the issue.

"I didn't mean to upset you."

"You didn't, Evelina. At my age, I love new things, and you've been like a breath of fresh air. Promise me you'll come to visit me more often."

I hesitate because I'm not sure if that's what Dell wants.

"I..."

"Please forgive me if the day was a bit crazy. I shouldn't have let the boys go so far with you."

"That's not it. In fact, I loved every second. On my birthday last year, I was with my grandmother. It was very sad because her battle against illness was nearing its end."

"What did she have?"

"Congestive heart failure. Do you know what that is?"

"No."

"It's a condition in which the heart is unable to pump blood properly, leading to fluid buildup and progressive deterioration of heart function."

"My God, I'm so sorry, dear."

"It's okay. She rested."

"Wait, you said on your birthday last year... Evelina, today is your birthday?"

I feel my cheeks flush.

"Yes. I'm turning twenty. I even asked Dell if he would need me because, if not, I was going to take a walk to celebrate. But I'd much rather come here. I love to talk."

I can't decipher the expression on her face, but I don't have much time to think about it because soon, my husband's voice thunders behind me.

"Why didn't you tell me it was your birthday, Evelina?"

Chapter 28

Evelina

"I didn't think it was important," I say awkwardly. "It's very important. I'm taking you out to dinner."

There's no point in talking to my stupid heart and telling it not to race because this must be how Dell would act with any acquaintance who was celebrating a birthday.

I can feel my heartbeat in my throat.

"You don't have to, but if you really want to, I'd love it."

"Dinner?" I hear Vernon mock. "I have a better idea. I know of a party tonight that could be an excellent celebration for my sister-in-law."

"I don't think that's a good option." Dell glares at his brother, who I now know is the youngest, giving him a look I understand as a warning.

Why? Doesn't he want to take me to meet his friends? Is he afraid I'll make a blunder?

No, it can't be that. Dell knows my background and now also knows I tend to overshare and don't always behave as I should, so if that were the case, he wouldn't invite me to dinner.

The temptation to tell Vernon that I don't want to go to any party because I prefer to spend more time alone with my husband is great, but I think it's dangerous to be alone with him. Dell has already made it clear what he wants from me, and if I allow it, I'll be used and discarded like last night's clothing.

"If I can choose, I prefer the party. I've never been to one, and I've never celebrated my birthday like this."

"I think the hammer has been struck, brother," London interjects. "Evelina has the right to choose how to celebrate her day."

In a bizarre way, the strangest and most aloof of the Westbrooks seems to have taken a liking to me.

Not that he smiled or even showed an openness to friendship, but he has defended me twice now, which I believe is not something very common in his personality.

"What kind of party are you talking about?" I ask Vernon, not paying attention to my husband's closed expression.

"A good party." He smiles with a mischievous look but disguises it when he remembers that their aunt is also present.

"I'm going to need a dress. Can you drop me off at a mall?" I ask Dell and can't resist adding, "I promise I won't run away again."

He doesn't laugh, but I don't mind. I know that in some way, losing control of the situation drives him crazy, and that amuses me.

Besides, celebrating my birthday has made me excited.

AN HOUR LATER, WE ENTER a store with a wonderful scent. I would be very intimidated if it weren't for the fact that Dell is holding my hand.

When we left Wilma's house, he told me he would come with me. I could have played the independent card and said no, but it's nice to have a man who is used to sophisticated places guiding me on what to wear.

As we walk through, the heads of shoppers and salespeople turn to look at us, and I have no doubt it's because, besides being handsome, Dell is very well known in the celebrity gossip columns, from what I could research.

No one with looks like that goes unnoticed by a woman with warm blood running through her veins.

Several minutes later, I'm in a dressing room trying on a short red dress with an open back, almost to my butt, and only a bow tying it around my neck. The neckline is quite pronounced, creating almost a valley between my breasts, but I feel beautiful.

Also insecure, because I don't want, on my first appearance among Dell's friends, to look vulgar.

"Are you alright, Mrs. Westbrook?" the saleswoman asks from outside the fitting room after several minutes pass and I still haven't decided what to do.

She brought me nearly a dozen dresses, in addition to skirts and blouses. I liked everything, but since I have to choose only one outfit, if I could, it would be this one.

I'll probably spend almost every penny I saved on it because just by the feel of the fabric, it shouldn't cost less than a thousand dollars, but the extravagance will be worth it. I have no clothes to wear today.

Even though my bag, the same one I left with the man I thought would lock me in a cage, Dell's former driver, was delivered to me last week along with my belongings from my old apartment, there was nothing there I could wear to a wealthy party. They're casual pieces because Fantini told me he would get me everything I needed in terms of clothing when I arrived in New York.

"Mrs. Westbrook?"

"Could you come in for a second?"

Of all the salespeople in the store, this was the only one who didn't look at me with a disguised air of superiority, and I wonder if Dell chose her to help me on purpose. If that's the case, my ogre husband has a sensitive side.

"Is everything alright?" she says, pulling back the curtain. "Oh, it looks beautiful!"

"I loved it too, but I'm afraid it might be 'too much,' you know?"

"You're newly married, right?"

"Yes, how did you know?"

"Everyone in Manhattan knows the Westbrooks. We would know if you'd been married for long. Now, let's focus on your dress. I don't want to pry into your personal life."

She has no idea how messy my "personal life" is.

"Do you think it's excessive?"

"No, but I can call your husband in here for his opinion. I think that would be best. I'd hate to give a wrong suggestion and cause a fight between you two."

"I'd appreciate that."

I know he's sitting in an adjoining room, where I heard the salesperson who's helping me say that "no one would bother him there."

I was aware that the Westbrooks, besides being gorgeous, must also be very well-known, but I had no idea they were treated like celebrities.

Not even two minutes pass before I hear his voice.

"Do you need me, wife?"

He's performing, of course. He must have said that for the people present in the store to hear, but even so, hearing his voice call me "wife" short-circuits my body.

"I'm not sure if the outfit I chose is suitable for the party."

Without any warning, he pulls back the curtain, and when we're face to face, I feel my legs weaken at the way Dell looks at me.

"Is it too much? Did I overdo it in the choice?"

Chapter 29

Dell

The damned territorial and jealous selfishness in me orders me to say yes. To demand that she only wear this dress in my presence and without panties, so I can fuck her against a wall, just lifting it, while I eat her hard and spank her ass.

The dress is more of a strip of fabric than anything else, but it looks perfect on her, even though I'm sure the damned neckline will leave me obsessed all night long.

I can't tell her she doesn't look stunning just because I feel jealous. Besides not being a liar, I won't let her feel sad just because I don't want anyone else to see what I consider mine.

Is it an insane thought? No doubt. Can I control it? No way.

"You look beautiful," I say, stepping into the booth and closing the curtain behind me.

My temptation does a three-hundred sixty-degree turn, but there's nothing seductive in her expression. Evelina looks insecure.

I put both hands in my pants pockets because the urge to pull her to me is practically uncontrollable.

"What's wrong?"

"I don't want to look vulgar and embarrass you. It's already enough that I came out of Eric's cake in just my panties and bra."

I step closer to her and curl a strand of her hair around my fingers.

"Let's make something clear. You wouldn't embarrass even a king. You are the most beautiful woman I've ever met. Everything about you is perfect."

I see a flush spread across her cheeks.

"Are you telling me this because you want to take me to bed?"

"I want to, I won't deny that, but I'm not an animal and I won't attack you or use dirty tricks to convince you. You don't like casual, and that's all I could offer you. However, regarding the dress, I'm being sincere. You look perfect."

"Thank you."

"I don't want us to be fighting for this time we'll spend together. Let's stick to your original plan and be friends."

"And on top of that, I'll have seduction lessons from the best. I'll observe how you act at the party today to make the women fall for you."

"I don't have a seduction manual, Evelina. I see something I want and I take it. That's it."

She turns her back to me, but even though she's now facing the mirror, she doesn't look at herself yet, keeping her gaze focused on the floor.

My gaze travels from her blonde hair down to the bare back I can only see partially, as it's covered by her hair, and finally, I reach her delicious ass.

I want her to lean her hands against the mirror and eat her pussy with my mouth. To hear her scream my name so loudly that the whole damn neighborhood would hear.

"Ah, yes, I get it. Thank you for giving your opinion on the dress today, Dell. I'd appreciate it if you helped me every time you think I'm dressed inappropriately for the event you're taking me to, or even guiding me so I don't talk too much."

"Don't be so nervous."

"I'll try. Can you call the saleswoman, please? The dress doesn't have a tag, and I estimate it's about a thousand dollars, but I don't want to be embarrassed if it's twelve hundred, so I'd rather ask first."

A thousand dollars? I doubt there's a piece in this store for less than ten times that value.

"Don't worry about that. I'll give it to you as a birthday present. Take whatever you want."

"No. I'm not going to buy the rest of the clothes I tried on because I prefer to wait for that personal shopper. What if I mess up and take something inappropriate?"

I don't say anything. I walk even closer to her, and as if she feels the heat of my body, she shivers, though she doesn't make eye contact with me.

"Choose a gift for today, Evelina. It's not enough to just give a dress to my wife," I say, brushing the hair from her shoulder and touching her bare, velvety skin with the tip of my finger.

I intend to take everything she tried on, but I want her to receive something more because I should have paid attention to the documents and noticed it was her birthday. I feel guilty for this oversight.

I feel her tremble under my touch, and I should stop, but I keep sliding my hand down her arm.

"Anything?" she asks.

"As long as it's not illegal or involves you running away from me."

Finally, her face lifts, and her eyes meet mine through the mirror.

"Kiss me. Let's not do anything beyond that, but kiss me, not as if I'm a woman you think you'll have sex with in a few minutes. Kiss me as if we've just met and you think I'm precious, Dell."

What is she asking me? To act as if I could fall in love?

I should refuse, say that I wouldn't know how to do that, because, for me, physical contact is directly linked to sex.

The two examples of love stories I have in my family went very wrong.

The tragic marriage of my grandparents and the death of my mother, which left my dad unhappy for the rest of his days.

Instead of pulling away, however, I turn my wife to me and touch her face with both hands.

"You deserve much more than I have to offer."

"I know, but right now, it's your kiss that I want. I'm feeling like a princess, and even if just for this moment, I'm choosing you to be my prince, Dell."

Her eyes shine with a mix of hunger and challenge.

"Kiss me," she repeats, but with a touch of vulnerability now that becomes irresistible to me.

I know I should refuse, that all we have is just a deal, but in this moment, all the logic I use as a compass in my life is consumed by desire.

I don't kiss her like I did last week, where only lust commanded me. I do my best to give her what she asked for, taking her lips as if she were a delicate, perfect crystal.

I lean into her slowly and am surprised to find that it's not hard to kiss her this way, too. Evelina is addictive in every version.

She opens her mouth, accepts my tongue, and melts as I pull her to me by her ass. Her hands touch my shoulders, arms, chest, and without any warning, the initial tenderness explodes into a fierce passion.

I bury my hands in her soft hair, holding her still so I can take what I want, and she moans against my lips.

Evelina's mouth is sweet and receptive, tastier than any other I've ever experienced, and I know we just crossed a dangerous line because there's no way I can spend a year by this woman's side without making her mine.

Chapter 30

Evelina

I am consumed by contradictory thoughts. While I know I made a mistake by asking him to kiss me, because I doubt any man will ever be able to turn me into the burning fire he is making me feel right now, I am certain that I could not live the rest of my life without knowing what it's like to be consumed by him.

When he kissed me last week, there was passion and desire, but I think, even in my inexperience, that Dell was acting on autopilot, as he does when he wants a woman.

Now, however, I am sure he knows that it is me, Evelina, his pretend wife who is here, and that makes everything so much more enjoyable for me.

The way Dell kisses me, even in his "gentle" mode, is rough and dominant.

His lips are incredibly warm, and that heat makes me dizzy and needy. As the kiss deepens, I feel a shiver of pleasure run down my spine, every cell in my body reacting to his closeness. It's as if the entire world has stopped, and all that matters is the two of us.

His fingers glide through my hair, sending waves of electricity across my skin.

My heart beats so hard it becomes a little painful, and when I touch his neck, I can feel his racing pulse, vibrating against my fingertips.

The passage of time is irrelevant. Minutes or hours may have passed because all that matters to me is the mouth of the man with whom I will live a pretend marriage.

"Mrs. Westbrook, do you need a shoe to go with the outfit?" I hear the saleswoman ask from the other side of the curtain, and I immediately take a step back, as if caught in the act of doing something wrong.

Dell doesn't pull me back into his arms, but he doesn't need to. I feel tethered to him as if a powerful bond unites us.

"I think that..."

"My wife will want them, yes," he interrupts me. "We'll take everything Evelina tried on, along with matching shoes."

"Thank you, Dr. Westbrook," the woman replies, and I swear I can "see" her smile in her words.

Surely, Dell has made the woman's commission for the entire week.

"You didn't have to. Didn't you say you'd call a personal shopper to see me? What if she doesn't like what I chose?"

"You liked it, that's what matters," he says, waving his hand as if my arguments are nonsense. "Now, let's stop talking about clothes. Was all you wanted from me for your birthday a kiss?"

I swallow hard, knowing relatively what he's trying to say.

My inner coward tells me to say yes, that I'm more than satisfied, but I've never celebrated my birthday as an adult, and I want to take a risk.

"And what if it's not?"

I get all goosebumps as he lowers his face towards my ear, his beard brushing against my lobe. Dell gently pulls at the skin with his teeth, and I nearly combust.

"I'll give you my gift tonight. We're going to the party to celebrate your birthday. You have a few hours to think about whether you want to go home and sleep afterward or if you want to celebrate my way, wife."

"OH, MY DEAR, WHAT A great mess you've gotten yourself into!" Fantini says as I get dressed for the party.

Hours later, my pulse is still racing from Dell's words, but I've decided that I will enjoy tonight. Just this once, I will be happy without thinking about the consequences, and then I can go back to normal.

But what is my normal? I have no idea. I've never lived a period since entering my teenage years where I didn't have responsibilities, bills to pay, or worry that Grandma might pass away at any moment, leaving me completely alone.

I learned during this time that love, even the most sincere, which is what I felt for her, can also be selfish. Sometimes we forget the pain of others because all that matters is our own.

The fear of being alone.

I'm twenty now, and I think it's better late than never to start living. Until the day breaks, I'll enjoy everything I have the right to.

"I know." I force myself to stay in the conversation. "In my defense, I can only say I was trying to keep myself safe. I didn't know you or him well."

I saw that there was a missed call from her on my phone when we got home, surely due to the message I sent her, so I decided to call, mortified but knowing it was the right thing to do.

"And you put yourself in even more danger. How did Dell react? He contacted me. He was very worried about you."

"He reacted well, given the circumstances."

"Ah, wonderful! Now, enough of talking about sad things. Where are you living? Did he put you in a nice apartment?"

"Yes, actually excellent. I'm on the third floor of his triplex apartment."

"What? Evelina, mon Dieu! That wasn't the plan. My dear, I shouldn't interfere, but I like you too much to watch this happen before my eyes without warning you. Men like Dell Westbrook..."

"Today is my birthday." I interrupt her like a coward because I don't want to hear her tell me I'm being foolish for getting involved with him. I know that very well, but I want to enjoy tonight.

"I'm sorry." She shows that she understands my diversion from the conversation. "Happy birthday, dear. Let's hope I'm just being an old fool and overly worried. Will you call me if you need anything?"

"I will, Fantini. And once again, forgive me for not explaining my escape."

"Water under the bridge. Play your part, get out of this rich and scarless relationship, and I'll be sure it all went well."

Scarless hearts don't seem so difficult. I just have to face my pretend husband as a pretend passion, and I think I'll be fine.

Chapter 31

Dell

"She took the part about having fun seriously," Vernon says, gesturing toward Evelina, who is dancing with some "friends" she made at the party practically since we arrived.

"It's her birthday." I pretend not to care that my wife is shining like a bright beacon amidst the fog of Manhattan's high society.

Besides being gorgeous like a goddess, Evelina is charming, which has turned her into a wink from the queen of the party.

She hasn't done anything to annoy or make me jealous. I even made sure every male in the place knew she was mine, and yet I feel irritation spreading across my skin as I watch her act as if I don't exist.

And since when did I care about that? It's not the first time I've brought a woman to a party, and I've never cared if she had fun on her own.

With Evelina, I feel like a Neanderthal wanting to claim his woman.

"I could never do that," he says.

"What?" London asks. "Get married? We're both in the same boat."

"No, that middle ground. No one needs to be an expert in relationships to know you two are hot for each other, Dell. And then what? Just let her loose? What if she wants to hook up with some guy?"

"She and I have an agreement," I say, not clarifying that until dawn, she will be mine because that's no one else's business.

On the way here, Evelina made it clear that we only have today, and what, in any other partner, would seem like a winning lottery ticket, given it's with her, pissed me off that even before anything happens between us, she's sure she'll be immune to me the next day and won't want *more*.

"What? Behind closed doors? Because if I may say so, you should clarify that to the guys who are drooling over her. In six months, a year, whatever timeframe you set for the marriage to end, with Evelina rich and if she wants to live among Manhattan's high society, there will be lines of our friends waiting to be with her."

"What are you? A fortune teller? Evelina wants to open a candy store and live quietly in a small town."

"Dell, your wife can hide even on a deserted island. With that kind of beauty, she'll attract attention wherever she is."

I down the whiskey in one go. My mood, which has already been shit since we arrived, worsens with images of Evelina looking fucking gorgeous, married to an idiot who will fill her with his babies.

The mental image isn't pleasant, though I can't quite guess why.

"I have an agreement with her with a deadline. As soon as I manage to calm the Tempus Council, there's no reason for us to stay together anymore."

Evelina

"SHALL WE GO TO THE bathroom?" one of the redheads I've befriended asks.

"Let's go. I really need to."

I felt awkward when I arrived. A little intimidated, but soon the girlfriends of Dell's friends made me feel at ease, perhaps because he wasn't discreet at all when he arrived, announcing that I was his wife.

I'm sure this is part of the game, the reason he needs to get married, although there are still some pieces missing from this puzzle.

"You dance really well," the blonde with us says.

"You really think so? It's my first time at a party."

The two look at me as if I've just landed from Mars. And who can blame them? They both know, because I said so, that I'm turning twenty today. I doubt they would understand that in my teenage years, I was struggling to take care of my grandmother, who had no one else.

"You have a funny accent. Where are you from?"

I'm not feeling very fond of her at this moment.

Funny accent? Yes, I have an accent because I'm not a native American, and English is not my native language, but I didn't like the way she said it.

"I'm Russian. I was born in Moscow."

"Ahhhh," she says, exchanging a look with the redhead.

Did I misjudge these two? Are they just bitches after all?

I'm not the most patient person in the world. I also didn't receive the refined education of a princess, so I decide to go in with both feet.

"Could you explain what that 'ahhhh' means?"

"Nothing much," the blonde says. "It's just that so soon after the scandal with the stripper on the yacht, it makes perfect sense he got married quickly. They say that affected the Westbrook family business's stock."

I shouldn't be upset; after all, Dell never deceived me. I knew I was part of an arrangement that was important to him, not just because I already understood that there was some issue involving Tempus, but also because no one would pay ten million dollars at the end of a marriage if they didn't desperately need a wife of convenience.

"Do you work in the stock market, by any chance? Because that's the only thing that would justify gossiping about my husband's company. Did you lose money on some stock play?"

"Wow, don't be so aggressive!" The redhead puts her hand on her chest.

"Aggressive? You two are the rude ones. What kind of person gossips about a husband to his wife?"

"It's not gossip, Evelina. Everyone knew something was behind this marriage as soon as Dell announced it today. We were just the most sincere and curious to ask you."

"Don't talk about my husband in front of me."

It doesn't matter that I'm sure Dell is a shameless jerk; I will never allow anyone to speak of him that way.

"Honey, half this party has already fucked the Westbrooks," the blonde says. "No, wait. To be honest, I think *everyone here* has fucked everyone, except you, who is Russian, of course, and lived in Moscow."

That's the last straw.

"My grandmother used to say that a diploma doesn't take the ears off a donkey. What that means is that having a formal education doesn't make you a better or less stupid person. I would finish that saying. Having money, as you obviously do, doesn't mean you have class. Gossiping is ugly, low, and vile. But doing it in front of a newlywed is the end. Don't come near me again, or I swear I'll tell

Dell what you tried to do by turning me against him. And you must know him well enough to know that my husband won't like that one bit."

Chapter 32

Evelina

After venting my anger—yes, anger because I know what just happened: they wanted to put me in my place because they think I'm not worthy of being married to Dell, while all they probably received was a night in his bed—I stomp out of the bathroom.

Instead of heading in the direction where I know my womanizing husband is, I head in the opposite direction.

The two idiots I just left had taken a tour with me around the house when we arrived because apparently, they are friends of the owner, so I take the opportunity to slip out the back and breathe some fresh air.

A terrible idea, because only when I'm outside do I realize that the night is too cold and that I forgot my jacket inside.

I'm about to go back in when I bump into a man as tall as my husband.

"Excuse me."

"No problem, love."

He doesn't step out of my way, and irritated with the stranger, I cross my arms over my chest to show that I'm not in the mood for flirtation.

Maybe he wasn't present when Dell introduced me to his friends.

"Could you please move out of my way?"

"You don't seem very keen on going back to the party."

I lift my head to look at him.

"I'm taken, so if you're trying to hit on me, be warned that I'm not interested, and spare us both the embarrassment."

He throws his head back and laughs. He's a really handsome man, the kind who attracts attention without even trying.

"I know you're Westbrook's wife, Evelina. I just don't understand how he managed to keep you hidden from the rest of the world."

I notice, when the stranger looks back at me, that although he laughed, he didn't just smile. There's something cold about him. I can't explain it. It's not a feeling of being in danger when around someone evil, but I'm also sure that if life were a movie, he wouldn't be the hero of the story. In fact, he closely resembles the way Dell looks at things.

It's as if he were analyzing me, trying to uncover all my secrets.

"Are you going to tell me what upset you so much that you left the party without a jacket on a chilly autumn night in New York?" He lets his eyes wander over me, but I would say it's almost clinical, not as if he's genuinely interested.

"I'm a bit temperamental. I act before I think. Two women, who probably are your friends too, laughed and mocked my accent. Now, please let me pass."

He takes off his blazer and hands it to me.

"You don't want to go back in there. Wear this and take a walk to calm down."

I bite my lower lip, weighing my options.

If I go back in now, Dell will notice something happened, and if I tell him, he'll be sure I turned green with jealousy.

And am I not? The image of him having sex with a woman on the yacht fills my mind now. Besides, the bitches said he's done the same with practically every woman here. How could he bring me to a place like this?

"Thank you." I decide, accepting the stranger's blazer. "I just need to cool off, and as soon as I'm not in the mood to kill someone, I'll go back and return the blazer." I was about to walk away, but I remember I didn't ask his name, so I turn back to the man. "You know I'm Evelina Westbrook, nice to meet you, but I don't know your name yet."

He takes the hand I offer.

"I'm Seth Jasper Seymour, Evelina, and I have a feeling we're going to be good friends."

"I make friends easily, but that means we can be 'acquaintances,' Seth. To be friends, it will take time."

And I won't stick around long enough for us to get to that point—I finish in my mind.

I walk away from him without looking back, and as I walk, I breathe in the cold night air.

Today was only the first time I went out with Dell, and I've already had a taste of what awaits me. How am I going to deal with this for an entire year?

Dell

"EVELINA DIDN'T COME back?" one of the women who was dancing with my wife, whose name I have no idea of, asks.

"Wasn't she with you?"

"She went to the bathroom with us, but after that, I don't know where she went. Or rather, I saw her going outside the house. If I'm not mistaken, with Seth."

"What the hell are you talking about?"

"Oh, look, I'm right. There's your wife." She looks behind me and then back at me again. "Whose blazer is she wearing if you're still wearing yours, Dell?"

Before I can check what the crazy woman is saying, I hear the voice I hate most assert:

"It's mine. You should take better care of your wife, Westbrook. The poor thing was freezing out there, and being a gentleman..."

He leaves the rest of the sentence hanging, and I don't wait for him to finish. I lunge at the bastard.

I vaguely perceive that the music stops and the lights come on, but I don't care. It's not the first time Seth and I have come to blows, although the last time it happened, we were still teenagers.

I land a punch on him, he responds with another, and we're about to roll on the floor when one of his friends holds him back, just as I'm sure Vernon is doing with me.

"Get close to my wife again, and I'll kill you, Seymour!"

"I don't usually go for taken women, Westbrook, although we know your family has a history of stealing friends' girlfriends."

"You son of a..."

"Dell, no!" My wife steps in front of me. "Nothing happened. I just wanted to cool off, and he lent me his coat when he saw me going out into the cold night."

She takes off the blazer and hands it back to Seth, but I'm still seeing red.

I shake off Vernon and leave the room because I know if I stay here, I'll go after the son of a bitch again.

Chapter 33

Evelina

"What just happened here?" I ask in shock, though I realized a little too late that Dell and Seth, for whatever reason, are enemies.

"You can't get close to Seth anymore, Evelina," London says in a dark voice, shaking his head.

"I realized they're enemies, but..."

"*Enemies?* Our families have been rivals forever, but that's not what I'm talking about. Provoking each other is normal for them, but what happened today... Dell never loses control, or he would have killed Seth a long time ago. Apparently, my brother is very territorial about you, so do us all a favor and don't let Seth get close again."

"Nothing happened. I need to talk to Dell."

"I don't think it's a good idea to go after him right now, sister-in-law," Vernon says.

"Dell would never do anything against me. I'm sure of it. I just want to explain things to him. To tell him it was all just a misunderstanding."

I step away from both of them and head in the direction he went. I think I'm heading toward the bedrooms of the mansion. Dell explained to me when we arrived that the owner, Kingsley, is their childhood friend.

I pass a few couples who are looking at me with curiosity now.

God, are they thinking we're forming some twisted kind of love triangle?

That's just what I need! Instead of helping Dell, I'm making his situation worse because I'm almost certain his need to get married has something to do with Seth.

I don't think twice before opening the doors of the rooms after a quick knock.

In the first, there's no one.

In the second, a couple who seem quite drunk are arguing loudly.

I open two more doors before I see, with great relief, my husband's broad back. He looks out at the night, but even from a distance, I can see how tense he is.

"Dell, nothing happened," I say, entering and locking the door behind me. He doesn't turn around. "I'm sorry. I had no idea they were enemies, and..."

When he finally faces me, his expression is dark.

"You are *my* wife."

The way he says it feels so real, so true, that I'm left breathless.

"I am."

"*My* wife, Evelina. If you're cold, it's *my* damn coat that will cover you." He steps closer. "If you want to eat, I'll go to the kitchen and prepare your dinner. If you want to be fucked, I'll give you everything and much more than you ever dreamed of."

His rudeness doesn't shock me because I remember London's words.

"Apparently my brother is very territorial about you, so do us all a favor and don't let Seth get close again."

My intuition tells me that right now, I should follow the path of desire. It's the only way I'll be able to calm him down, leaving this fight behind.

"You haven't given me my birthday present yet."

"This isn't a good time to play with me, Evelina. I'm on edge."

"And I'm not playing. I told you earlier that we would have today. I'm here, Dell. I don't know what you have in mind, but I'm willing to find out."

Dell

THE STORM INSIDE MY chest, born from hatred for Seth, calms down, transforming into desire.

Evelina drives me crazy in a way no woman ever has.

I feel volatile and irritated because I don't like being so tied to someone who is practically a stranger.

I still can't shake the image of her wearing that son of a bitch's coat, even though I'm now sure, from the expression on her face, that Seth played with my wife, and Evelina was nothing more than an innocent pawn in his chess game.

And yet, knowing he didn't touch her, that I have no right to be so possessive about her, I can't make the jealousy disappear from my chest.

She doesn't flee as I approach; on the contrary, without any idea of how much I want her, she takes a step forward, like a prey choosing to surrender to the predator.

For a moment, silence hangs between us.

Our eyes don't release each other, and when I stand before her, I extend my hand.

"For one year, you are mine."

"No. For *tonight*, I am yours. It's my birthday, and I want my present."

I touch her impudent mouth with my fingertips, the same one that doesn't accept my command like all the others did before her.

Without giving her a chance to escape or a hint of what I'm about to do, I pull her in for a kiss.

There's a rawness to my demand, an urgent hunger as our tongues intertwine in a lewd ballet of uncontrollable desire.

Her softness meets my strength, and our lips press together and devour with wildness.

Evelina

THE SENSATIONS HE IGNITES in my body make me burn with passion, a tension that grows with each passing second, bringing a pulse to the center of my thighs.

His hand glides to the nape of my neck, tilting my head to take everything from my mouth. Our breaths meld together, becoming one.

Dell grips the hem of my dress, and my heart races even faster.

"I'll start here because I can't wait, but I'll finish in my bed. Later, I want you naked and free to scream my name while I fuck your little pussy, wife."

Chapter 34

Dell

Evelina's cheeks are flushed as I lift her into my arms and carry her to Kingsley's suite bed.

She looks like a flower: soft, rosy, surrendered.

Her eyes, however, tell a different story. There's fire in them; in fact, they're like two little flames dancing in her blue irises.

At this moment, I don't care about the agreement or the fact that Evelina lives with me, which could become a problem starting tomorrow. I want her more than I've ever wanted anyone in my life, and nothing could stop me from having her.

I lay her down, and her dress, already too short, rides up even further, revealing her thighs.

I take a step back to look at her, and her breathing becomes heavy.

I lift what's left of the fabric with both hands and go wild when I see the tiny red panties, the lace at the front unable to hide the blonde fuzz of her pussy.

"Is this what you want? Because I'm dying to taste you, woman, but not if you're not sure you want this."

She nods with a movement of her head, her eyes shining with the same lust I feel.

I pull her toward me, holding her by the ankles, but not getting onto the bed as well. Her ass is almost off the mattress.

I no longer hide the hunger I feel for her. My hands slide up the inside of her thighs, the tips of my fingers savoring the sensation of her warm skin, and the closer I get to her pussy, she trembles for me, biting her lower lip, trying to control herself.

I touch her panties, and Evelina is so wet I can feel it even through the barrier of the fabric.

"Damn, baby, I want to drink you for days."

I free her from the lingerie, and like the pervert I am, I bring it to my face to smell it.

I tuck it in my pocket and look at the half-naked woman lying there, waiting for me.

My unplanned wife.

Her body is enough to bring a man to his knees.

Narrow waist and wide hips. Evelina is like an hourglass, curvy from the hips down.

There's something in her face, however, that makes me slow down, even though I'm dying to taste her.

I remember how she asked me earlier today to treat her as if she were precious.

I lower myself, fitting between her legs, and kiss her again.

I untie the neck of her dress and let my lips trail from the curve of her shoulder to her breasts, sucking on a nipple while my hand finds its way between our bodies.

Evelina bites me when I touch her clit, which is hard and swollen. My mouth waters when I imagine feeling it on my tongue.

I alternate between kissing her mouth and sucking on her nipples while continuing to massage her pleasure point, and only when I make her come for the first time and feel her relax do I go for my food.

When I finally have her naked, wet pussy in front of my face, I lick it, relishing its taste.

"Dell..." she whimpers.

"I want to make you scream my name, wife, but for now, I'll satisfy myself with your moans."

I feast on her with my tongue while teasing her clit with my thumb.

"I could stay like this for hours, Evelina. You're so damn delicious."

Before long, she's moaning loudly, begging for more, raising her pussy to meet my mouth.

When I slip a finger inside her gently while sucking her clit, her body trembles violently, and Evelina feeds me with her pleasure.

I suck it all down, drinking her completely, and it doesn't feel like enough.

I kiss her belly and rise, sucking on her breasts.

"Come with me, wife. I need you in my bed."

"Don't call me that."

"Call you what?"

She's got her eyes closed.

"Wife. It's a beautiful name that shouldn't be used mockingly."

The biggest irony? I wasn't being mocking. It came out naturally, and now that she's pointed it out, I'm completely confused.

I put her panties back on, but she doesn't let me close the dress; she adjusts it herself.

"That's why people love sex," she says, a beautiful smile, like a satisfied cat. "I'm still floating."

Something in what she says puts me on alert, even though I can't pinpoint what it is.

She sits on the bed, her eyes directly on my cock.

"Oh! You don't..."

"I'm not going to have you here. I only made you come because I was dying to taste you. You're far more delicious than I could have ever dreamed, but let's go to..."

Fuck, did I just say *"let's go to our house"*? Except that's not *our* house; it's *my* house, and Evelina is a temporary guest.

"Dell?"

"Let's go."

"No. What happened?"

She gets up from the bed.

"I don't want to be a jerk. Remember when you told me to treat you as if you were precious? It's easy to do that, Evelina, because you are. You have a hell of a temper, but even that makes you even more perfect."

"Why do I feel like this is the part where a 'but' comes after?"

I hold her face and kiss her forehead.

"But nothing is going to change. Don't think that just because we're living together... and married..."

She pushes me away.

"I'm not going to think anything. When this year is over, I'll thank God for getting rid of you."

"I didn't say that to hurt you, but I'll never tie myself down to any woman."

She smiles, but her eyes are sad.

"You know that thing you said less than two minutes ago about me being precious and perfect? You just reduced your compliment to nothing by making me feel like all the others you've had. Go to hell, Dell, with all your experience and cynicism. I would never want to be forever with someone like you. A bastard who sees women as merchandise on a supermarket shelf."

"Evelina..."

"Thanks for your 'gift.' You're really good at what you do. My legs are still shaky from the pleasure you gave me. I'm sorry I can't reciprocate. Maybe you should grab one of your merchandise women to satisfy you." She glances at the wristwatch I gave her today from a jewelry store. "It's still early. Maybe there's still time to find a partner tonight. Now, I want to go to the place I'm temporarily living, Dell. See how quickly I learn? I didn't even call it 'my house.'"

She rushes out of the room, and I go after her because for the first time, hurting someone hurts me too.

Moreover, none of what she said is true. I don't want another. There's no way another woman could satisfy me like this.

"I didn't mean to treat you like merchandise. I was trying to do just the opposite."

I hug her from behind before she reaches the stairs that lead to the first floor.

She doesn't try to fight me off; she lets me hold her, but her words are icy.

"I want rules, Dell. Clear rules, not ones that only work for you. I'm going to reread the contract we signed and analyze it item by item. Aside from living on the third floor of your apartment, I will follow them to the letter. You'll have to tell me when you need me, and what happened now will not happen again. I'm worth more than that."

Chapter 35

Evelina

Almost three weeks later

I don't leave the third floor when he's home, and since the night of my birthday, Dell hasn't requested that we appear together. The most that happens between us are text exchanges, always initiated by him, and my replies are short and formal.

I'm going crazy with nothing to do, and when I know Dell is away, like today, for example, I go down to his floor to whip up some sweets because that kitchen is much better equipped than the one on the third floor.

I swear I must have enough frozen desserts to feed an entire city.

Aside from calls to Katya and Fantini, I have no one else to talk to. Even the hope that Wilma would invite me for a snack has vanished because when I asked Dell about his great-aunt in one of our dry text exchanges, he told me she had gone away to spend a few days in the Hamptons because she loves the beach.

I've never been the type to invade someone else's space, but I swear if she called me, I would invite myself to keep her company.

I know that the problem isn't just loneliness. If that were the case, I could solve it by taking some online courses. Dell's house may currently feel like a prison, but it's an incredible prison to be in because it even has a gym.

What I really miss, and I hate myself for it, is how much I long for him.

A bastard, womanizer, detached, and yet, with all those flaws, he managed to penetrate my heart.

Every time we exchange messages, when I say goodbye, I stare at the screen of my phone and see "dots" being typed. They're slow dots, and there's not a single occasion when my heart can maintain a normal rhythm as I wait for what he'll say. In the end, though, he always signs off with a *"take care, Evelina."*

I throw the dish towel on the counter and cover my face with my hands, controlling the urge to cry.

I can't keep going like this. I need to talk to Dell about getting a job. Spending another eleven months in this situation is going to drive me crazy or make me fall into depression.

Dell

"NO, I DON'T FEEL LIKE going to any damn party."

"Damn it, Dell, stop being such a stubborn mule and sort things out with her, then. Even I, who don't believe in love, passion, or any of that bullshit, can see that you've been completely unhappy since you two fought," Vernon says on the phone as I step into the elevator to my apartment.

"We didn't fight. Evelina demanded I never touch her again, and I'm respecting her space."

"*What the fuck! You know exactly why she asked for that. I'm not the best advisor when it comes to love. Maybe you should ask our friend Martín, who's happily married, for advice, but if you want a layman's opinion, any woman in her position would have done the same after you... whatever happened in Kingsley's bedroom, I think any woman would send you to hell if, after you two hooked up, you told her that 'despite living together and being married, you'd never tie yourself down to any woman.' That's the worst kind of shit to say to your wife.*

I could argue that she isn't my real wife, but the fact is hearing Vernon say that feels even worse than when I said it myself.

The most fucked-up thing of all is that not a second has passed since that night that I haven't missed her. Several times, I've gone up the stairs determined to fix things between us, to tell her she was right the first time we spoke when she called me an ass.

When you live your life without ties, sex, beauty, and physical attraction become commonplace. In one thing, Evelina is right. I cataloged her within me as "just another" woman in my universe, even though I knew from the start that wasn't the case. Not only because I made her my wife, but because she intrigues, irritates, and fascinates me all at once.

"I don't want anything permanent."

"*No one does, if I may say so. I think most men, if asked whether they're willing to put a noose around their necks, will say no. I'm one of them, but we can't deny there are success stories. Your friend Martín and his older brother are proof of that.*

"I need to hang up."

"*Dell, I never thought I'd say this to you, but she's not just another one. You're completely enchanted by your wife. The biggest proof of that is that it's been damn three weeks, and you haven't even mentioned Seth's name. You didn't even get angry when he tried to provoke you at the meeting last week.*

"Goodbye, Vernon."

"*You're stubborn as hell.*

"I never denied it, but that's not what's keeping me from approaching her. I don't know how to fix things between us. I ruined her birthday night."

"*Take her on a trip. Screw the agreement, Tempus, any of your business. Focus on her. Make winning Evelina a project.*

"Have you turned into a damn Cupid now?"

"*No, but I love you, brother, and even though I'm sure something like that will never happen to me, I realize you've been hooked. The longer you take to realize this, the greater the chance you'll lose her forever. I'm not talking about forever, Dell, I'm talking about 'let's see where this goes.'*

I stand at the door of the apartment after he hangs up.

I know what I want. The temporary wife in my bed.

In my life.

And after?

I have no idea, but we both have a year to figure it out.

Chapter 36

Dell

I was preparing to take a shower and then go after her, but I'm caught off guard by the smell of food in the air, and when I follow the direction it's coming from, I find Evelina in my kitchen, wearing only a short pair of shorts and a top, her hands covering her face as if she's... crying? Did I do this to her?

I drop everything I have in my hands to the floor and walk toward her, but Evelina seems so lost in herself that she doesn't notice I'm getting closer.

"You're not just another one, and that's what scared me."

She uncovers her face, looking sad, but thank God, she isn't crying.

"Dell, I'm sorry, I shouldn't be here."

She tries to flee, but I grab her by the arm. I think she's so anxious about our unplanned meeting that she didn't register anything I said.

"I don't know what to do with you, Evelina, because I like to have my life planned out, but you're not just any woman. I want you, and it doesn't please me that this desire to be with you, in bed or outside of it, has become uncontrollable. I think about you all day, and I wish I could take back the words I said to you that night. I've never regretted anything in my life, but I can't forgive myself for hurting you, especially when..."

"When what, Dell?"

"Nothing I said was how I was feeling. I've learned to keep things simple when it comes to women. You're unique; something I've never experienced happens inside me every time I touch you."

"I don't..."

"If what you said that night still stands, if you don't want me to touch you, this is the moment to tell me, Evelina, because I'm dying for you, dreaming of your mouth and your body."

Evelina

I'M TREMBLING AS HIS fingers remain closed around my wrist, and I thank God I've already turned off the stove, because I suspect that one more minute in Dell's presence and I'll forget my own name.

Dell says he misses my body and mouth. I'm starving for him.

"I don't want to feel used."

"Let me touch you again, and I'll show you how perfect you are. I'm not using you, Evelina; I'm crazy for you."

The latent tension between us is so strong that it leaves me breathless. Dell's gaze consumes me, demanding and dominant, and I know that the step I take now is a point of no return.

"I want to be touched by you. Reach every part of me, Dell. Show me what it means to belong to you."

At this moment, I don't care how many women he's kissed or had in his bed because right now, in this kitchen, the giant Westbrook is entirely mine.

Dell

HER EYELASHES LOOK like a long, dark layer of silk, and when Evelina lifts her gaze to meet mine after surrendering to me, I'm immersed in her doll-like features for a few seconds.

"I thought about you every damn second we were apart. I'm so obsessed that I ended the business trip three days early because I wanted to at least know you were just a few steps away from me. Wanting you is driving me crazy, Evelina."

When my mouth finally finds hers, I feel as if I'm coming home.

I can't remember the last time I didn't possess something I wanted, or went without a woman, but I stayed away for her benefit, putting her feelings and the determination not to hurt her above my desire.

However, kissing her again, I know I've just lost the game.

Her delicious mouth, paired with the whispers of pleasure as I invade her with my tongue, makes me send to hell the reasons why I know this between us could go very wrong.

I lift her and set her on the kitchen counter, my hands pulling her head and ass, bringing her closer to me to steal as many kisses as I can from her.

I pinch her lower lip between my teeth, and her body moves, coming into contact with my cock, hard as steel.

Our mouths explore each other, the kiss is a battle of teeth and tongue.

After what feels like hours, I pull away so we can breathe and take the opportunity to ensure we're on the same page, that Evelina isn't just swept away by the moment.

When our eyes meet, I get the answer I was looking for.

I see her bite her lower lip and her little hand stretch to touch my face. The movement makes her nipples stand out against her top, intensifying my hunger to have them in my mouth.

The strength of the attraction between us seems to fill the air with our desire, creating a cage where we both willingly enter, trapped by lust.

I notice a vein pulsing in her neck, and my body reacts in a primal way.

I pull her closer by the waist.

I can feel my woman trembling, her nipples pushing against my chest.

Her face is flushed, and when I take her mouth again, Evelina returns the kiss as if, like me, she can't control herself.

There's no longer any disguise for our mutual hunger.

I slide one of my hands down, squeezing the flesh of her ass, and with the other, I open the button and pull down the zipper of her shorts.

"Lift your hips. I need to taste you, and then we'll take a shower. I just got back from my trip, but I don't want to be away from you for a second."

She obeys me, and soon, she's in just her panties and top.

I grip her hips and feel the fabric of her panties between my fingers. I pull her to me, rubbing my erection against her covered pussy.

I tear the lingerie off with a tug and toss it on the counter.

I take her thighs, resting them on my shoulders, inhaling the sweet scent of her arousal.

"My delight."

My wife is breathless and moans when I touch her folds, one finger playing with her clit.

I bury my face between her thighs like a starving animal, and at the first contact of my tongue, she screams and locks her legs around my neck.

I've never felt such desire. I don't just want to fuck her. I want to devour her whole. Lick her entirely.

I look up as I feast on her, and she has her hands flat on the surface, completely focused on me.

I swirl my tongue on her clit, unable to decide between having her right here or just continuing to indulge in her sweet pussy.

I slide my middle finger inside her, not going too deep, and start a gentle in-and-out motion to help her get used to the intrusion, because even my finger feels huge compared to how tight she is.

I make her come and drink her honey, but I don't stop.

I keep feasting on the center of her thighs, and I go wild when I notice the marks my hands and beard have left against her pale skin.

Before long, she's not just receiving; she's letting go, naughty and fiery. She holds my head, caressing my hair, but also as if she's asking me not to stop.

I slide my fingers inside her canal but stop every time she moans in surprise.

"Evelina?"

"I think this is a good time to tell you that I'm a virgin, Dell. I've never done this, so if you're not interested because..."

"*A virgin?*"

"Yes, I lied. I never..."

I silence her with my mouth.

Possessiveness, hunger, lust—I'm a dangerous combination at the moment because all that comes to mind as I carry her to the bathroom in the suite is the certainty that the woman I desire most in life is all mine.

Chapter 37

Dell

I turn on the shower without stopping the kisses. I set her on her feet, finish undressing her, and lifting her up, I lick her nipples because tasting Evelina is like a compulsion.

I let the water fall on her, and as I watch her naked and wet, waiting for me, I strip down without breaking eye contact.

Evelina has the power to turn me into a primate. An irrational being wanting to claim the woman.

I pull down my boxers, and her gaze falls to my cock. She doesn't hide her curiosity, and when I step closer under the water, she touches my abdomen.

"I like how hard you are."

"Was that a pun?"

She turns red.

"No. I was talking..."

Jesus, she's beautiful.

"I'm just kidding, baby. I got it. Touch me. I want your hands on me."

Instead of accepting my command, she lowers her head and smiles. Then she grabs the soap.

"You said you wanted to take a shower. Turn around, Dell."

I turn and brace my hands against the wall, accepting her game because my desire has already crossed the threshold of self-control, and maybe going at her pace will be less dangerous because the last thing I want is to hurt her.

I close my eyes when I feel her soft palms sliding over my back, ass, and thighs. I know she's crouched down because she's reached my ankles.

"Face me now, Doctor Westbrook."

"I have a better idea." I take the soap from her hand and lather it up in mine. "Let's wash each other."

Thirty seconds. That's how long it takes for my plan to go to hell because unlike my wife, who is a good girl and took the idea of bathing me seriously, my hands simultaneously find their way to her pussy and breasts.

And once I touch paradise, I can't pull back.

I rinse her off, lower my head, and take her medium-sized breasts into my mouth.

I suck, switch to the other, and then attack the first one with my tongue.

Addictive, sweet, delicious. Evelina is my downfall.

I lift her, and she screams in surprise, then laughs as I make her straddle my shoulders, her sweet pussy right in front of my mouth.

"Hold on," I order as I lift her slightly and plunge my tongue into her opening.

The remnants of embarrassment she showed in the kitchen are overshadowed by desire, and Evelina grinds against my face.

I make her come as I suck her clit, and when her tremors subside, I lower her down, turn off the shower, and, both of us dripping, I carry her to bed.

I don't give her any rest or pause. I lie down, bringing her with me, sitting her on my face, determined to make her come again. But Evelina isn't a doll to be manipulated. She's fiery and, catching me off guard, slides down my body, settling on my thighs.

"You've given me pleasure with your mouth a few times. I want to learn to do the same for you."

"You don't owe me anything. I'm crazy for your taste. Don't think you have to reciprocate and... damn!" I moan as she interrupts me, trying to wrap her tiny hand around my cock.

"I'm a virgin, but I'm also a reader. You have no idea what we women can learn from books, Dell, so just tell me if I'm doing something wrong."

She licks the tip of my cock, and that's when I realize Evelina is a kind of addiction I've never dealt with. I've been with many experienced women, but none have ever driven me as crazy as watching my Russian learn how to please me.

"Wait a minute. Come here."

I move further up the bed, leaning against the pillow, and bring her along. I grip her hair in my fist, keeping her head where I want it.

"Open your mouth and suck your husband's cock, Evelina."

I pinch her nipple with my fingers, and instead of just tasting, she swallows my head completely.

I moan loudly because damn, it's delicious.

"Use your tongue," I command, as I bring her delicate hand to stroke my cock.

She starts slowly, giving timid licks, but it's not long before she's eagerly taking my half-hard shaft into her mouth.

"I can let you suck me all day if you want tomorrow, baby, but not right now. I'm dying to feel you inside me."

I pull her onto my lap, kneeling, and kiss her.

Evelina, naughty, leans on my shoulders and grinds against the head of my cock. I should stop her, but besides being a delight, knowing she's learning drives me insane.

"I need to grab a condom, beautiful. I assume you're not on the pill."

"Actually, I am, because my period... well... but anyway, I prefer that you use one."

I like the way she talks about sex so naturally, without any embarrassment, but on the other hand, I feel dirty because I perfectly understand what she meant.

Being a virgin, Evelina wouldn't pose a risk to me since she's never been with anyone. I, however, can't say the same. Even though I've always tested myself and never had sex without a condom, I don't want to start a fight over it, even though the desire to feel her without protection is almost impossible to contain.

I lift her, leaving her kneeling on the bed, and go out to get the condom. When I return, I'm completely hypnotized by the blonde sorceress, all mine, waiting for me just as I left her.

I pull her by the neck and kiss her while my hand touches her pussy.

It doesn't take long for me to make her come with my fingers, and I turn her around, positioning her on all fours but facing a full-length mirror in my room.

"As much as I'd love to kiss you while I enter you for the first time, I don't want to hurt you, baby. I'm too big. I need to prepare you."

I see her flushed face reflected in the mirror, and I know that half of it is lust, but part of it is also embarrassment because Evelina looks perfect, but so naughty, her beautiful ass up, hair falling in front of her breasts, waiting to be taken.

I grip her hip with one hand and touch her clit with my fingers.

She's very wet from her recent orgasm, and when I fit myself at her entrance and begin to push, she lowers her head, moaning.

"No, my goddess, you're going to look at us the whole time. You'll remember today forever, wife; the day I made you mine."

In this position, I can have more control to avoid hurting her, and holding her waist, I pump gently, letting the head of my cock feel her warmth.

She moans and pushes her body back, responding desperately to my thrusts.

"Don't do that. You could hurt yourself."

I play with her clit and re-enter her. I spend a long time eating her out slowly, gently, to get her ready for me, but each time, I go deeper, always stopping at the barrier of her virginity.

I have her hair twisted in my fist, forcing her to lift her head.

"You're beautiful. Will you tell me if it hurts?"

"I want more."

I eat her out for more than a minute, and only when I'm sure she's ready, I pull out of her and lay her back on the bed.

I awkwardly position myself over her, but Evelina locks her legs around me.

Her hands pull me in for a passionate kiss, and my ability to wait disappears.

It's no longer just desire; it's need.

I suck her tongue, melding our mouths into a deep dive.

I slide my lips down her neck and bite one breast as I re-enter her.

I start to push, and she's so wet that she opens for me, her pussy sucking me in.

I feel the barrier of her innocence and pause for a few seconds.

"Tell me if it hurts too much," I ask just before kissing her and entering her completely.

She lets out a distressed moan.

"I'm sorry."

"I knew it would hurt. It will pass. Don't stop," she moans as I graze my teeth against her nipple.

I pull out and thrust again, and she squirms.

I force myself all the way inside her, filling her with my cock. I kiss her, staying still, although I'm dying to fuck her the way I want.

After a while, Evelina spreads her thighs, welcoming me fully, allowing me to penetrate even deeper.

I rise up, resting on my elbows, and thrust into her, feeling her flesh around me.

It's slow sex by my standards, but I penetrate deeply every time I traverse her tight body. Soon, she's with me, undulating beneath me.

I kiss her mouth, nibble her neck, and both breasts without stopping my pumping in her pussy, and she digs her nails into my arms, whimpering my name.

Her eyes are open now. Her pupils dilated with pleasure. The pain is forgotten.

I pull all the way out and then back in, possessing her completely.

I clench my jaw because, out of desire, I'd put her on all fours again and fuck her until I hear our bodies slapping together. The lust this woman ignites in me makes my balls tighten with desire, a hunger that borders on insanity.

I capture her lips, kissing her as if the sweetness of them is my source of life.

I bring her legs to my forearms and penetrate her hard and deep.

She trembles but accepts everything, scratching me as I become wilder.

Her pussy is wet, and I go wild at the sound it makes every time I pull out and enter her again.

I suck her breasts, touch her clit, and Evelina surprises me with the intensity of her climax.

She moves like a tigress, screaming loudly, reveling in her pleasure.

She feels so good.

My cock thickens as a warning that I won't be able to hold back, and I kiss her once more just as a strong orgasm hits me.

The connection I feel with her makes my heart pound in my chest.

I should pull out, but instead, I hold her gaze. Her eyes are still closed.

"I want more of you."

Evelina takes a moment to open her eyes, but when she does, I see uncertainty in her blue lakes.

"You pushed me away a few weeks ago."

"Because I didn't know how to handle you. I still don't, but I don't want this between us to end."

Chapter 38

Evelina

I hear his breathing as he sleeps. I dozed off too, but despite making love twice, I don't feel tired. In fact, I'm electric, as if someone has plugged me in and given me maximum charge.

Dell's arms hold me against his chest, and I rub my face against his hard flesh. I love his scent, or maybe it's our mixed scent that I adore.

My God, I had no idea sex could be this delicious. I will never forget what happened tonight.

Thinking about it reminds me that I have a deadline to leave, and that it might be better if I indeed forget about him, about us.

I push the sadness away because I don't want to anticipate the pain. I've lived so little in my twenty years, and I'm getting the chance to enjoy a relationship with a handsome man. Why should I sulk in the corners as if everything has already come to an end?

Maybe, in a few weeks, I'll be tired of him. I'll realize that beyond sex, there's nothing more we have in common — I try to deceive myself.

I think I doze off for a bit, but when I wake up, as if to confirm that what we experienced was real, I raise my hand and touch my husband's beard.

I let out a little squeak of surprise when he grabs my wrist and nibbles my finger.

"I thought you were tired."

"Are you?"

"No. I'm hungry for you, but we can't fuck again because I'll hurt you if I do, so what's left for us is to eat food instead."

"Oh, you came back from your trip and didn't eat anything."

He lifts me up as if I were a feather.

"No, but you were making something, right?"

He sets me down on the closet floor while he looks for a pair of boxers to wear. He lends me one as well as a t-shirt. When I don't respond to him even after getting dressed, he comes closer.

"Weren't you cooking?"

"Sweets."

"What?"

"I'm a pastry chef. Specialist in wedding cakes. I've made more sweets in the past few weeks than in my entire life. If you look in the freezers around the house, you'll see there are various types of frozen cakes."

"Why?"

"I was anxious. Missing you and to keep myself from going crazy or grabbing you, which I thought would be embarrassing, I decided that working on sweets would be the most harmless alternative."

"Did you want me?"

The way he says this, as if he's not sure, stirs something in my chest that makes my heart constrict because it shows a nuance of vulnerability.

"I thought you knew that."

"I thought you hated me," he says, touching my face and leaning down to kiss my mouth.

"I hated you that night. Unfortunately, it didn't last long."

"I ruined your birthday, but I'll make it up to you."

"I don't want you to do anything out of pity."

"Oh, wife, maybe you need to get to know me better to understand that I don't feel pity for anyone. What I'm saying is that I want to make it up to you in some way. Let's travel."

I rise on my tiptoes and try to kiss his chin, but I don't even come close. Dell lifts me up.

"Take what you want."

"Your mouth."

Before long, I'm pressed against the wall and the temperature rises between us. And then, suddenly, when I'm already burning for him, Dell kisses my forehead and then the tip of my nose.

"No. I won't hurt you in any way, Evelina. You're so tight, and you'll feel pain tomorrow, not the good kind."

"I don't know if you realize, but when you say those dirty things, even if you're being sweet, it makes me even more turned on."

He kisses me again, and I feel the rigidity of his sex against me, indicating he's holding back a lot. Dell wants me, and knowing that he thinks more about my well-being than his own pleasure makes me realize that what we have isn't just attraction.

"In a few days, I won't let you sleep, woman, because I'm crazy for you. But not at the cost of your pain."

I hold his face.

"How is this going to work, Dell?"

"Both of us?"

I nod.

"You've been in a relationship, so..." He pauses. "Wait, you and your abusive ex-boyfriend... you never...?"

"There's no ex-boyfriend. I was running away from people who were after my brother."

His lawyers confirmed that there were no pending issues in my name regarding the fire at the café, but I never told him or Fantini the truth.

Dell sets me down on the floor, and his face is serious now.

"Why did you lie?"

He seems genuinely offended and looks at me with suspicion. I can't deny he's right, and still, I feel myself deflate inside.

I had every intention of telling him about the Bratva, but in light of this, I decide to keep that information to myself.

"My brother was involved with dangerous people. They came after me at the bakery. Then they set the place on fire. I was terrified. I left my life behind and ran away. When I met Fantini and she offered me a chance at a marriage contract to get out of Europe, I didn't think twice."

He steps closer and embraces me.

"You will always be safe with me, Evelina. I will never let anyone touch you, but don't lie to me again. I don't handle lies well."

I feel very uncomfortable with the conversation, and even though it's the last thing I want to do, I give a weak smile and try to pull away to exit the closet.

In Dell's world, the villains are other businessmen. In mine, they're assassins who won't hesitate to set buildings on fire. How can I expect a magnate to understand what it means to have a toxic brother who handed me over to mobsters?

"No." He doesn't let me go.

"This will never work between us. We've satisfied our curiosity about each other, but now..."

"We satisfied our curiosity?" He pulls me by the waist. "I'm not a curious boy about sex, Evelina. I'm obsessed with you. I desire you, and I'm throwing my rules as a single man out the window because I want to pay to see what this is between us."

"We didn't agree on this."

"I don't agree with anyone. I'm a heartless bastard who only lives for business and to prevent my grandfather's enemies from gaining power at Tempus, but somehow, you've reached a part of me that's closed off to everyone else, and now, I won't let you go. Don't be a coward. You want me too."

I get angry. I hate that he can read me so well. The words of denial rise in my throat, but I can't say them.

"I want you," I say instead. "I'm afraid of getting my heart broken, but I want you, Dell. It's possible that I might hate you later, that I might even hate myself for letting you hurt me, but I won't run, and if I do, bring me back. Because you're the one I want."

Chapter 39

Dell

"I want you to tell me more about your brother," I ask while we eat one of the cakes she made during the week, still somewhat frozen and with the consistency of ice cream.

Evelina made a sauce for it, which is exactly what she was cooking when I arrived, and after warming it up a bit, she poured it over the dessert.

I've never been much of a sweets person, but I swear to God I've never tasted anything better in my life. The woman is a sugar fairy.

Sitting on a high stool at the kitchen island, side by side, she remains silent, which isn't typical for her. Evelina enjoys talking, so all I can think is that there's still something bothering her about that bastard of a brother.

"I think I've told you everything."

She looks sad, and I wonder if it's because she doesn't want to think about him anymore after what he did, or because there's something she still hasn't revealed.

"No, you haven't told me."

She sighs and sets her fork down on her plate.

"Let's just say Pyotr isn't one of the good guys in this story, Dell."

"I've already noticed that. But we both know it goes much deeper. My younger brother is what most would call a bad boy, Evelina, but London would never put the family at risk with his actions. Pyotr was selfish and irresponsible. You could have been in that store when it caught fire."

"They knew I had left, and I think that's precisely what pissed them off."

"*They?* Who are they?"

"Why should I tell you everything about me, and you don't do the same? One example is that you've never explained to me why you needed to get married."

"It's a complex issue."

She stands up, looking upset.

"You say I'm unique in your life, but you treat me like everyone else because nothing in the world will convince me that you made confessions to your temporary women, Dell."

"Don't mix things up; the reason I needed to get married has nothing to do with us."

"Fine."

She turns her back to me, placing the plates in the dishwasher.

"Evelina."

"I'm not going to force confessions, Dell, but if we're going to keep things this way between us, if there are going to be secrets even about why you sought a wife, don't try to force me to reveal everything about my life."

She was passing by me, but I grab her by the arm and pull her onto my lap, seating her sideways.

"The guy whose coat you borrowed that day, Seth, is my enemy. Or rather, our families are."

"A family feud?"

"Yes, that has lasted for generations."

"I'd like to know more about it, and I swear it has nothing to do with wanting to meddle in your life or your family, but rather because of your fight with Seth the other day."

I stand up with her in my lap and carry us to the living room sofa. I lie down with Evelina on top of me.

"My great-grandfather founded Tempus. He and Seth's great-grandfather were friends. Not acquaintances; real friends, like brothers. My great-grandfather made it on his own. He didn't come from a wealthy family or have a refined education, but he had an unmatched talent, which was the art of watchmaking that he learned from a Swiss craftsman."

"And how did he meet a Swiss craftsman if he had no money to travel?"

"Destiny, for sure. Do you know anything about the state of Connecticut?"

"Where your great-aunt lives?"

"Yes."

"I don't know much about it. Before coming to the United States, I had never heard of it. I learned, upon arriving here, that it's where millionaires who work in Manhattan prefer to live."

"Millionaires with families. It's a good place to raise children, I guess. That's where I grew up. Back to my great-grandfather, he was poor, from a village in Connecticut. Seth's great-grandfather, on the other hand, always had money. That Swiss craftsman moved into a house next to my great-grandfather's parents, and since my great-grandmother was kind to him during an illness, he became friends with my family."

"Was your great-grandfather already born?"

"Yes, he was a teenager but already ambitious at that time. He wanted to escape the life of proletarians that my great-grandparents had and become rich. The Swiss not only admired his ambition but also changed his destiny by teaching him the art of watchmaking. In no time, the disciple surpassed the master. My great-grandfather was meticulous, patient, and had real talent for creating watches.

He started as a small business, but soon everyone wanted to own a Tempus."

"And how does Seth's family fit into this story?"

"As I already explained, the Seymours have always been wealthy. Seth's great-grandmother was impressed by the watches my great-grandfather made and ordered one for her son. And that's how it all began. Seth's great-grandfather, the son of that woman, became fascinated with the watch and offered partnership to my grandfather. They became inseparable. Brothers, in addition to being business partners, and later, when they married and had children, that friendship endured."

"I don't understand. If there was such a strong bond uniting your families, how could everything have gone so wrong?"

"I'll get there. My great-grandfather always held the majority share of Tempus, but Seth's great-grandfather was the second major partner. Just as it happened with their parents, the children of both men, Randolph Seymour and Obadiah Westbrook, became inseparable until my grandmother entered the equation. I won't go into details; I'll just tell you that Seth's grandfather caused a death followed by suicide. He had an affair with my grandmother, and that made my grandfather, who was completely in love with her, kill her and then himself, leaving my father orphaned."

"My God! And Seth's grandfather?"

"He lived for many years. He got married that same year. Started a family, but destiny intervened again. He died in a helicopter crash a few years later. The man who raised Nigel Jasper Seymour, Seth's father, is not his biological father but rather his stepfather. Seth's grandmother remarried. As you can see, we have shattered families because of two traitors—my grandmother and Seth's grandfather—who couldn't control their lust."

"It doesn't seem that simple, Dell. The story has many nuances."

"Nuances?" I kiss her forehead and then pull her off me. I stand up because this is the kind of forbidden subject, just like the death of my brother, and someone from the outside could never understand. "There are no nuances, Evelina. If you have a brother, it doesn't matter if he shares your blood or not; you don't look in the direction of his wife. And if you do, you see her as a sister too, not someone you want to fuck. My father made me promise that I would never allow a Seymour to be a major partner or even the CEO of Tempus."

She looks uncomfortable.

"Why don't you just buy Seth's share?"

"Because the bastard will never sell to me. He hates me just as I hate him."

"And what does that have to do with the marriage story?"

I know she won't like the answer, but I don't like lies. Hiding something is not the same as lying. Until now, she didn't know my reasons for seeking a convenience wife, but Evelina is asking me a direct question, and I have no way to hide this from her.

Chapter 40

Dell

"I was filmed having sex with a woman on a yacht. I'm almost sure it was a setup by Seth. The Tempus board wanted my head after that, which means, to put it bluntly, they would vote in favor of my replacement as CEO of the company my great-grandfather founded."

She looks at me with a neutral expression, and I have no idea what she's thinking, but soon I get my answer, not with words but when she stands up and starts walking toward the stairs that lead to the third floor.

"Where are you going?"

"I need to sleep a bit."

She doesn't wait for me to argue. She runs out, but I catch up with her easily. We arrive at the small living room before her suite.

"You can't run away every time you confront my past. I didn't live in a monastery until I met you, Evelina."

"Don't worry, that didn't even cross my mind."

"Then why do you seem mad at me?"

She finally turns to face me.

"You fought with Seth that day because you saw me as a possession, something that belongs to you and that your enemy touched. It had nothing to do with any feelings you have for me. I'm not an object, Dell."

"A possession? Yes, I won't deny that even though I can't understand how you got under my skin so quickly, I am possessive of you and considered you mine even before we had sex, but I don't classify you as 'something'. I was burning with jealousy and didn't like the feeling."

"Jealousy? I had no idea who he was! I know we don't know much about each other, Dell, but look at me and tell me that if I had known you hated him, I would have even approached him? I have a lot of flaws. I'm impulsive and I might talk more than I should, but if there's one thing I value, it's loyalty."

A stranger. Evelina is nothing more than a stranger in my life, and yet, I believe every word she says, even though trust isn't something I easily offer to people.

"I never doubted you. I was crazy with jealousy because you were wearing his blazer."

Her expression relaxes.

"Very jealous, Dr. Westbrook?" She smiles, stepping back a few paces, and watching her flee makes my blood boil immediately because I know Evelina is playing with me. I know her well enough to see that she's turned on.

"Only with you. You're my wife."

"A fake wife."

"A convenience wife."

"It's the same."

"My woman." I move forward, and she backs away again.

"Too bad you can't show how much I'm yours right now."

I watch, hypnotized, as she brings her hands to the hem of her shirt and pulls it over her head.

"What are you doing?"

"I suddenly felt hot. I think I'm going to take a shower."

"You're a tease, Evelina."

"Never," she says with a smile and tries to turn her back to me, but I pull her toward me.

I take her to the armchair and turn her to face me, making her climb onto my lap, her hands on the backrest.

"I don't want to hurt you."

"I don't care if it hurts a little. I'm burning all over for you."

I smack her firm butt and lean down to bite one of her cheeks. I part them and push my tongue into her already wet pussy.

She completely surrenders to me, pushing her sex into my face and moaning for more.

"I won't come inside you, but I want to feel you. I've never had sex without a condom."

She looks over her shoulder.

"Promise."

"You have my word."

I receive a nod, and I can't wait to fit my swollen, pre-cum slicked head into her tight entrance.

I'm on the verge of losing control because eating Evelina without protection, our arousal mingling, is the most erotic thing I've ever experienced.

My fingers tighten on her waist as I slowly enter her, overtaken by the most obscene lust.

I move just a few centimeters, only letting her have a taste of what's to come, and Evelina squirms, anxious.

I pull her by the neck, lift her, and kiss her mouth, burying my cock deep inside her at the same time.

My self-control crumbles, and with a grunt, I possess her ravenously while the mantra "my wife" pounds in my mind.

The rhythm of our bodies, coupled with the certainty that she is mine, drives me into a spiral of madness. Evelina responds, insatiable, to every thrust.

When she comes, I pull out of her and mark her back with my warm semen. I spread my pleasure over her skin and kiss her again.

"I want to come inside you. Set a deadline for feeling safe, but I need to know what it feels like."
"Why?" she moans as I start to finger her pussy again.
"Because you belong to me."
"Are you mine too?"
"Until one of us wants to say goodbye, I am yours."

Evelina

"UNTIL ONE OF US WANTS to say goodbye, I am yours."

That sentence was what prevented me from agreeing to move into his room.

Dell was upset, argued, but I stood firm.

Yes, maybe he feels a little more than desire for me, but in his mind, I'm still temporary, and I don't want to be kicked out if he gets tired of me first.

"It makes no sense," he says, kissing my hair from behind.

We went to my suite, and even though my bed is much smaller than his king-size one, I feel like I'm still in control of myself by not moving downstairs.

"It makes sense to me. Do we need to fight about this?"

He stays silent for a few minutes and then spins me around to face him.

"You're going to sleep with me every night. In my room, in yours, in the kitchen. Anywhere, you will be mine, so why fight it?"

"Because my intuition tells me you've always had everything easy in your life, Dell. Maybe I came along to dismantle your certainties."

Dell

Two weeks later

"I'VE NEVER SEEN YOU calmer, Dell. You guys, my boys, always seem to be chasing something, as if you never stop to breathe, but I think our Evelina has done you good," *my great-aunt says on the phone.*

Our Evelina.

Yes, every day she feels more like mine, and that seems to have extended to the rest of the family too. Even London seems protective of her.

"I know what you want me to say, Wilma, and the only thing I can assert right now is that our marriage is as real as it can be."

"So it means there won't be a deadline after a year?"

"I don't know if I'm cut out for a *forever*. We've never talked about it either, but I can tell you I can't see myself sending her away from my life for a long time."

"She's yours, Dell, just as you've been taken by Evelina too."

"We don't know each other."

"And you'll have time for that. The initial marriage deadline seems perfect because it's when love blossoms or ends for good."

"Why haven't you ever married?"

"What?"

"You heard me. You could have married, and yet you dedicated your life to taking care of my father when your sister died and then, to us."

"I had a love in my life, but it wasn't reciprocated. You know what that means, Dell? When our heart chooses someone, there's no room for substitutes."

I think of my father and how he never got serious with a woman after my mother died.

"Maybe our family has no luck in love since the only one that lasted for a while ended in tragedy."

She falls silent, and I feel like a heartless jerk.

"I didn't mean to hurt you, Wilma. I know that despite everything, my grandmother was your sister."

"I'm not hurt. I got used to seeing people look at me because I was, at the time everything happened, the sister of the treacherous wife. I'm almost a hundred years old, Dell. Maybe today, if my sister had done the same, getting involved with another man, it would have just ended up in court and finished in an expensive divorce. No scandals or so many hurt people."

I doubt it. The kind of love my grandfather felt for her was what makes a man lose touch with reality. A kind of spell. He wasn't just in love; he breathed her.

"Forgive her, Dell. It's been a long time."

"I can't. Her actions changed the course of our family, turned me into what I am today. You gave us all the love you were capable of, Wilma, but the bitterness and hatred are part of the Westbrooks, and I don't think that will ever change."

Chapter 41

Dell

"I'm looking forward to meeting your wife, Dell," one of the advisors says after a meeting. "You've chosen well, son. Your lady seems lovely. Any idea when heirs will be on the way?"

I glance at my brothers and notice they're both suppressing smiles.

The vultures of the Tempus board seem determined to make me a respectable man.

I've always been sure I didn't want children, but now, the prospect doesn't seem so bad, although I'm not convinced that, given our family history, it's a good idea to bring more Westbrooks into the world.

I think of my father, a man who only knew pain and sorrow from the losses of my grandparents, his wife, and one of his sons.

Not even his marriage to my mother, according to Wilma, could bring peace to his heart. Despite being very much in love with her, as he himself confessed, the sordid history surrounding our family existed like a shadow over him.

Would Dad have liked to be a grandfather? Maybe. Who knows, perhaps that would finally make him feel that our family could start the story again, free of the stains of the past?

"I don't think Westbrook is thinking that far ahead," Seth mocks. "A recent marriage can end in the blink of an eye."

I place both hands on the table, my knuckles turning white from the force I'm using to control the urge to leap across and beat the hell out of him.

I see Ellington Bixby making a subtle "no" with his head. It's something that's quite common in our meetings. He always seems to know the exact moment I'm about to explode.

This time, I decide to ignore the provocation. Seth knows he's losing ground, and his move is like bait to make me throw my self-control to hell.

"We haven't thought about it yet. Evelina just turned twenty. You'll meet her at the charity dinner my family hosts annually in a few weeks."

"Maybe we could even host a breakfast for you," the same man who seems eager for me to become a father says.

Have I suddenly turned from an almost excommunicated man into a saint?

I doubt these same men judging me have been faithful to their wives their whole lives. At least while I was out screwing around, I was single.

"I need to talk to my wife about it, but I don't think it'll be a problem. Evelina loves to talk."

A few minutes later, the meeting that seemed never-ending finally comes to a close.

After the usual small talk, everyone leaves, but of course, my personal demon stays behind, along with Ellington Bixby.

"I'm not in the mood for your shit today, Seth," I warn as I put my notebook away.

"My shit? This isn't a game, Dell. I'm going to take you down. I know this marriage is nothing but a sham."

"Seth, control yourself," Ellington says to him. "In fact, you both, hasn't it gone on long enough for you to understand that you're not teenagers anymore?"

He's been friends with both our grandfathers forever and even witnessed the romance my grandmother had with Seth's grandfather when they were still too young to know what they wanted in life.

Ellington is persistently trying to get Seth and me to put the past behind us, but neither of us is backing down because I'm sure we'll carry this grudge to the grave.

"I'm not doing anything other than keeping control of my family's business, as it should be. Apparently, the Seymours aren't satisfied with stealing other people's women. They also want the business."

"You know perfectly well that without my grandfather, Tempus would have never been more than a backyard workshop. I know what you did, Westbrook. A bastard like you would never marry for love. I'll prove it and bring your reign in my company to an end."

I smile.

"Worry more about your back, Seymour. Have you ever heard that karma is a bitch? Prepare yourself. I don't know the word forgiveness. And the warning I gave you that day still stands. Get near my wife again, and I'll finish you. Keep Evelina out of this. Don't use her to destroy me, or I swear to God, the time for playing nice will be over."

"WHAT'S WRONG?" SHE asks hours later when we're sprawled on the kitchen floor after having sex while my wife was testing a mousse recipe.

"How do you know something happened?"

"Because I've learned to read you a little bit."

"Seth."

"You fought again?"

She traces patterns with her fingertips on my chest.

"The same old thing. He's an idiot who will never stop tormenting me, and the feeling is mutual."

"But was there something specific?"

"He brought your name into our argument, saying he knew our marriage was a sham, which it was at first."

"At first?"

"I don't know if I'm the ideal husband, but I want to try, Evelina. I like having you with me. I'm addicted to you, and that's so much more than I've felt before. I'm not even sure I felt anything before you came into my life."

Evelina

I FEAR HE MIGHT HEAR my heart.

I'm certain Dell isn't the type to make declarations, but what he just told me is far beyond what I ever dreamed of hearing.

"You don't like feeling something for me."

"The men in my family don't fall in love moderately, Evelina. They destroy everything in their path."

"I'm not afraid of you, Dell." It's almost uncontrollable, the desire to say that I'm in love with him, but I hold back.

"You'll never need to be afraid of me. I'm crazy about you. Just don't betray my trust, Evelina."

I prepare to tell the whole truth about my coming to his country.

"I would never..."

He holds my face and kisses my mouth.

"I know, baby. You're good and honest. There's nothing Seth can do to ruin our relationship. The worst that could happen is him finding out you're involved with some criminal organization," he says jokingly, but I feel my blood run cold.

"Why?"

"Because it would cause Tempus's stock to plummet. Nobody wants our company's name linked to misdemeanors or crimes. But you don't have to worry about that, sweetheart. Let's forget that loser and plan our trip. Have you decided where you want to go?"

Chapter 42

Evelina

A Few Weeks Later

"I can't believe I won't be able to go to your wedding," I say to Katya on the phone.

"Don't worry about that, dear. We're getting married in a little town. It's more of a celebration of our love anyway. No guests."

"I'm truly happy for you, Katya. It's amazing that you've known each other your whole lives and didn't realize how much you loved each other. Or rather, that you didn't love each other as siblings only."

"I think we did know, but we were both in denial. I was afraid of missing out on life, of being with him and then regretting not having experienced more. It took me getting my heart broken, dealing with a handful of scoundrels throughout my life, to finally understand that Juhani was my love."

It's a story full of ups and downs. He was married and became a widower. The typical *friends to lovers* scenario filled with misunderstandings that we see in books. The only problem is that in real life, outside the pages of a brochure, the pain is also real and the happy ending is not guaranteed.

"What matters is that you're together now. And speaking of weddings..." I pause, gathering courage to tell her about my relationship with Dell. A relationship I still don't know how to label. "I need to reveal something to you."

About a month has passed since our first night together, and although I've remained firm in my resolve not to move to the lower floors of the apartment, it hasn't mattered much because we sleep in the same bed every night.

Dell comes up and without any ceremony, makes himself at home in my room.

I sometimes feel a bit foolish for continuing to insist on this arrangement, but I'm trying to protect my heart.

"What's wrong? Don't tell me those men..."

"No, God forbid."

"Oh my God! I almost had a heart attack just now."

I know she might feel hurt for not telling her about the marriage, but when I came here, I had no choice. Telling the truth would annul the contract, because Fantini was very clear about that. On the other hand, staying in Finland would put Katya and Juhani's lives at risk.

However, I've already gone out publicly several times with Dell, and by some stroke of bad luck, a photo of us might end up reaching her. And I know that if it happens, it will hurt deeply.

"Don't freak out, please. Listen to me until the end."

"I'm starting to freak out right now, Evelina. Haven't you ever heard that telling an anxious person to calm down is like pouring gasoline on a flame?"

"I got married."

"What?"

"I met someone and..."

"Oh my God! Who is he? Why didn't you ever tell me about him?"

"I met him when I arrived in New York. He's a friend of Fantini."

"Wow, what a scare. Well, everything's fine then, right? The fact that you've only been in New York for a little over a couple of months doesn't matter."

"Don't be ironic or grumpy."

"I'm not trying to be mean, but I worry about you. I'm really sorry for what I'm about to say, Evelina, but I don't believe in fairy tales. If you don't want to tell me the truth, that's okay. But do you remember the photos of Fantini you showed me in the newspapers? She's an ex-rich girl. I read everything about her family. However, she lives in the glamour, which tells me that either she received an unexpected inheritance or she's doing something illegal."

"She doesn't do anything illegal. You have my word."

"Something unconventional, then?"

"I really can't talk about that, Katya."

"I'm sorry. I didn't mean to be indiscreet or make you feel bad, but just tell me: are you happy?"

I sigh as I look at the sunset outside, in my luxurious concrete prison.

Am I?

I feel happy when I'm with Dell at night or when we go out, but living in this house being supported by a millionaire was never part of my plans, even if this mogul is gorgeous and sexy.

"You don't have to answer. Your silence says a lot."

"It's not that. I adore him, but I feel like a doll, being dressed up and taken care of."

"My dream."

"Don't be silly; your fiancé loves you."

"If you're dissatisfied, why not talk to him about it?"

"I'm planning to do that, but he's traveling."

"Hmm... is he a businessman?"

"He's not a mobster," I joke, but then realize it was a terrible joke.

"There are mobster businessmen."

"Yes, I know. My husband is a businessman."

"Look at us, from being pursued by the Bratva to becoming married ladies in the blink of an eye."

I laugh for the first time during our tense conversation.

"I adore you, Katya. I hope to see you soon."

"When the farce of my marriage ends and I have my own money to pay for tickets for you and your love to visit me" I complete silently.

"I do too, Evelina. Don't worry about what I said; it was just concern. I think the older we get, the less adventurous we feel."

She has no idea how right she is about there being much more to this story of my marriage than I've told.

"Don't feel bad. Friends say what they're thinking to each other."

A few minutes after we say goodbye, I'm still gazing at the sunset.

Soon, I'll have to get ready for a charity dinner. Wilma will be there too and has already called me twice to ask if I thought I would look prettier in a light blue or cream dress.

Tonight's event should be fun because every time my aunt and I meet, which has been quite often, I have a good laugh. Other than that, the social commitments we have to attend are tedious and predictable, and I get the feeling that Dell hates them too.

I'm about to get up when the intercom rings.

I also have a unit in the kitchen of my floor. I asked Dell why he bought an apartment with another one independent on the third floor, and he told me he closed the deal as an investment about two years ago, but never intended to stay here forever.

Apparently, the apartment belonged to a famous rock singer who lived with his mother, even as an adult, and to avoid mixing her in the parties he threw, he sent her upstairs. In fact, the walls of my room are soundproof, so I can only imagine what kind of "parties" he didn't want his mother to hear.

"Hello?"

"Mrs. Westbrook," the doorman says. "How are you? Flowers just arrived for you here."

"Flowers?"

"Yes. There's a card too. Can I have one of the building staff bring them to you?"

"Yes, please, thank you."

Dell has given me a lot of jewelry during our time together, but never flowers.

I smile as I go to the lower floor, but I feel strange when I see a bouquet of calla lilies.

They are my favorite flowers, and just that makes my blood run cold because I'm sure I never told Dell.

"Thank you," I say, tipping the staff member.

I close the door with weak legs and grab the card to check who it's from.

"If the dead could speak, your brother would have sent his regards, but before leaving he told me how much you liked these flowers, Evelina. Thought you could escape from me? It's only a matter of time before I lay my hands on you."

Chapter 43

Evelina

"You look beautiful, my daughter, but the perfection of your face doesn't match those sad eyes. What's happening?"

I look at my husband's aunt, all smiles in her new dress, makeup, and hair done, and wonder what she would say if I told her the truth: that I think the Russian mafia has found me.

Across the charity dinner hall, I see Dell talking with some businessmen, but all the while, his eyes are on me. From the moment he told me he had never felt anything for a woman before meeting me, everything changed between us.

It's as if he had given me the opening to enter, which also scares me a little because I have no doubt that, like everything in life, being his chosen one, for however long it may be, comes with a heavy load of expectations.

I massage my temple, feeling sharp pains at the sides of my head.

God, I need to tell him about the note, but I lost my courage after Dell joked about me being related to a crime organization.

I observe the men around me, many of whom Dell introduced as members of the Tempus Board, those who have the power to remove him from his position as CEO and hand it over to Seth.

They seem formal, and it has nothing to do with their age; it's as if they are very traditional to the point that I feel super awkward, not knowing how to act, both around the men and their wives.

"I'm tense, that's all. It's my first time at such an event."

Half of what I said is true. I do feel anxious, and not even the weekend Dell took me to spend in the Hamptons fifteen days ago allowed me to relax.

How will I manage to sleep after the note I received?

"It doesn't look like it. The trip you took was too short. Why don't you convince Dell that you should go somewhere wonderful for at least fifteen days?"

"It would be paradise," I say distractedly.

"What would be paradise?"

I didn't even notice he had approached, but I shiver when I feel his hand on my hip.

"Wilma is saying we should travel."

"Evelina is tense, and if you want my opinion, it's because she's locked in that apartment all day alone."

"Are you?" he asks, sounding confused.

"I always worked. I feel useless."

"Why didn't you tell me this before?"

"Maybe because you, my dear, are like a steamroller. You take charge and act without asking," Wilma says.

I feel guilty.

"He had no way of guessing, Wilma."

Dell pulls me close to his body.

"My aunt is right. I have been careless. A friend of mine from Argentina invited me to his birthday at the family vineyard. What do you think of the idea? We can stay a few weeks away, getting to know that country."

It's like receiving a balm after days of agony. I can postpone telling him about the note a bit longer. Maybe this trip will bring us even closer, and when I tell him everything about my past, Dell will already be sure that my brother and I are completely different from each other.

Yes, because after thinking a lot, I came to the conclusion that what was said in that note is a big lie. Pyotr is not dead. I'm not important enough for the Bratva to still be hunting me.

I think it was Pyotr who sent me the flowers. I texted Katya, asking her to inquire about my brother with our former neighbors, and one of them said they were sure they saw him strolling down our old street some time ago.

"I would love to," I finally respond. "But I don't know how to speak Spanish."

"No problem. They all speak English."

"Go, Evelina," Wilma says. "Have fun for me. Give my regards to Rosario, Dell, and..."

She stops speaking and looks over my shoulder. As I turn, I see Seth entering with a red-haired woman beside him.

"What is he doing here?" I ask.

"The institution was founded by our grandparents when they were still friends. Dismantling it would take too much work," Dell says through clenched teeth.

"And besides," Wilma continues for him, "neither of them would give up the association. Dell and Seth have always fought over everything."

There's a lot of sadness in her voice, and when I turn around, her face matches the melancholy tone.

"Why do you seem to lament the fight between the two? Oh, forgive me. I'm being indiscreet," I say when I remember that her sister was the pivot of the tragedy because she got involved with both friends simultaneously.

"It's nothing, dear. I've gotten used to this pain."

"Dell, could you come with me for a moment?" one of the Tempus directors calls him, and after giving me a kiss on the mouth, he walks away, but I still notice that as he walks, he looks over his shoulder to make sure Seth isn't approaching me.

"I wish they would stop this."

"Why don't you hate Seth? It seems like all the Westbrooks do."

"I'm not a Westbrook. I'm a Carrington, and the women in my family have a weakness for the Seymours."

At first, I think I didn't hear right, but when I look at the elderly woman, I realize her face carries the purest expression of love.

"I don't understand."

"Seth's grandfather was my first and only love, but he only had eyes for my sister, Calantha."

"Oh my God, Wilma, so much sadness in one family! Do your great-grandchildren know?"

"No. And to be frank, I don't even know why I shared this, Evelina. Maybe because you remind me a little of her."

"Do you have resentment towards your sister?"

"No. I miss her. I would give anything to be able to tell her how much I loved her."

Chapter 44

Evelina

Argentina

Three weeks later

"You live in paradise," I tell Tess, Martín's wife, a close friend of Dell.

She smiles at me while keeping an eye on her little girl, Magdalena, who is playing with her cousins a few steps away from us.

"Do you like country life?" asks Lorena, the wife of the older Benítez.

"I don't know. I've always lived in a big city, but I liked being here. I haven't felt this at peace in a long time."

After a trip to Buenos Aires, where we met the rest of the Benítez family—the matriarch Rosario and her husband, Urtiga, as well as the youngest brother, Simón, a surgeon, who keeps his thoughts to himself, although if I could guess, he is attentive to everything around him—we came to the farm they have on the outskirts of the capital.

Both she and Lorena are wonderful. Friendly, simple, and pleasant, very different from the women I met in Manhattan who are part of the Westbrook social circle.

Tess also told me that they have another farm in Texas, because although, in theory, her and her husband's main residence is in Buenos Aires, they both love being in the countryside, close to the horses they raise. Martín retired a few years ago and is still considered the greatest polo player who ever existed.

"But if you could choose?" Lorena asks.

I'm sure neither they nor their husbands have any idea that my marriage started as a farce.

And is it real now?

I'm not sure.

"I prefer smaller places. Manhattan is beautiful, but where Wilma, my husband's great-aunt, lives, is a perfect place for..."

I stop myself because I was going to say "to start a family."

Jesus, Evelina, where is your head? You don't even know if this marriage has a future, let alone think about kids!

"A perfect place to live when the family grows?" Lorena completes, as if guessing my thoughts.

"Yes, for a couple who desires them, I think it would be much better to live in a house away from the hustle and bustle of the island."

"Why do you seem uncomfortable when talking about this?" Lorena insists. "Haven't you two talked about children?"

"No. My relationship with Dell is complicated."

Now, both of them laugh.

"Trust us, Evelina, our marriages didn't start like a fairy tale," Tess says. "In fact, perfect relationships that follow a straight and precise timeline mostly happen in romance novels. In real life, people make mistakes, suffer, regret, apologize, and forgive."

I smile, thinking that she is clearly in love with her husband, and maybe because of that, despite seeming to have a relatively realistic view of a love story, she is also very romantic.

"Our relationship is based on physical attraction."

"All start that way, but do you see yourself with Dell in the future?"

"Yes, I see myself with him forever, but it doesn't only depend on me. There are many issues that could put our marriage at conflict."

"Like what, for example?"

"I have a brother, and he is not a good person. I left Moscow because of something he did, and now, I suspect he is trying to reconnect with me."

"Are you afraid of him?"

"If you had asked me that a while ago, I would have been sure the answer was 'no,' but now, I'm not so sure anymore."

"Tell Dell."

"I will, soon, but right now, Dell has his own problems to deal with." I smile and get up because I don't want to confess anything more, and I also don't wish to be rude to the two of them. I think that perhaps a friendship is forming between us. "I didn't come here to make you sad or worried about my life. Let's take a walk on this beautiful farm. I've never seen a cow or a horse in person. Can you show me?"

About an hour later, I notice Dell stepping away from the porch, where we were all sitting, to answer the phone.

I watch him from a distance and can tell, just by his body posture, that it's something related to Seth. When it comes to his enemy, Dell changes.

He is smiling, though, so it must not be something bad.

I get up and walk toward him as soon as he finishes the call.

"Is everything okay?"

The ironic smile widens as he types something on his phone and then hands me the device.

It takes me about five minutes to read the entire article.

"Is what's written here true?"

"And what does it matter? I'm happy to turn his life into chaos, even if it's a temporary hell."

I think about the conversation I had with Wilma at the charity dinner, and that she also told me that Dell had no idea that he loved Seth's grandfather.

"Your hatred can hurt the people around you."

He pulls me into his arms and kisses me on the mouth.

"The only people I truly care about are you, my brothers, and Wilma. As for the rest, suffering is part of life."

I come very close to telling him that it's exactly about the aunt I'm talking about, but Wilma never told the truth to her great-grandchildren, and this is not my secret to reveal.

Chapter 45

Dell

New York

"Would you like to live in a place less busy than Manhattan?" Evelina asks as she wakes up and goes to the panoramic window of our suite.

After we returned from Argentina, without saying a word, she simply moved her things here.

I have a controlling temperament. Ordering and being obeyed is part of my world, but I've learned that the sweet as honey Russian has a strong character, and I'm fascinated by these contrasts in her personality.

"I never thought about it. Why?"

"Nothing. Just a conversation I had with Lorena and Tess where they asked me about it because they saw how happy I was on the farm."

I get up and wrap an arm around her waist.

"All my businesses are here."

"I'm not holding you to anything. Besides, we don't even know what will happen to us in the future. It was just a comment."

I don't like the idea that she might be preparing for an end. I don't see a future without Evelina in my life.

"We could find a house in Connecticut."

She spins in my arms, and I can read dozens of questions on her face.

"A house?"

I nod, while thinking that the surprise I prepared for her might not work as well as I expected if she really wants to leave the island.

I've noticed that she has been introspective. With me, she acts as always. Passionate and delightful, but I notice that sometimes she stares off into space as if her mind is elsewhere.

I thought it could be because of the jerk of a brother, so I concluded that Evelina needed to have her life back, and what better way to do that than by working on her sweets?

I had three stores in mind to buy where she could set up the bakery, but I sensed she would like the one located on a quieter street.

Evelina's question about leaving Manhattan now only confirms that she doesn't really like the island's hustle.

I intended to surprise her since the store I bought as a gift was the one that needed renovation the most. But with her desire to leave, I might have overstepped.

"Yes. If you want, you can start looking, but I would advise you to wait a little.

"Why?"

"Maybe you'll change your mind about leaving."

"I like when you say 'we're leaving,' husband."

"Because that's what will happen if you decide to leave, my Russian. You're tied to me, and you'd better remember that."

Dell

"HOW LOW CAN YOU GO, Westbrook? Involving a child in our fight? But what could I expect from someone from your family?" Seth says, passing by me in the Tempus hallway.

"As low as you paying that exotic dancer to beg for us to fuck outside the yacht. Which means there are no limits to what I would do, except kill you, to see you in the gutter, where you belong."

"Metaphorically speaking, right? I have more money than time left on this damn planet. I could stop working for several lifetimes and still be a billionaire. You'll never see me in the gutter, Dell."

"Yes, it was a metaphor. When I say 'gutter,' I mean being kicked out even as one of the directors of Tempus. What do you think will happen at the next Board meeting? They don't tolerate scandal, Seth, especially from someone who isn't really an owner, but a usurper."

"There will be payback, Dell. I'm going to deliver that with interest. You can bet on it. Enjoy your days of happiness in your fake marriage. It has a countdown."

The bastard found out that Evelina is my weak spot and doesn't hesitate to push that button.

Before I realize what I'm doing, I lunge at him.

I don't reach him, and Ellington Bixby intervenes, stepping between us.

"Not here, guys." He sighs, as if exhausted. "In fact, nowhere. Neither of you is old enough for this kind of thing. I was friends with your grandparents, and nothing makes me happier than having you, Dell, and you, Seth, still in charge of Tempus. But I swear to God I will recommend to the Board that both of you be removed if a scene like this happens again."

"This time he crossed the line, Bixby," Seth says.

"As much as when you approached my wife to hit me at that damn party. I warned you, Seth, but I'll say it again. Evelina is off-limits. Don't cross the line because I swear to God, if it happens, not even the risk of losing my position as CEO of Tempus will stop me from killing you."

"I'm not afraid of your threats, Dell. I'll do whatever it takes to destroy you. If you're sure of her love, why worry? A woman who truly loves her man doesn't cheat."

The reference to my grandmother is clear, and only the risk of hurting Bixby, who remains between us, prevents me from punching him.

"She may have been disloyal, but your grandfather had no honor, Seth. You don't touch another man's woman."

For a second I see him waver, but soon the expression closes again.

"Go to hell, Westbrook. My grandfather saw her first. If anyone should feel ashamed, it was Obadiah Westbrook, a murderer."

"Stop!" Bixby says and suddenly puts his hand on his chest.

Immediately, Seth and I help him. Perhaps the first thing we've ever done together in life.

"Call the doctor," I ask as I easily carry the elderly man to my office.

Two hours later, with the counselor hospitalized with a heart attack scare, I propose a temporary truce, or at least in front of him.

Bixby was friends with our grandparents and suffers witnessing our hatred.

"Only in his presence," Seth agrees. "But every one of the promises I made you today still stands, Dell. Wait and you'll see."

Chapter 46

Evelina

Days Later

"What are you up to?"

"Nothing much. Just felt like cooking."

"Because I can't stand being cooped up anymore" I complete in silence.

Dell has been tense because the scandal involving Seth's name has brought repercussions, which has made me postpone my conversation about my brother.

He comes home irritated and only calms down after we make love for hours.

He is affectionate and passionate, but I see in his eyes how tormented he is.

I don't know how someone can live like this since childhood, and even understanding the trauma of his father, how hard it must have been for a child to find both parents dead, I don't think it was fair that Heywood Westbrook placed such a heavy burden on his son's shoulders when he was still a boy.

By recounting his pain of having been the one who found his parents dead, my late father-in-law made Dell's revenge against the Seymours mandatory. He grew up with no choice.

None of the other Westbrook heirs knowing the truth also prevents my husband from sharing the load he carries.

Dell is good and honorable. To spare his brothers, he let them think that his hatred for the Seymours stems only from the love triangle between their grandparents and Seth's grandfather, but from what I know of him, I know it also comes from knowing that his father, from the moment he found Calantha and Obadiah Westbrook dead at home, had his childhood decimated.

"Why do I feel like you're not telling me everything, Evelina?"

"I don't like your tone," I say, irritated and guilty at the same time. Dell is very perceptive. "I can't stand being cooped up inside the house anymore. I'm not a doll, Dell. I wasn't raised to be one. Since I can remember, I literally put my hands to work. Our freezers are already overflowing with frozen sweets."

"What do you want to do?"

I feel very awkward about what I'm about to say, but the alternative is to stay silent and be treated like a supported wife. There's something my grandmother always repeated:

"No matter what your profession or life choice is, you need to have a goal."

Mine has always been to make the most beautiful wedding cakes in the world.

However, from the moment those men entered my shop in Moscow, it's as if my dreams have been suspended in the air.

"I know we have an agreement, but I need to have something to do or..."

"Or what, Evelina?"

"We never talked about the future. What will happen when our year is up? I want to pursue my profession. I'm sorry if it's not glamorous or will embarrass you in front of your friends, but it's what I know and love to do."

"I would never be ashamed of you. When we get home later, we'll talk about it."

AN HOUR LATER, I AM walking through the food department store.

It's like an amusement park for me, especially the candy section, because they have products from all over the world.

Suddenly, I feel watched and glance back, certain it's one of the bodyguards. I asked them not to come in with me. There are two, besides the driver, and every time I leave the house, they follow me like shadows.

Dell hasn't said anything, but I think he believes Seth might harm me, as things between them are getting worse.

Although I sympathize with my husband regarding the Seymours, I don't think Seth would be capable of something like that. In fact, Dell wouldn't like to hear this, I'm sure, but I believe that Seth and he are very similar. Two sides of the same coin, but not in a negative connotation.

Both heirs, Westbrook and Seymour, carry the stigma of avenging their ancestors and are lost in a sea of hate, but they are both good men.

I glance back again when the feeling of being watched persists, but I see no one.

In the next half hour, I distract myself looking at jarred sweets and thinking that it would be ideal to reopen a café while I can form a clientele for my cakes.

Suddenly, someone grabs my arm and pulls me to a part of the store where there isn't a living soul.

The shock is so great that at first, I can't even scream.

"Let me go."

"Shhhh... calm down. It's me."

"Pyotr, what are you doing in Manhattan?"

"What do you think? I came to see you."

I pull away from his grip.

"I don't want to see you. I haven't forgiven you for sending those men after me."

"I didn't do it on purpose! They threatened to kill me and to let me go, I said you could pay the debt."

"You're a liar!" I say with disgust, feeling a lump form in my throat because I no longer recognize this man in front of me as my brother. "You destroyed my life!"

Blood doesn't make anyone siblings. Dell and Martín aren't biological brothers, and they love and respect each other.

"Don't be dramatic. I did you a favor. If they hadn't gone after you, you would have stayed in Moscow, on that filthy street, selling your pathetic cakes. And now, look at you." He takes my hand. "Just these gold and diamond rings you're wearing must be worth over a hundred thousand dollars."

They're worth much more because they are family heirlooms, but I'll never let him know that.

"Let me go, or I will scream."

"If I were you, I wouldn't do that. In fact, if you're smart, you'll do what I say. I need money."

"As always. You're a bum. You only care about gambling. Will you never grow up?"

"Evelina, lower your tone with me, or I'll leave here and go straight to the newspapers."

"What?"

"You heard me right. You'll do what I say, or I'll go to the press and say you're the one addicted to gambling and ran away from Moscow because you didn't pay the mafia."

I feel bile rise in my throat.

"No one would believe that! A quick search would show it's all a lie. My life story speaks for itself."

"I know, silly, you've always been boring, never knew how to enjoy, but by then, the scandal will be formed. What do you think your millionaire husband will say when his wife's name appears in the newspapers?"

"How do you know I'm married?"

"The old-fashioned way. I put your name on the internet. When you disappeared from Moscow, I figured you'd run away to Europe, but look at the surprise. Now I have a millionaire sister."

Chapter 47

Evelina

"I never thought I would say this, but I hate you, Pyotr. I can't love you anymore. You've turned into a monster."

"I've turned into one?" He laughs. "I'm not to blame if you kept seeing the teenage boy in me, Evelina. I grew up and learned to prioritize myself."

"Being a selfish liar, a scoundrel, and dishonorable is now called prioritization?" I look at him with disdain. "Katya was right; those men going to the café after me was a rigged game. You sent them there knowing I would never be able to pay off that debt. How could you? I'm your blood. Didn't you care what they would do to me?"

He shrugs.

"You're beautiful. The boss I owed was looking for a Russian wife. I thought it would be the perfect arrangement."

"You're insane. We're not in the Middle Ages. How could you think of 'arranging' a relationship for me against my will?"

I think about the irony of my situation. In having to flee from the men my brother owed, I ended up falling into a similar type of relationship. The difference is that my husband has more honesty and honor in the pinky toe than my brother does in his whole body.

"I'm not crazy, I just have a plan: I want to retire before thirty."

"I'm worried about you, brother. You've clearly lost your mind. How could you retire if, as far as I know, you've never worked a day in your life?"

"You're going to provide that for me, Evelina."

"What?"

"I want money. Five million dollars. That will be the price of my silence to avoid causing a scandal in the newspapers. I've researched your husband. Despite being a womanizer, from what I've seen in the headlines, he's never been involved in anything dishonest. He owns several companies worldwide. What do you think will happen to the shares of all the Westbrook companies when a scandal involving your name explodes in the media?"

"My God, Pyotr, you urgently need psychiatric help."

"What I need, and will have, is money. I know you, Evelina. You must be in love with the man. You hold the key to your happiness in your hands, sister. Give me the money I'm asking for, and you can live your fairy tale."

"Never. I will tell Dell everything."

"I have a partner."

"What?"

"Someone who knows about you and your husband. If you turn your back, with a touch on my phone screen, that person will leak the news to the media. You have two days to make a decision, Evelina. But don't play with me. I'm serious. One slip-up on your part, and I'll ruin your love story."

Hours later

"WHERE ARE WE GOING?" I ask, straining to keep a neutral tone when inside I'm still trembling from my encounter with my brother.

Dell got home, and even though our phone conversation felt strange, he's excited now.

"I was going to take you to see something, but if you're not in the mood, that's fine."

It's like watching a gas balloon pop.

"No. I'm sorry. I want to go."

He takes off his blazer and pulls me into a hug.

"What's wrong?"

"I have a headache."

It's a partial truth. I really have had a headache thinking about how I'm going to tell Dell that I need five million dollars.

But, on the other hand, wasn't this our agreement?

My God, I don't want to do this, but what choice do I have?

"Is it just the headache bothering you?"

The question makes me pull away from him and take a step back.

"What else could it be?"

"The bodyguards told me you spent almost an hour in the gourmet food store."

"I didn't know there was a timed limit to be there."

"You came back without any bags, Evelina."

"If you want to imply something, just say it outright."

"I'm not implying anything," he says, sounding irritated. "I'm asking you what happened that made you stay in a store for so long and not buy even the chocolate you love from there."

"Dell, I'll say it again. If you want to accuse me of something, just speak up."

He steps closer, and his expression is dark, furious, and more serious than I've ever seen.

"Don't lie to me."

"What?"

"If you ever want to leave this marriage, just say so, and it will be over. But don't betray me."

"You must be crazy."

"Then tell me why you took so long in that store."

"Let's do it differently. Why don't you put a chip in me like a pet you can track?"

"You won't be able to turn the tables. I know you're hiding something from me."

Guilt crushes my chest like a one-ton stone.

"You're paranoid."

I turn my back and leave him alone in the living room because I'm sure if I stay, I'll start to cry.

How could everything be going so wrong? If I don't fulfill what Pyotr asked of me, he goes to the newspapers, and that will not only destroy my marriage but also prevent Dell from honoring the promise he made to his father because surely the board will replace him as CEO of Tempus.

I hear his footsteps behind me.

"I know you're not telling me everything."

Because I fell in love with you and would rather let you go than ruin your life. And that's exactly what will happen if I don't do what my brother commanded.

I look at him, and it's like a curtain falls before my eyes because now I understand what he's thinking.

"My God, Dell. I would never betray you. How could you even consider that? I love you. I hate myself for being so foolish and for falling in love with you, but I love you."

Chapter 48

Dell

I waited for this. For one of us to put into words this madness that explodes whenever we're near each other. But without any familiarity with feelings other than desire, I didn't know how to name what I feel for her.

I walk up to my wife, forcing her back until she leans against the wall of our suite, where she fled.

I have one hand open on her throat, keeping her gaze from drifting away from me.

"Repeat what you just said. Not the part about the vow. Tell me about your love. About our love."

Evelina

I SWALLOW HARD WHEN I feel the tension in him because it smells of danger, but also passion.

"I love you. I don't care if it wasn't what we agreed on and... what? You want me to talk about our love?"

He doesn't answer. He just kisses me.

He devours me with fury and need, a feeling revealed through our caresses, poured over our bodies, so intense that it's almost tangible.

Dell doesn't take my clothes off.

He rips them off in seconds, and then his go too.

I tremble with anticipation. Desiring his possession. Silently pleading for him to make me forget the past and swear that all that matters is the two of us.

"Say you're mine and no one else's," he commands as he lifts me up, his hands under my thighs, a finger testing the moisture of my sex.

"I'm yours. Wife, lover. The woman who loves you, Dell."

Dell

SHE GIVES ME EVERYTHING, and it's good that she does because I won't settle for anything less than all of her.

Her body, her love, her life. Everything belongs to me, just as I will lay the world at her feet.

The desire I feel with Evelina always straddles a fine line with insanity, but this time it's mixed with the certainty that what I feel for her is love.

I consume my woman with my mouth. I swallow her sighs and moans, and when I penetrate her, I test how wet she is with long strokes to prepare her, because soon, I'm fucking her with ferocity.

She whimpers, raising her hips, sinking hard onto my cock, feeding my hunger and desire.

"You're a turn-on. My naughty wife."

Standing, I angle my body, driving into her with passion.

Evelina is so light that I can hold her up with one hand while I possess her and touch her clit with the other.

"Ride, wife. Show me how well you've learned to mount your man."

I fuck her hard, and her little pussy, already completely slick, takes all of my cock.

I suck on her nipple as I penetrate her deeply. I push with greed while pulling her into me.

Her body pulls me in, and my hand massages the rigid knot, pressing her clit enough to make her beg to come.

I hammer hard, going in to the limit of my balls.

She bites me.

Her hands grip my neck, pulling me closer.

She keeps her gaze locked on mine, and soon her hips move, restless, her pussy welcoming me, sending tremors of pleasure down my spine.

I nibble on her ear.

"Be a good girl and come hard for me. As a reward, I'll fill you with my seed, woman."

The words make her tremble, and when I caress her clit, I feel small spasms around my shaft.

The beats of my heart are as powerful as a hurricane, knocking everything around it down.

Erasing what I thought I knew about relationships, creating a new universe where she is my queen.

And when Evelina finally comes for me, I kiss her and spill inside her. My orgasm is so intense that it spills into both of us, but I don't want that; I want my seed inside her, and I take her to bed, bringing her legs over my shoulders and keep thrusting, pushing my pleasure deep inside her body.

"You are mine."

"I know. I always knew, Dell."

The next day

"WHAT WERE YOU FEELING yesterday?" I ask as I watch her prepare breakfast for both of us.

I know everything is fine because we spent the night awake, filled with fucking, kissing, and talking.

Evelina told me about her childhood and adolescence, and how much she loved her grandmother.

I shared how it was growing up with brothers and even managed to talk about Lee, though I didn't delve too deeply into the topic.

"I don't like feeling financially dependent on you," she says, not meeting my gaze, probably because she's embarrassed to touch on the subject of money. "I've always worked. I'm used to paying my own bills."

"You have no bills to pay here. Everything is included in the stay," I say, just to provoke her.

"You know what I mean."

"From the moment you moved in here, I opened an account for you, Evelina. There are twenty million dollars in it. Unlimited credit cards too. Didn't you ever open the envelope I handed you the day after I brought you to this apartment?"

"No. I thought it was a copy of the contract to remind me not to run away."

"Come here, love."

I watch her turn off the stove where she was making pancakes for us and then come over to me. I spread my legs and fit her in between them.

"I don't want to seem mercenary."

"The money is yours."

"That's not what we agreed on. It was supposed to be ten million at the end of the contract."

She seems uncomfortable.

"Spend it on whatever you want. I don't mind. Buy clothes, baking molds. Or maybe, open a shop."

She was looking down, but now she meets my gaze.

"A shop? What are you talking about?"

"I have a surprise for you, but I'm not telling you today." I close my eyes, irritated. "I'm going to need to travel."

"Where to?"

"To the other coast. I'm having problems with one of my companies in Seattle."

"Will it take long? I'll be anxious to know what my surprise is."

"Self-interested."

"Very. I married you for your money, Westbrook." She covers her face with both hands. "Forgive me. I should never have said that, not even joking. It's not funny."

I kiss the tip of her nose.

"I know you wouldn't do that. I trust you, Evelina."

"I love you, Dell. Never forget that."

Chapter 49

Evelina

"My eyes are swollen from crying, and I promise myself that I will meet my brother this time and never again."

"He will get the money he wants, but first he will have to leave the United States. Only then will I make the transfer. That's what I told him on the phone yesterday when he called me. However, he demanded that I give him ten thousand in cash today, so I had no choice but to withdraw that money from the bank."

"He agreed to leave the country; after all, he would have to be crazy to give up five million dollars. I threatened him and said that if he blackmailed me again, I would tell Dell everything and let my husband deal with him."

"The truth, though, is that I don't know how Dell would react if I revealed the truth to him. He is very suspicious, and now he is finally giving me some room in his life and heart."

"Two days ago, he traveled and is not expected back until the weekend, but even so, I hate having to act behind his back, even if I'm trying to protect him."

"After what Pyotr did to me, handing me over to those men in Moscow, I wouldn't doubt it if he went even further."

"I lower the hood as I enter the hotel where I agreed to meet my brother, acting like a criminal, since I sneaked out of the house away from the bodyguards."

"I could never justify to Dell a stop at the bank to withdraw ten thousand dollars, and surely his employees would tell the boss about this 'stop' to get money."

"Although the idea of seeing Pyotr makes me want to vomit, I focus on the fact that this will be the last time I meet him. There is nothing left between us."

"Feelings, or even memories. I can no longer remember the boy from my childhood. Pyotr has turned into a despicable man, whom I am increasingly hating."

"The hotel is cheap."

"I head straight for the elevator after checking the room number on my phone one last time."

"The smell of cigarettes fills the hallway as the elevator doors open. I go to the odd side and soon find myself standing in front of room three."

"I ring the bell just once, and finally, I am face to face with my only living relative."

"I know this will be our last meeting, so I memorize all his facial features before saying anything."

"Was Pyotr always like this? A soulless bastard? Or was it something that happened throughout life that changed him? I will never know."

"Don't look at me with that pitying face, Princess Westbrook. I hate bitches who think they are superior."

"I don't let him see how much his insults hurt me."

"Here's your money, Pyotr," I say, handing him the bundles of cash I carefully kept in my huge bag. "I meant it when I said that if you blackmail me again, I will hand you over to Dell."

"I don't intend to do anything, Evelina. You can rest assured, but before you go, I want to talk to you."

"We have nothing to talk about."

"He sighs."

"I know you'll never want to look at my face again, but at least don't hate me so much."

"You just called me a bitch."

"Forgive me."

"Spare me your lies."

"I'm not doing this for me, but for Grandma. She wouldn't want us to part on bad terms."

"It's too late, Pyotr."

"Please, have a coffee with me, and then I will never bother you again."

"As long as you leave the door open."

"What?"

"You heard me. Don't close the door. I don't trust you."

"Fine," he says, sounding hurt, but I can no longer believe anything that comes from him.

"I pass by him, keeping as much distance as possible so as not to touch him, but barely step into the room and I know I made a mistake because I see a syringe approaching my neck.

"Pyotr, what have you done?" I ask as I feel my legs lose strength and my bag fall to the floor.

"You're an idiot if you thought I would settle for five million dollars, Evelina. I was approached by someone powerful, and he offered me six times more to bring you into a trap, little sister. I hope you enjoyed your fairy tale because tomorrow your husband will never want to look at your face again."

Seth

About an hour later

"WHY MEET HERE? THE hotel is a dump," I say as I take a sip of whiskey.

"Why not? We needed privacy, and it had to be a place that wouldn't attract attention. We both want the same thing: to destroy Dell, and he can't suspect that I came to meet you or my plans will go down the drain."

I focus on the person in front of me while pretending to believe what he is telling me.

I didn't get to where I am for nothing. I have the blood of the Seymours running in my veins, and I'm naturally suspicious, so I wonder how I never suspected that they might have been playing me and Dell simultaneously, feeding our mutual hatred, which has always existed, with even more resentment.

I paid the exotic dancer to screw him in public. He unearthed my past. Neither of us is playing fair.

I want Tempus. He doesn't want to leave the CEO position he's held for years. Our war will never end. However, the meeting with this person today feels like something beyond that.

I see in his features that he has a plan, which is basically to pretend that we are friends and that he is on my side to destroy Dell.

No, you don't just want to destroy Dell, you want to destroy both of us. Why?

"What do you have to tell me?" I ask because I'm not in the mood for this shit. I intend to get out of here as soon as possible and then figure out what else this being is planning against us.

I raise the whiskey glass for another sip, but my hand trembles, and I can't bring it to my mouth.

At the same time, I hear a moan, as if it comes from an adjoining room.

I turn to face the person who invited me to this meeting, but my eyes close, no matter how hard I try to keep them open, until finally, my eyelids weigh irrevocably, and darkness takes over.

Chapter 50

Dell

I had already intended to return early. It's what I do whenever I can because any time away from her feels too long.

I laid my head back in the airplane seat, anticipating the moment I would have her naked beneath me. The moment I would arrive home and be greeted with a passionate kiss. The moment I would inhale the scent of my wife.

At the door of our apartment, I press the device, and I don't know how it doesn't break, given the fury I feel.

But I can't break it because it holds the proof that I made the biggest mistake of my life by letting my guard down around her.

When I think I'm calm enough to enter, I enter the code that will unlock the door, but the lights are off.

I head to the kitchen, as if my mind is playing a trick on me, telling me that everything will go back to the way it was, that nothing I just saw happened.

Evelina isn't there either, so I go to our bedroom and finally find her.

It feels like a *déjà vu* of a scene we've lived through so many times. She stands in front of the panoramic window, looking outside.

I close my eyes for a second, and even though she might hate me for this weakness, I want to immortalize the moment, because this will be the last time I am with the woman I made my wife.

Nothing will ever be like it was, and everything we lived was a lie.

"Evelina."

She slowly turns to me, and I can see from her face that she is scared.

"Dell, we need to talk."

"No, what you need is to disappear from my sight."

"What?"

"I know everything."

"It was a setup. I swear it's not true. Wait. How would you know?" she sounds confused. "See? It's the biggest proof that it was all a plan."

"I don't believe you."

"Dell, I know you're angry because you hate Seth and..."

"Don't say that bastard's name in our... in *my* bedroom, fuck! What happened, huh? You wanted to keep playing your game with your lover, but he decided to stop? Of course, he would stop. He got what he wanted!"

"You don't know what you're talking about."

"I don't?" I unlock my phone and throw it on the bed because even though I hate her in this moment, I still love her, and being near her feels like having a knife stabbed in my chest.

I see her walk with her head down to the bed, but I can't be moved; it's all an act. Evelina is a traitor just like my grandmother was.

Seth won, because Tempus is nothing compared to what I'm feeling for having been deceived by the woman I wanted to spend the rest of my days with.

She looks at the screen, and I notice she shudders as she scrolls through the images because I know what she saw in the first one.

The diamond ring that belonged to my grandmother alongside the wedding band my father bought for the woman he loved, on Evelina's finger, while her hand rests on the abdomen of that bastard.

Apparently, they're both asleep, but of course, it was all a setup by Seth, the final blow to destroy me.

"Dell, I would never do this to you. I love you."

She drops the phone as if it burned her.

"Tell me that's not you in the picture, Evelina. Try to convince me you weren't in lingerie on a bed with my enemy."

Evelina

I CAN'T HOLD BACK THE tears, although I sense they will do me no good. Dell is unmoved by weakness because he is a fortress.

When I woke up a few hours ago in that hotel bed with Seth, I initially screamed in panic, believing he had violated me. However, even when I pushed him away and started yelling that I would call the police, he didn't move.

I got dressed and fled, certain he was asleep. In my confused mind, all I could think about was that I needed to get out of there because I remembered my brother's last words before I passed out: he told me that someone had paid him six times more than I would have if he helped me end my marriage.

When I encountered Seth, I was sure it was him, but I thought they were setting a trap, that Dell would arrive and catch us together, so I ran.

I got home, calmer now, and realized something was wrong. Seth was drugged too. I have no idea who set this up, but it must be an enemy of both who wants to turn us against each other.

I tried to call the hotel and gave the room number to an attendant, saying that a friend of mine was there.

I was afraid that, since he hadn't woken when I left, he might have overdosed, but with great reluctance, the receptionist told me the guest in room three had already left the hotel.

I felt relief knowing he hadn't died, but at the same time, I was scared of why my brother wanted us both together if it wasn't for Dell to catch us in the act.

Now, I know.

Someone photographed us.

"I can't. I was there, in bed with Seth, but it's not what you think. I..."

"Get out."

"Dell, I know you're angry, but let me explain. It was all a setup. My brother drugged me and..."

"Your brother drugged you? Your brother is in Russia, Evelina."

"Please, let me explain. I didn't tell you everything. My brother is no good; he set me up. He came here and..."

"And threw you on a bed with Seth? That bastard sent me those photos, Evelina. He wanted me to see. In the first one, you have..."

"Please, don't say it, or you'll never be able to take those words back. I know what was in the first one. I swear to God, Dell, it's all a setup. I wouldn't touch another man, much less while wearing your family's jewelry."

"Read the message I received on my phone with the photographs, Evelina."

Reluctantly, I pick up the device again.

"I don't need her anymore. All yours now, Westbrook, but I must say you have good taste. She's a delight."

"I'm going to kill him when I find him, so if you're thinking of looking for him when you leave here, I swear you won't be with him."

"Dell, I'm not your grandmother. I've hidden some things from you. I ran because my brother got involved with the mafia. They're the ones who set my café on fire."

"You're a compulsive liar. You lied about the abusive ex-boyfriend, and now you're throwing the Russian mafia into this story? Did they also force you to jump into Seth's bed?"

"*Seth's bed?* It was a dive hotel. I went there to meet my brother!"

"Get out of my house. Take whatever you want. The money I deposited in the bank will still be available to you, but I don't want even a tissue of yours here. All I need from you when you move out is your address so my lawyers can contact you to discuss the terms of the divorce."

"I love you, Dell. I know you're hurt, so I'm going to a hotel so you can cool off, but I'm not going to give up on you."

I don't care if I'm crying or humiliating myself because I can feel he's hurting too.

And then he says the words that change everything inside me.

"I don't want you anymore. Get out of my life."

Chapter 51

Evelina

A week later

"You don't need to stay here, my dear. Come to Marseille with me," Fantini says as I open the door to the small apartment I rented.

The day I left Dell's house, I was so dazed that I spent the night in a hotel near where I used to live. A frightening dump, but the only thing I could afford.

I had about a thousand dollars in savings when I moved in with him and never spent a dime. That's the money I'll use to support myself until I can get a job. I don't want a penny from him, and I've shredded the credit and debit cards he opened in my name. I threw everything in the trash.

I spent that entire night crying and feeling completely alone, but the next day, I knew I needed to take action. I don't have a prince to save me. I'm the princess in this story, but I'm also my own guardian and warrior. I have to take care of myself.

I made a step-by-step list of what I needed to do to remove the Westbrook surname, and the first logical step was to find Fantini.

With the internet provided by the hotel, I spent hours on the phone, via Skype, with the Frenchwoman responsible for bringing me to the United States.

This time, I told her everything in detail, and the first thing she did was tell me to move to a decent place.

I told her I intended to pay her back as soon as possible, but she said I had more to worry about right now than money.

I accept the embrace she offers.

"The offer is tempting, but I don't want to give Dell any more reason to think I'm a gold digger. I don't want a penny from him. If I leave, he'll think I'm running away to get more from the divorce."

"Evelina, he called me."

"I don't want to hear it."

It's not the first time she's tried to bring up his name. We talk every day, and when I told her everything the day after I left Manhattan, she cursed him with foul names, but I noticed that in recent days, she's been trying to soften what happened.

"But you need to."

"No, I don't need to. All I want is your help to get divorced. I won't see him or talk to him. Please, I'll sign anything, as long as I never have to look at him again."

"Dell offered a generous settlement, but he demands a meeting with you."

"The time for him to demand anything is over. More precisely, when he kicked me out of his life."

"You're hurt, but don't be emotional. You're entitled to a generous portion of his money. Dell said you aren't returning his messages."

"I keep my phone off and... Oh my God!"

"What happened?"

"I withdrew ten thousand dollars from the bank and gave it to my brother. Is that why he wants to talk to me? Is he going to accuse me of theft?"

"Your brother is a miserable wretch who deserves to rot in jail, but believe me, ten thousand dollars to the Westbrooks is equivalent to a cup of coffee, Evelina."

"Then I don't understand what he wants from me."

"We'll only know if we go to this meeting."

"Would you go with me?"

"My dear, I'm not leaving this country until you're divorced and safe financially."

"I won't take a penny from him, Fantini."

"Dell is offering a hundred million dollars in exchange for meeting with you. A mere meeting, dear."

"No. Not even if it were a billion dollars. I don't want to look at him again. Dell broke my heart. He stomped on it. I know the photos were horrible, but what about everything we lived? Doesn't that count? I'm not his grandmother. I would never betray him with anyone, especially not with the man who is his greatest enemy."

She looks at me as if she thinks I'm making a mistake, and I know she thinks that regarding the money, not because my heart is broken. Fantini is a practical woman above all.

"Is that your final word?"

"Yes, it is."

She sighs dramatically.

"Then I have an idea."

"An idea?"

"Convince me that you're the best wedding cake baker in the world, and I'll invest in your business."

"What?"

"I have more money than time left to live, dear. I want to do something good instead of looking back on my deathbed and only seeing two hundred thousand dollar handbags and expensive shoes in my closet. But first, let's move. Choose a city where you'd like to set up your business, and we'll relocate there."

For the first time in days, I feel alive.

"Are you for real?"

"I am, indeed. And a sinner too. I lied to you when I said I didn't believe in fidelity. I loved only one man, and to him, I was faithful, but I had my heart broken just like yours is now. I know what it's like to be young and alone. I had the advantage of being rich; you don't. Pretend I'm your fairy godmother."

Dell

"*She doesn't want any meeting or is interested in your proposal, Mr. Westbrook,*" Fantini says on the phone when she answers.

"Evelina isn't leaving this marriage if I owe her anything. I want to settle the score."

"*For that, you would need the power to turn back time and fix what you did, Dell, which is impossible. Evelina told me the whole story, from the beginning, and one day she will realize she lost the love of her life because even over the phone, I can tell she is suffering. She wants nothing but the divorce. Set your terms and do it as quickly as possible.*"

"Why the rush?"

"*Because when it's over, she will be free to love and be loved. Her life is none of your business, Dell. You don't deserve to hear this, but I will say it anyway. Evelina won't be alone. I will support her like a mother would. Ease your conscience, which must be heavy. And stop making offers for a meeting. She doesn't want to see you for any amount of money in the world.*"

Chapter 52

Dell

"I don't care what she wants. We're not going to end this marriage like two fugitives from the law, Fantini. We started with a contract where both parties knew what they were getting into."

"*You can't force her, Dell. Not even with all the money you have, you can't make Evelina look at you.*" Her words are like a knife in the middle of my chest. I shouldn't have to force the woman I love to be with me, but wasn't it I who pushed her away? "*She's not a criminal on trial. Evelina just wants to forget you ever existed in her life. And if your concern is about the ten thousand dollars she had to withdraw from the bank to pay her brother's blackmailer, rest assured. I'll replace the money.*"

"Ten thousand dollars?"

I have no idea what she's talking about. All I know is that Evelina never touched a penny of the large sum in the account I opened for her.

"*You know about Evelina's brother, but you probably don't know about the Russian mafia that made her flee Moscow.*"

"There's no mafia. The night she left, Evelina told me about it, and I went to check. I hired people in Moscow to confirm the story. It was her brother's lie. Pyotr Volkova is a petty thief."

"*How do you know?*"

"You have no idea how far I would go to find out the truth, Fantini, and that includes hiring people who don't walk on the right side of the law. It's likely that the men who tried to scare her, if the story she told you is real, were just her brother's associates trying to extort money from her."

"*Let's clarify something. She didn't leave. You kicked her out after months of treating her like a queen. Evelina went back to the neighborhood she lived in because all she had in the bank, being hers, from the savings she made before meeting you, was a thousand dollars. She spent the night crying in a filthy hotel. Only after she spoke to me did I relocate her to an apartment.*"

"She had money in the bank to buy a place if she wanted."

"*Your money, which she didn't want to touch. Maybe you should leave your throne and step into the streets, walk among common people, decent human beings, Dell. From what I'm seeing, this conversation is pointless. Have a good day.*"

"Keep talking to me, Fantini."

"*For what?*"

"I need to know."

"*Evelina fled Moscow because she was sure the Russian mafia was after her.*"

She explains the whole situation from the beginning, probably how Evelina relayed it. The newspaper report about her café and then the phone call from Pyotr Volkova on the same day asking for money from her sister. Then the appearance of the men and her escape to Finland.

I hate that everything she says makes sense. No matter how much I don't want to believe this surreal story, it seems true.

"The mafia wouldn't send warnings. If Pyotr Volkova 'sold' her to someone, they wouldn't give a deadline. They would have taken her from day one. Either he was bluffing, or..."

"*What?*" she asks.

"Or he actually intended to negotiate her, but to someone else. Some pervert who thinks a woman can be bought."

The thought makes me sick. Thinking of my wife in the hands of someone who would treat her like an object assures me I would become a murderer if I laid hands on that unfortunate soul.

The night Evelina left, I spent the night drowning my sorrows with my brothers, with a bottle of whiskey.

There was no conversation among us. I didn't show them the pictures. I just told them what had happened, and they stayed with me.

Yes, they were with me, as they always had been my entire life, but my wife, on the other hand, had no one. She found herself utterly alone in a hotel with no security.

I feel like I've been punched in the stomach, as her tear-streaked face that night flashes in front of me.

"It doesn't matter anymore. She's safe now. I won't let anything happen to her."

"It's not your duty to protect her. It's mine."

"*You should have thought of that before you kicked her out. Evelina doesn't want anything to do with you, Dell, and certainly, she doesn't want your help. I'd say she would prefer to go to jail for some scam her brother is involved in if it spills over to her rather than accept any assistance from you.*"

Her voice remains flat when she says this, and it doesn't seem like something spoken to hurt me, but rather what she believes to be true.

"Finish telling me about her brother. I have men searching for him around the globe, but we haven't found him anywhere."

"*Evelina wanted to tell you about the supposed mafia and also about Pyotr, but you were caught up in your war with Seth for power at Tempus, as she explained to me, so she was afraid you would kick her out thinking she would jeopardize your business.*"

"The faith I had in the love I feel for her was minimal."

"*And the opposite isn't true, is it? The fact is that Pyotr started blackmailing her. He sent her flowers at her apartment pretending to* be the mafia, but this time, Evelina didn't believe it because even for a young girl like her, the Bratva chasing her in Manhattan was a bit much. The bastard didn't give up. He followed her on a day she went to a department store. He said he wanted five million dollars; otherwise, he would go to the papers and claim she was involved with criminals, which, of course, would cause her company's stock to plummet."

"I wouldn't care about the stock. I'd do anything to keep her safe. If she had trusted me..."

"Do you admit you were wrong?"

"I want to hear the whole story first."

"You're very stubborn, Dell, and only because I believe you truly love her, I'll tell you. Evelina prepared to give him the money, but she also warned him it would be the only time, and if he insisted on it, she would tell you the whole story, even at the risk of losing you. In that last meeting, at the same hotel where the photos you saw were taken, Pyotr drugged her. Evelina woke up in a bed, only in lingerie, with Seth next to her."

"I'm going to kill him," I repeat what I've been telling myself since the night the images were sent to me.

Seth has disappeared. He's not in the country, and I can't find him anywhere.

"*I don't know if Pyotr was in cahoots with Seth or not,*" she says, indifferent to my threat "*but Evelina believes he wasn't.*"

"What?"

"*She told me Seth seemed to have been drugged too because when she woke up almost naked next to him, she freaked out. She started screaming, and even then, he didn't wake up.*"

"And who would do something like that? There would be no interest for Pyotr to involve Seth in this. Besides that, Evelina's brother didn't know about my enmity with him."

"*She told me that before drugging her, Pyotr revealed that someone had paid him six times more than the five million dollars he would receive from her. I don't know what your problem is with your partner, Seth, but maybe you should pull back a bit on your hatred and consider that you both might have a common enemy. And that this person, man or woman, wants to destroy you both. Now, the reason they want this, I have no idea, and it's none of my business. I'm accepting to talk to you on the phone to tell you that Evelina wants the divorce. If you don't arrange it, I'll find a lawyer with her, and we'll do it ourselves."*

"It will have to be a contested divorce. I won't grant it until I clarify this story."

"*It won't make a difference. You've lost her, Dell.*"

The words hammer in my brain as I finally accept that I made the biggest mistake of my life.

"*No, I haven't lost her. If Evelina is hurt with me, it's because she still loves me. I'm going to fix everything between us.*"

"Good luck with that, but don't get your hopes up."

Chapter 53

Dell

After I hang up, I see my brothers staring at me.

"You're fucked," London is the first to speak, since the phone is on speaker.

Even though he's the angriest and most vengeful of us three, he has had a strong connection with Evelina from the beginning, and from the moment he learned what had happened, instead of aligning with my anger, he strangely remained neutral.

"I can't believe Seth is innocent," I say.

"It makes sense, considering he disappeared," Vernon says. "If Seth were behind this, why wouldn't he be here gloating about having destroyed your marriage?"

"Because he knows I'd kill him."

"No," London says. "It doesn't fit with Seth to run away. He'd love to see you suffering for losing your wife, especially in a situation of betrayal."

"Seth is now a secondary problem. He can't disappear forever. He has family and business here."

"Yes, your bigger problem is accepting that Evelina will listen to you, which I find hard to believe will happen."

"She loves me."

"You love her too, yet you sent her away."

"The scene of our grandparents' betrayal replayed in my head. Exactly the same."

"What?" both of them ask at the same time.

I look at my brothers. I've tried to spare them the pain their whole lives, but now, they are adults and deserve to know the truth.

I stand up and walk to the safe. I unlock it and take out a single photograph. The same one my father showed me when I was still a child.

I hand it to Vernon first, who looks at it and then passes it to London.

"How is this possible?" my middle brother asks, rubbing both hands over his face.

"Our father found this image over our grandparents' bodies when he was still a child. Apparently, someone sent it to our grandfather, and that triggered the tragedy."

I don't need to look at the photo again to understand what it is. It's the exact copy of the pose in which Evelina was with Seth, but instead, it was my grandmother with his grandfather.

"Why didn't Dad ever tell us about this?"

"To spare you. He was the one who found our grandparents' bodies."

I see London's eyes glinting with a bit of madness in them. I know, without him having to say, that he's remembering the day he found Lee dead. It's as if our family is destined for tragedy.

"He should have shared it with us," Vernon says.

"Dad asked me not to. He spent his whole life tormented by the image of seeing them both dead."

"He had no right to ask you that. It was too much for you to carry alone."

"It's done. Years have passed. I learned to deal with it."

"You didn't, Dell. The image of our grandmother's betrayal, combined with Dad's narrative of finding them dead, has marked you forever. Now I understand why, of the three of us, you hate the Seymours the most."

"The story is too strange, Dell," London says. "And I'm starting to believe that Seymour has nothing to do with it. The person who supposedly set this up not only would have to know all about the betrayal between our grandmother and Seth's grandfather. They would also have to..."

"Know about the photograph," I finish.

"And how would they know about it? Unless they were the ones who photographed Grandma and Seth's grandfather in the act of betrayal, or they set it up to be caught, just like what happened with Evelina and Seymour."

"What are you saying?" I ask. "Do you think there was never any betrayal?"

"I think the person who orchestrated all of this, both in the past and today, is old enough to have had the opportunity to interact with our grandparents. That's practically certain," London says. "And in that case, we need to find out why."

"Yes, because if it's true, there are only two names that would be close enough to have been able to conspire something like this," Vernon states, and I know exactly who he's talking about.

"Wilma or Ellington Bixby."

Evelina

Ridgefield — Connecticut

SEVERAL DAYS HAVE PASSED since Fantini arrived, and now I have my life relatively back on track.

We moved to an apartment in a town called Ridgefield, with about thirty thousand inhabitants, safe, picturesque, and beautiful.

Fantini and I are looking for a store so I can set up my bakery. After tasting my sweets, she advised me that this would be the best way to start a business—offering my creations to the locals and letting them spread the word until I build a good reputation among customers.

It sounds like a good plan, and although my heart is still broken and bleeding, at least I've been able to sleep a little more.

Fantini told me about her last phone conversation with Dell, and although she said he insisted on talking to me, I remain steadfast. I don't want to see him because I still love him, and my pride can't handle any weakness if I break down crying in front of him. I don't feel strong enough yet.

I look at the empty store we're thinking of renting.

It's dusty and abandoned and needs a good renovation, which I plan to do myself, just like I did in the café in Russia. I don't want to overburden Fantini's help. I know how to paint and clean. I can also deal with clogged plumbing because my grandmother taught me everything. She wasn't the type of woman who sat around waiting for the world to serve her.

I sigh when I think that I'll have to spend about a month just painting and cleaning the place, but at least I already have the furniture and the counter since, like the property I rented in Moscow, this was an old food store.

Yes, I'll have a lot of work ahead, but I can already see my shop ready, customers sitting at the tables enjoying my recipes, voices chatting and laughter filling the air.

I will be okay — I promise myself. — *I've survived a lot, and broken hearts don't kill.*

And it's precisely at this moment, when I start to feel better and stronger, that my past comes back in the form of the voice of the man I love.

"You can't run away from me forever, Evelina. We need to talk."

Chapter 54

Evelina

In one swift movement, I turn to face him and simultaneously step back until I feel the counter of the shop against my back.

I see an expression that seems to be pain cross his face.

"Don't be afraid of me. I would never hurt you."

I lift my chin, all the hurt I've accumulated over weeks exploding all at once.

"Try again. And I'm referring to choosing a different kind of promise because you've already succeeded in hurting me."

"Evelina, let me talk."

"No. I don't want to see you anymore. I was better off before I met you, Dell, because alone, I knew I didn't have anyone. I hate having experienced love, a family, and then having all of it taken away from me. I apologize for not being honest from the start and for not telling you how dangerous my brother was. I was wrong, but you categorically sent me away, and even if we can forgive each other for our mistakes, I won't put my heart at risk again."

"Your heart is mine."

"It's not," I insist, as the store seems to spin around me. "Just go away. All I want from you is a divorce."

"I won't, Evelina, until you truly forgive me. You are the woman of my life, my only love, and I won't give up on us until you convince me that you don't love me anymore."

"Loving you means nothing. I offered you my heart on a platter, and you stepped on it, shattered it to pieces. I would have to be very stupid to give you the chance to hurt me again."

"I'll do whatever it takes."

"You didn't believe me. You needed Fantini to tell you everything to accept that I would never betray you."

"You set a trap for yourself. I was wrong. I was cruel and unyielding, but some time before, Seth swore he would destroy my happiness."

"To hell with Seth and this cold war you have with him! I never wanted to be part of your game. I'm not a pawn to be moved at your whim."

"I've never seen you like this. You are my life, wife."

"Don't call me that."

"You are my love. I'm here asking for your forgiveness and a second chance."

"No. Go away."

He steps closer to me, and I grip the counter even tighter, mostly due to the physical weakness that has been attacking me for days and feels more intense than ever, rather than fear.

I know he wouldn't hurt me.

I'm angry for having hurt me so much, but that doesn't mean I've stopped seeing who he is or erased from my mind and heart everything we've lived.

"Let me stay."

"Stay?"

"Nearby."

"Are you crazy? I'm not moving in with you again. I have self-respect."

"I'm not asking you to do that, just not to push me away."

It's like having one of my dreams come true when I would wake up wishing that everything that happened between us on the day of my departure from Manhattan had been nothing but a nightmare.

But it wasn't. Dell kicked me out of his world without a second thought.

"You mean to say don't push you away like you did with me? If you want my forgiveness, you have it, Dell, because despite being hurt, I acknowledge that I had a part in our separation, but I can't forget you telling me that you didn't want me anymore and..."

My eyes begin to close. It's as if someone gave me a strong sedative, which I know isn't the case.

I've been feeling unwell. Dizziness, racing heart, swelling in my legs, but I thought it was all due to pain and suffering. At this moment, though, I'm no longer so sure about that. My body feels strange.

"Go away," I ask again, but my voice sounds different to my own ears.

"Evelina?"

I don't realize that Dell already has me against his body or that my hands are gripping his shirt until I feel his breath on my face.

"Dell, I think I need to go to a hospital. I haven't been feeling well."

"What's wrong?"

"Maybe it's the same problem my grandmother had. She had high blood pressure, suffered from congestive heart failure and..."

The words die in my throat as his face, the shop, and the world disappear.

Dell

"WHAT DID THE DOCTORS say?" London asks in the hospital corridor.

He was the last to arrive. Vernon and Fantini, whom I informed as soon as I brought Evelina in for treatment, are with us as well.

I run my hands through my hair, desperate. If it were up to me, I would have taken her by helicopter to be treated in Manhattan, but the fear that something serious might happen to her during the journey, given what she told me about her grandmother's heart condition, made me hesitate.

I stand up, pacing back and forth.

"They don't know anything yet."

"She looks so healthy, my poor girl," Fantini says, her eyes red from crying.

The Frenchwoman has really bonded with Evelina, and for that reason alone, I already like her.

"She didn't complain of any pain? Dizziness?"

"No. I don't think you really got to know your wife well, Dell. Evelina is made of steel. She learned to raise herself. She took care of her sick grandmother when her useless brother only wanted to party."

Pyotr Volkova. The bastard who, like Seth, is off the radar. The man—if you can even call that draft of a human being a man—who has made it onto my enemies list.

I sense a movement out of the corner of my eye, and when I look in that direction, I see a doctor approaching.

"Who is the closest relative of Mrs. Westbrook?" he asks, and I feel a buzzing in my ears, not wanting to believe he could tell me he wasn't able to save her.

Like a sequence of photographs, I replay our story.

The first time I saw her through the monitor in Finland and how her boldness fascinated me.

Her coming out of the cake at Jack's house and how I carried her away over my shoulders.

The moment I made her mine and when she told me she loved me.

Then, like tiny video clips, our day-to-day life emerges in my mind.

Homemade sweets and love on the kitchen floor.

Me awake at dawn, watching her sleep, keeping her locked in my arms.

The smile she gave me when she wanted to tease me.

"She can't be dead!" I shout, feeling each word pierce me like daggers driven into my body simultaneously. "Don't tell me she's dead!"

I've never cried in my life.

Not even when I was a child and my father told me about my grandparents.

Not when, years later, I understood that my mother left too soon.

Not when Lee was gone or even when I found my father's body.

Now, however, I feel tears welling up in my eyes.

The sensation is strange because I wasn't raised to give myself the right to cry.

I don't care. I let the tears come anyway, here in the middle of the hospital corridor because the thought that it might be too late is unbearable.

"I am her husband," I say defiantly, as if telling him not to dare say ex-husband, because my wife cannot have passed away.

"She is alive," the doctor says, and at that moment, I would give him all my fortune just for delivering what I needed to hear. "But I would like to talk to you both together."

"Is Evelina awake?"

"Yes, please follow me, sir..."

"Dell Westbrook. Her husband," I repeat like a proud fool, grateful at the same time for having a second chance.

Chapter 55

Evelina

"I don't want him here," I say as soon as I see the man who attended to me when I woke up from my fainting spell being followed by the giant I married.

The doctor looks confused and awkward.

"Ma'am? But I thought Dell Westbrook was your husband."

"He is, but..."

"Could you leave us alone for a moment, doctor?" Dell asks.

The doctor looks at me, and I know he's waiting for my consent. I nod.

"Don't upset her," he warns Dell. "As I told you a moment ago, I need to speak with you both. It's very important."

He leaves, and only then do I face my husband.

I'm not sure what I expected, but it certainly wasn't the expression of pain on his face.

"Hate me. You have the right to do so, but let me hold you for a minute because I've never felt fear before today, and the thought that you might have died terrified me."

My pride tells me to push him away, but I can't. The love I feel for Dell is my strength, but it's also my weakness.

"One hug," I concede, and in less than a second, I'm trapped back in our world again.

It's painful and comforting. It's frightening and also home. It's hurt, but it's also love.

Dell holds me as if he'll never let me go again. He squeezes me and kisses the top of my head. For a moment, I resist.

It doesn't take long, though, and I'm holding him back. And like a straight line, a natural walk, our mouths meet.

It's a kiss full of longing, despair, pain, loss, and reunion. But on my part, there's still so much hurt left, so even though my whole body pleads for the opposite, I pull away from him.

Dell doesn't stop me. He fulfills his part of the bargain, even though I'm sure neither of us wants this distance.

"You are mine."

"Not anymore."

"You'll be mine forever. Just as no other woman will touch me while I breathe."

His words are strong because I know his history and how much he enjoys sex.

As if he could read my mind, he says:

"I didn't go out with anyone. I don't want another. I'm your husband," he says, showing that he's still wearing the ring, and our eyes fall together on the nightstand beside the hospital bed, where the staff that attended me placed my jewelry. "You didn't stop wearing yours either."

"Because I'm still your wife, but that's going to change soon."

"I want a chance. You owe me that. When you ran away from me, you broke our agreement."

"Are you going to throw that in my face?"

"I will. You broke our agreement and asked me to believe in you. I didn't know you, but I kept it with me. I want the same in return. No promises for the future. No touching you unless that's what you want, but let me stay by your side."

I'm torn, but it's not an equal division. My pride and anger don't even come close to the love I feel for him.

I look at Dell's face and notice he's lost weight. His beard has grown; even his clothes are wrinkled.

Yes, he's suffering too, and somehow that lessens my bitterness a bit.

"Do you believe me?"

"Yes, I believe," he says without hesitation.

"Why only now?"

"It wasn't just now. The moment you left my house, I knew I had made a gigantic mistake. I called you, as you know. I searched for you all over the island."

"To ask for a divorce."

"No."

"You offered me a hundred million dollars."

"I was still in denial, but I would have offered you ten times that just to have the chance to breathe the same air as you."

"I don't know if I can, Dell. I'm too hurt."

"I won't rush you. It'll be on your time, just don't send me away."

I decide to change the subject because it's much easier to talk about anger than about us. I'm confused and ashamed of myself for not being able to give him a definitive no.

"And what about Seth? He wasn't involved in that, Dell. I know you hate him, but when I left the hotel, he looked faint. Just the fact that I was confused and panicking made me run away, but I think I should have called an ambulance."

"He would have hated it if you had done that. Like me, Seth doesn't like to show weakness."

"You don't have any weakness."

"You're mistaken, wife. You are my weakness. A little while ago, out there, when the doctor came to talk to me, I thought..." He diverts his eyes from mine and shakes his head.

"What?"

"I thought he was going to tell me you had died, Evelina, because of your grandmother's heart condition. I thought you had the same. I survived the death of my family, but I would never recover if I lost you."

I feel a lump of emotion forming in my throat, but I don't let it linger.

"I'm alive."

"And I will thank God forever for that."

"Finish talking about Seth," I ask, trying to disguise how much it affects me that the cold CEO, the magnate who has always had everything he wanted, is so emotional over the mere possibility of my death.

"Someone set me and Seth up. You were used as a pawn. I think they paid your brother to take you to that hotel."

"Did you talk to him?"

"No. Seth disappeared, and I think I know who he went after."

"Who?"

"Do you remember Ellington Bixby?"

"The sweet old man who was friends with your grandfather and Seth's?"

"Yes, that one. I think he's responsible for this. Now there's not even certainty that my grandmother was really the mistress of Seth's grandfather. It could only have been him or Wilma, the only two people who were close to my family and Seth's when our grandparents were alive."

He fumbles with his blazer and takes out a photograph. Looking at the image, I'm shocked. It's exactly the same pose I was in with Seth at that hotel.

"My God!"

"It could only have been orchestrated by Ellington Bixby or Wilma."

"But what would either of them gain from this?"

"I haven't figured that out yet, and at the moment, it doesn't matter. All that matters is that you get better and give me a second chance."

"I'm not going to push you away, but you can't even try to hug or kiss me against my will."

"I just want to breathe the same air as you, wife. Until you grant me your forgiveness, that will have to be enough."

Once again, the intensity and meaning of his words make me shiver, but before I can say anything, we are interrupted by a knock on the door, and then the doctor appears.

Chapter 56

Dell

"What did you just say?" Evelina asks, and my eyes automatically drop to her belly.

"You're pregnant. Given the situation I witnessed upon your husband's arrival, I'm not sure if this is good news, but I would like to give you some very serious recommendations regarding your pregnancy and..."

"Free me from the agreement for a moment," I ask her, stepping between Evelina and the doctor, turning my back to the man and ignoring his presence.

"What?"

"I gave my word that I wouldn't touch you against your will. Release me from the deal and let me talk to our child."

"I think you both need a moment alone," the doctor says, and I hear the door close, but my attention is on her.

Evelina has tears in her eyes and nods at me.

I lean over the hospital bed and press my face against her belly. I stay like this for a long time because I don't know what to say, but soon, the words come out naturally.

"Your father is a proud bastard, baby. He makes more mistakes than he gets right in life, but here's a promise: I will love you just as I love your mother until my last breath on Earth."

I continue talking to our son or daughter, and some time later, I feel her hands in my hair.

"I'm not promising that I will forgive you, Dell, but I will give you a new chance to prove that not only do you know you were wrong, but that you will never do something like this again because the next time you push me out of your life, you won't hear from me again."

I rise up, my face at her level.

"You won't regret giving me a chance, wife. I love you, my woman, and I will prove to you that I learn from my mistakes."

"The previous agreement still stands. You can only touch me if I say yes."

"I will never disrespect you, Evelina. You are my queen, and from now on, you will be treated as such."

"That shop where you found me—I was looking to rent it because I loved it. In fact, I love everything about this town. I'm not leaving Ridgefield. I won't abandon the world I started to rebuild to follow you."

"I'm the lord of my universe, woman. I can do anything. I will work from here if necessary, but you can be sure that I won't leave your side. And about the shop, I know. During the hours I spent waiting for the doctor to tell me what was wrong with you, Fantini told me about your plans. I bought that shop for you. It's yours now. I've already transferred the money. All that's left is for you to sign. I want every dream of yours to come true. I rushed it; I had bought another for you in Manhattan before we separated because it was only the night you told me that you would like to move to Connecticut that I realized you preferred living in a small town rather than on the island, but we can sell it and..."

"You bought a shop for me?"

"Of course I did. You are my life, Evelina, and I noticed that you were sad. I wanted... I *want* your smiles, and I will make it my mission on this planet to bring them forth more than tears."

"I was feeling useless, like a doll. I've always worked and missed it. Moreover, guilt tormented me for not telling you the truth about my brother's messes."

"We both made mistakes due to lack of communication. It won't happen again. From now on, tell me anything you want."

"Even if it hurts you? I still have a lot of resentment inside me, Dell."

"Dump it all on me, wife. I can take it. Just don't push me away."

"Would you respect it if I asked to leave?"

"I wouldn't force you to stay, but I would move to Ridgefield anyway."

She hides a smile, but I still take it as a promising sign since it's the first one she gives me after we reunited.

"Call the doctor back, Dell. He said he wanted to talk to us, and he seemed concerned."

Evelina

A FEW MINUTES LATER, I feel like I'm falling into a crater when the doctor says that my high blood pressure, which is apparently hereditary and of which I wasn't even aware, could pose risks to our son or daughter.

"I want you both to understand the importance of monitoring the mother-to-be's blood pressure during pregnancy. High blood pressure, even hereditary, as I suspect is the case with you, Mrs. Westbrook, considering your family history, can increase the risk of developing preeclampsia, which can occur after the twentieth week of pregnancy. This is something we need to watch closely, as it can affect the health of both the mother and the baby."

The moment the man started talking about my condition, forgetting the agreement I made with Dell, I intertwined our hands because fear made my blood run cold.

I didn't plan for this baby, but I want it so much.

"Please explain everything to us," my husband asks.

"With high blood pressure, there are increased risks of complications such as fetal growth restriction, premature birth, and in more severe cases, damage to vital organs of the mother. The most important thing is that, with proper monitoring, we can manage these risks. If you continue in the city, I would be happy to refer you to a good obstetrician, the best in the area, but if you want my opinion, you might consider returning to Manhattan."

"My wife likes it here. I can have a helicopter on standby for her whenever she needs to consult, but Evelina has already decided that Ridgefield is where she wants to raise our son or daughter. Give me the contact for that obstetrician in Manhattan, and I'll make sure he comes today."

The doctor smiles and nods.

Dell makes me dizzy with the speed at which he makes decisions, but he is right about one thing. I don't want to leave Ridgefield.

"Continue your explanation, doctor."

"As you will be staying in the city, and as I'm a general practitioner, I can continue to attend to you as well. We will work together to regularly monitor your blood pressure and, if necessary, adjust the treatment to ensure a safe and healthy pregnancy for you and the fetus. From what I can see, you have all the support you need to have a smooth pregnancy. If you have any questions or concerns, feel free to ask me."

It's as if the doctor has opened a floodgate because Dell bombards him with questions right away.

By the end of thirty minutes, my husband dictates a list, proving that he memorized everything.

"Let's go, doctor. To stay healthy during our baby's pregnancy, Evelina needs: to adopt a diet rich in fruits, vegetables, whole grains, and to use little salt, as this can help control blood pressure."

The man nods, and Dell continues:

"She needs to exercise regularly, as should be recommended by the obstetrician. She must not miss medical appointments so that we can monitor the baby's development. She shouldn't get stressed, so activities like meditation and yoga can be helpful. If the obstetrician recommends, follow the medication he indicates strictly. And she shouldn't get upset, which, in the end, falls under the part about not stressing out."

"Don't you need to write anything down?" the doctor sounds astonished.

"I have a great memory. Besides, we're talking about the health of my wife and child. I doubt that even in twenty years these rules will fade from my mind."

"My God, Dell," I say, embarrassed.

The man must think he's crazy.

"And what about sex?"

Jesus, he didn't just say that.

I feel my face flush, and I want to kill him.

"There's no contraindication, but keep in mind that in the later stages of pregnancy, you need to be more careful."

When the doctor finally leaves, several minutes later, I'm still mortified.

"How could you ask that to the doctor? We haven't talked about having sex!"

"We're going to live together again, Evelina. Now that I know your health is at risk, there's no way I can stay anywhere else knowing that at any moment you might need me. I'm only going to ask that you think about our history. You're hurt right now, but look into my eyes and tell me if you think we can coexist in a house without touching each other."

I don't respond because I know that if I disagreed, it would be a lie. I love him and everything that comes from him. His kiss. His touch. The way he possesses me. Dell is the man of my life, and...

Suddenly, something ignites in my memory.

Something I don't want to be true because if it is, he will suffer too much.

"Dell, I just remembered something."

"What is it?"

"It's about Wilma. You said the only people who could have set you and Seth up would be her or Ellington Bixby. The night of the charity party, she revealed something to me that I would never tell you, but given the current context, I don't want to keep this secret."

"What did she tell you?"

"Wilma said that Seth's grandfather was the love of her life. I don't know if that relates to the tragedy that unfolded afterward, but it might be good to check."

Chapter 57

Evelina

"So, have you forgiven him?"

Dell stepped out to give us some privacy, but I know it's also because he wants to give my news to my brothers. He told me that Vernon and London are in the hallway and want to see me.

"I don't have an answer to that yet, Fantini, but I want to try."

"For the baby? Because if that's the case, dear, know that I'll be by your side every step of the way. I'll treat your boy as if he were my own grandchild."

It's amazing how close we've become after I separated from Dell.

I wonder, recalling what she said about the man she loved breaking her heart, if Fantini dreamed of being a mother, of having a family.

"No matter what direction my life takes, I will always be your friend, and I'll be honored if you consider my child as a grandchild."

She kisses me on the forehead, and her eyes are filled with tears. For a while, we hug until we hear a knock on the door.

"Come in," I say.

First, I see Vernon. Then, the bad boy Westbrook in his inseparable leather jacket.

Without saying a word, they both come over to me. Fantini steps back to give them space since they're both so big.

First, Vernon kisses me on the forehead and says:

"Accept that bastard of our older brother back, and we'll be the best uncles your children could ever wish for. No, scratch that. *I* will be the best uncle for your heir, even if you don't want Dell anymore, but know that our brother is crazy about you, Evelina. He has suffered hell since you left."

"We will try," I say, because even though I want it to work out, our future is still a question mark.

He smiles as if he's already guaranteed the "victory."

Damn Westbrook arrogance.

It's London's turn to kiss me on the forehead, but before he sits back up, he holds my face.

"I'm looking for your brother. If I find him, I'll rip his head off for what he did to you."

There's no trace of joking in his expression when he says this, and I know immediately that he's speaking pure truth.

Maybe some time ago, his promise would have scared me for fear that he would hurt Pyotr, but knowing that my brother drugged me and especially that he did it when I was already pregnant, which could have harmed my baby, makes me hate him even more.

"I don't care, and even if that makes me a bad person, I couldn't care less. You three here aren't my blood, yet you're more my family than he ever was."

Dell

I NEVER THOUGHT I WOULD do this in my life, but after the conversation with Evelina earlier and her revelation about Wilma's confession, I have no choice, so I call LJ, Seth's older brother, and ask how I can talk to him.

"What do you want with my brother?"

He sounds suspicious because, despite the Westbrook resentment against the Seymours and vice versa encompassing the whole family, the tension between Seth and me is more palpable.

"You know about the hotel situation?" I ask because if Seth and I are alike as I imagine, he wouldn't hide anything from the surgeon.

"Yeah, I know. And if you think Seth would sleep with your wife, you must be crazy. I won't say he isn't a womanizer, but besides having many personal problems to sort out at the moment"—he says, perhaps referencing the scandal I caused by bringing a woman from Seth's past to light—"he doesn't mess with another man's woman."

"I know."

"What?"

"Seth, like Evelina, was drugged. They set them up, LJ. And it's someone who hates the descendants of our grandparents."

"What the hell are you talking about? Is that why Seth traveled?"

"I believe so. I think he's hunting Ellington Bixby, as the friend of our grandparents isn't in the United States either."

"Ellington Bixby? That guy is over eighty!"

"Yeah, I know, but I think he, my aunt, or maybe both are somehow related to the scandal that culminated in the tragedy in our families. That's why I need to talk to Seth."

"He isn't answering his regular phone. Now it all makes sense. Damn, that bastard didn't tell me anything! Is there any chance Seth is in danger, Dell?"

"I don't think so."

"I'll give you his second cell phone number, the one only family knows, but I'm not sure he'll answer."

Five minutes later, I hear the man I've hated my whole life ask:

"What do you want, Westbrook? I didn't sleep with your wife, and I'm after whoever set this up."

"I know."

"You know?"

"Yeah. And that you're hunting Ellington Bixby."

I tell him about Evelina's revelation that Wilma was in love with his grandfather.

"Do you think your great-aunt has something to do with all of this?"

"I wish I could say no, but I believe she does, and I'll find out soon."

"Will you tell me when you find out the truth?"

"The truth?"

"Aren't you thinking that our grandparents might never have been lovers and that this was just a setup?"

"That thought crossed my mind, but how did you come to that conclusion even before knowing about Wilma's love for your grandfather?" I ask.

"Because it was Ellington Bixby who invited me to that hotel. He supposedly wanted to help me destroy you, but why now, if he's been by your side your whole life?"

"Maybe because he's sick."

"It's a possibility, but I won't stop until I uncover everything. And if he had anything to do with what led to the death of your grandparents, I'll put him behind bars."

Chapter 58

Dell

Ridgefield

Days later

I postponed the visit to Wilma, not because she hasn't been well, according to Vernon. I don't have that kind of pity in my heart.

It was for Evelina that I decided to delay a confrontation with the woman who helped raise us.

I'm tired of breathing vengeance and retaliation.

Even if she is involved in the plot that harmed my grandparents, Wilma, along with Ellington Bixby, is part of a past filled with hurt and pain.

Evelina and the child she carries in her womb are my present and future.

I had a helicopter sent to pick up the obstetrician recommended by the local hospital's general practitioner to come to this town to see my wife, and the doctor, after reviewing her tests and examining her, repeated practically the same recommendations that the previous one had made, especially regarding the issue of high blood pressure. However, he requested that I take her to Manhattan because he wants to perform imaging tests at his clinic, where the equipment is much more modern than what is available at the local Ridgefield hospital.

I plan to change that, of course. If Evelina decides that the city will be our final destination, I will renovate the entire hospital at my own expense and turn it into the most modern in the country to ensure that she receives all the care she needs.

Although the doctor explained to me that the condition that caused her grandmother's death isn't hereditary, the issue of high blood pressure is.

The only thing that concerns me right now isn't Wilma or even the bastards Ellington Bixby and Pyotr Volkova. The former is being hunted by Seth, and I have no doubt he will find him. The latter is in London's crosshairs.

Thus, for me, the priority now is to ensure that my wife is protected and her health preserved. I will give every last drop of my blood to prove to her that I regret my past actions and that I will never doubt her word again.

I know, however, that it's not a one-sided fight. Evelina will also have to learn not to keep secrets.

"You didn't need to do this." I hear her voice say behind me.

"You said you wanted to paint the shop by yourself and not hire workers. All your wishes will be fulfilled while I breathe."

"Even if I ask you to leave forever?"

I take a deep breath.

"I will never leave forever. There's a part of me inside your body. I will be close until I die, even if you prevent me from touching it."

"Dell, I..."

"Don't say what you think I want to hear, wife. We have an agreement, and I'm trying to fulfill my part."

I don't turn to look at her because I know what I'll find.

She has fair skin flushed from the late winter cold, as if she applied dark blush on her cheeks. Her hair is loose everywhere, and a beanie makes her irresistible because my woman is beautiful in every version of herself.

In seductive dresses or jeans, coat, and boots, as I know she is now, Evelina will always be a temptation for me, and that's why, because my self-control regarding her is almost nonexistent, I have kept a safe distance from her.

I don't want to scare her with the intensity of my love and desire, pushing her too fast and making her tell me to leave the small two-bedroom apartment we share with Fantini.

Yes, I am a guest, and I wonder if my father, from the grave, isn't laughing at this, since we were raised to command, give orders, and never accept the rules of others. The Westbrooks are the ones who move the pieces of the game, not those who accept impositions.

A passionate Westbrook, however, as is my case, knows no limits to get what he desires, and what I want is our life back.

Does Evelina prefer to live in Ridgefield forever? Fine. I will transfer my life here. I will fly to Manhattan by helicopter when needed. There won't be an obstacle I won't overcome to be with her.

"Dell?"

I drop the paintbrush I was using to paint the shop I bought for her in town and take a few seconds to turn around because there isn't a damn time Evelina is near me that I don't want to take her and hear her scream my name while swearing that she loves me.

"You shouldn't be here. The smell of the paint can harm you."

"What's wrong?"

I finally turn to see her, and as I expected, she looks lovely in a pink puffer coat.

"I'm not made of iron, Evelina. I'm doing my best to keep my hands off you, and that's why this manual labor, which I've never done in my life, has been helpful."

"You've also been running at dawn," she says, going to lock the door.

Then she walks over to the counter, where she places a plate, removes the foil covering it, and I notice there's a cake inside.

"Shouldn't you be resting?" I dodge the topic, while my eyes are glued to her as she takes off her coat and beanie.

The shop has heating, so I know she won't feel cold.

Since I started renovating it, after watching several videos on YouTube and also talking to a contractor who did some work for me at my house in the Hamptons, she has been visiting me on a daily basis.

At first, she would stay for five minutes, barely speaking, but I knew her eyes were on me. Gradually, though, like someone approaching the cage of a wild beast, she gathered courage, the small phrases she said transforming into full conversations until now, she always comes in the afternoon and stays with me until I leave.

I installed a soft sofa that transforms into a bed in the room that will eventually become an office, for when she feels sleepy, which the doctor explained is one of the symptoms of pregnancy. I also arranged for the shower to start working because when I finish working, I prefer to clean up here, since the apartment where the three of us are living is very small, and I don't feel comfortable with someone who is practically a stranger—Fantini—inside the house.

Although the desire to touch her is practically uncontrollable, I confess that we've gotten to know each other more during these unplanned chats than in all the months we lived together, because with me working, Evelina seems more confident to reveal memories from the past in detail and also many of her fears.

She told me that she feels sad for not remembering her parents and that almost all her memories belong to the time when she was already living with her grandmother. Evelina revealed to me that from time to time she wonders if the woman who raised her can see what her brother has become from heaven, and that she believes she would be very disappointed if she were alive.

And most importantly, which made me sure she is very strong: my wife stated that she never wants to know her brother again, no matter what kind of sad story he tells when approaching her. If Pyotr Volkova comes looking for her again, she will hand him over to the police.

What she might not realize, perhaps, is that I won't rest until I put him behind bars or see him dead.

"I'm not tired. I tested a new cake recipe and brought some for you to try."

"Wouldn't Fantini want to do that?"

"She went to spend the day in Manhattan. She said she wants to do some shopping."

I notice there's no spoon on the plate, so I tense up completely when I see her stick her finger in the frosting and bring it to my lips.

"What do you think you're doing?" I grip her wrist, feeling my heart pounding violently.

"Feeding you."

For several seconds, we stare at each other.

"If you want to do that, let me taste that sweetness on your body."

Chapter 59

Evelina

"That's not what we agreed on," I say, dropping the plate on the counter and running to the office of the shop under renovation.

It's an act of pure cowardice because I know what I want, even though I'm fighting an internal battle against my pride.

My love for Dell, if it were a mathematical operation, would be of the most complex kind.

It took me just a few days, after we started living together again, to be sure that I want a real second chance for both of us, and although my heart belongs to him and is filled with an intense love for my husband, a part of me still resists yielding.

I enter the small room and place my hands on the solid wood table that Dell bought for me online. I loved it when I saw it in an antique store on the internet, and after mentioning it to him, two days later, the piece was here.

Fulfilling the promise he made to me, he hasn't tried to kiss or hug me again, but when we're near each other, the air becomes electric.

Today, I know that what I did was a provocation, but I wasn't sure where it would lead, and now, as I hear his footsteps approaching, my pulse races.

"You're afraid to lose control with me, so be the one to give the orders today."

I glance back and feel my mouth water when I see him looking more handsome than ever in worn jeans and a fitted college t-shirt, slightly frayed, yet still making him look delicious.

Maybe it's the pregnancy hormones, but the truth is, Dell is more irresistible to me than ever.

"Give the orders?"

I watch him place the plate with the cake he brought on top of one of the many boxes stacked in the office.

Then, he takes off his t-shirt, and I fear that my drool will spill onto the floor as I fix my gaze on his muscular chest and toned abdomen.

I haven't seen him naked in weeks, and I'm starving for him.

"What are you doing?" I repeat almost the same question he asked me moments ago.

"You said you wanted to feed me, but it looks like you're the one who needs to eat, wife," he says, and I see him lock the office door, even though the shop is already locked. Then he discards his shoes and socks. He takes off his jeans, and I feel a flutter in my stomach when I see his rigid sex bounce free, as he's not wearing any underwear.

Dell is all big, and that includes his cock. He's long and thick, and the desire that overwhelms me to feel him inside me again is almost painful.

He gestures towards the plate while walking over to the sofa.

He sits down, legs open, hand on his shaft, masturbating while looking at me.

"Come eat your dessert, woman. You're dying to suck me off."

I tremble on my feet, swaying like a leaf in the wind, until I can't resist and make a move to grab the plate.

"No, I want you naked."

I don't know what entity possesses me, but I don't hesitate to obey his command.

In no time, I have nothing on my body.

I pick up the plate with the cake, and my insecurity disappears when I see the passionate way Dell looks at me.

I kneel in front of him, and looking at him through my lashes, I take his hand from his hard member, insert a finger in the frosting, and start spreading it all over him.

I drop the plate and, without touching him yet, I lick the sweet cream from the swollen tip.

"Eyes on mine, wife."

I obey him and take him, starved. At first, I'm still a bit shy, but soon, desire takes over reason. In no time, I'm lifted. He doesn't let me finish, standing in front of me and, with an open hand, spreads frosting between my legs.

He lies back on the sofa and pulls me over his face, licking and sucking, taking every part of me because he knows he owns me.

Dell

I DEVOUR HER WITH A hunger that's been restrained for weeks.

Around us, the world seems to be on fire, or maybe we are the focus of the blaze. The air is thick with sexual tension.

I explore every inch of her pussy with my tongue and fingers, and when she orgasms, I keep eating her.

Only when she goes limp in my arms do I lay her back on the sofa, spreading her thighs and positioning myself between them, letting her feel the strength of my erection.

"Tell me you don't want to be fucked by your husband, and I'll stop. But if you need my cock taking you hard, kiss me in response, my wife."

She bites her lip, but I know her decision is already made when Evelina pulls me by the neck and spreads her legs even further.

My hands roam over my wife's body.

I recognize everything about her. Skin, scent, wetness, moans... She is my home.

Evelina whimpers in pleasure in my arms, and the temperature of our bodies rises, our hands exploring each other, losing themselves in every inch of one another.

I slide a finger into her warm, silky opening to prepare her for me.

Her legs wrap around me, our hands unite. Pussy and cock ready to be possessed and possessive.

The tip of my shaft brushes against her opening once because I don't want to hurt her, and I know it won't be a gentle fuck. I'm starving for her.

When I feel her ready, I can't wait any longer and enter her, deep and rough, taking her whole.

She moans in pleasure, and I kiss her mouth, simultaneously stroking her clit, sucking her nipples, pounding hard inside her without pause, making us both plunge into a sea of ecstasy.

Every drop of my blood vibrates with passion.

Our bodies surrender intensely, connected by a force greater than reason, the past, and the hurts.

I open my eyes and see her looking at me.

"I love you, wife. I will never let you forget that. Forgive me, and I will spend the rest of my life treating you like my queen because that's what you are."

"Don't hurt me again. I was wrong too, but you hurt me deeply. I will put aside everything, my pride in the name of the love I feel, but I won't give you another chance, Dell."

Her promise, and finally her forgiveness, break through my madness, and I penetrate her deeply. Our hips collide against each other.

I unite our mouths, fucking her with my tongue as well.

"You are mine. I can't live without my heart, Evelina, and that's what happened during the time we were apart. I am in love with you and will be forever."

I thrust deep and fast. She screams for more.

"That's it, call my name. I'm your husband, my naughty girl. Come on your man's cock."

She receives me into her body, fully surrendered.

I ride her, thrusting deep, and she endures, grinding, asking for it even harder.

Her orgasm is animalistic in strength, and I can't control myself, spilling inside her moments later.

An electric current runs through our bodies until, finally, we surrender to satisfaction.

"I love you, Dell. I don't want to have to pull away again."

"I won't repeat my mistakes, Evelina, and sending you away was the stupidest thing I ever did. It won't happen again. I will live to honor our love."

Chapter 60

Dell

Days later

I've heard some of my friends, the few who are already parents, talk about the joy of hearing their child's heartbeat for the first time.

I doubt any of them, however, have gone through the emotional rollercoaster that Evelina and I have been on these last few months.

From strangers, we became a couple.

From a couple, we became lovers.

From lovers, we were swept away by an overwhelming love that neither of us predicted or knew how to handle.

We jumped all the stages of a normal relationship and didn't learn to trust one another, but at this moment, with her in the doctor's office, her small hand grasped in mine as she waits, I don't think about the mistakes we made, the fights we had, or what could have been because no one on this fucking planet will convince me that we're not meant for each other.

My heart races, partly from the nerves of knowing that our child is well; partly because until I discovered that my wife was pregnant, I never thought about having a family, but now I want the whole package, to grasp with all my might the second chance that life is giving me.

I know we're still treading on eggshells, and the presence of Fantini with us in the house they rented, where I'm a guest, is proof that nothing is definitive between us at the moment. Or at least that's what Evelina thinks, because for me, there's nothing more certain on this planet than the two of us.

What we're experiencing these days is new for me. I'm agreeing to let her take the lead.

Staying in a house that isn't mine.

Taking unplanned time off from my work to care for Evelina's health twenty-four hours a day.

Accepting to live with a third person who is clearly surplus to our relationship, but on the other hand, I respect the care and protection Fantini has for my wife.

It's not how I like to live my life. I've always been in charge, but I will do anything to make her understand that my love is not fleeting, but deep and eternal.

Our reconciliation is still fragile, and I know I can't rush it.

"Dell, what are you thinking?"

"About how much I love you and how lucky I am to have you back in my life."

I bring her hands to my lips and kiss both.

"You're terrible at keeping your part of the deal, Westbrook. You seduced me," she says, not caring about the obstetrician's presence, who stifles a laugh.

"I love you, Evelina, and I'm compulsive when it comes to you. I couldn't resist."

"Let's get started, mommy and daddy," the obstetrician says.

Evelina and I barely breathe. Except for the hum of the machines, I think we could hear a pin drop.

And then comes the sound that, for me, has become the most precious in the world. In the form of little rhythmic beats, we hear our child's heartbeat for the first time.

The unique melody of the life we created fills the room, and it's as if the universe pauses, and a connection occurs between us and the baby.

My chest warms, and a happiness I never could have predicted takes hold of every drop of my blood.

I look from the screen to my wife and see tears rolling down her face.

The doctor explains to us, a few minutes later, that both according to the tests and the ultrasound, everything now indicates that the baby is in perfect health.

He talks again about the care she will need to take during the pregnancy so that her high blood pressure doesn't turn into preeclampsia and about the next appointment. He warns that he will prescribe vitamins.

"Look at that, we're going to have a champion here. A big baby, it seems," the doctor says.

"I wonder who they take after?" she jokes, and as the proud jerk that I am, I feel my chest swell.

"My wife, my child," I say, hardly caring that I'm playing the fool.

"Can we find out the gender?" she asks, disguising her excitement.

"Not yet. According to your blood test, you should be about twelve weeks along, mommy. If we're lucky, in another two, we'll be able to find out, but I think another ultrasound in such a short time is unnecessary, unless you're too anxious to wait."

"I can wait. How about you?" she asks me.

"Whatever you decide, my queen."

She blushes and smiles.

"He's a little seducer, Dell."

"I'm a man in love."

A little while later, it's all over, and we leave the office together.

"I don't want to leave you alone, but I need to go see my aunt. I can't put off this conversation any longer, Evelina."

"If you don't mind, I'd like to go with you."

"Are you sure about that? My gut tells me it won't be a pretty conversation."

"Wilma is our child's great-aunt. I don't know how involved she is in this sordid story, Dell, but I want to go with you." She pauses and instinctively hides her face in my chest. "I love her. I'll be very disappointed if she's the one who orchestrated everything against us, but I need to know the truth."

"I don't think it was her, but she has some involvement in everything that happened in the past. Against both of us, I want to believe she didn't do anything, but regarding Seth's grandfather, yes."

"I'm going with you. I'm not made of glass, and I want to be by your side. If the roles were reversed, would you let me go alone?"

"Never."

My phone rings, and after pulling her in for a kiss, I answer when I see Vernon's name pop up on the screen.

"Dell, you need to come. Wilma doesn't seem well and wants to see you. She asked for all three of us to come."

"Call a doctor."

"She refused. She said she needs to talk to us."

"I would have gone anyway, but by car. Now, I'll take the helicopter. I'll be there in an hour, at most."

Chapter 61

Dell

"I'm so sorry, Dell," my great-aunt says as I enter her suite, and even though she hasn't explained anything yet, I can recognize guilt on someone's face. "Would you give me a kiss one last time?"

London and Vernon are already here, sitting in a relatively distant armchair from her because I've always been Wilma's favorite.

I clench my fist inside my suit pocket.

Having pity isn't something I'm used to, and if she harmed Evelina in any way, I will never forgive her.

"First, answer me if you had anything to do with my separation from Evelina."

"I swear on everything sacred that I didn't. I committed one sin in my life, and I've paid for it my whole existence because once you unleash evil, Dell, it's like pushing over a line of dominoes."

I move closer and lean down so she can kiss me, and when I feel the lips of the woman who raised me, knowing she's about to say something that will change everything between us, it feels like a punch to the heart.

"Now you, Evelina."

My wife is much more generous than I am, as she leans down, kisses, and hugs Wilma.

"I've missed you," she says.

"I missed you too, my child, and I knew you would be together again."

I want to pull Evelina away from her, but I respect that my wife decides when to step back.

As soon as my wife returns to me, I lead her to an armchair near my brothers.

"Tell me everything, Wilma. I know it was Ellington Bixby who set a trap to destroy my marriage, and I also know he played games with me and Seth. He must have been doing this for years."

She nods and adjusts herself more comfortably against the pillows.

"It's a long story. But I will start with the part that triggered all the misfortune. I was the one who saw Seth's grandfather first when Calantha and I were still teenagers. But he only had eyes for my sister. The two fell in love at first sight. It was the kind of love you knew would last a lifetime."

What she says shakes me. I always thought their relationship was a teenage fling; otherwise, why would she marry Grandpa?

"Continue."

"Randolph Seymour and your grandfather, Obadiah Westbrook, were best friends, just as their parents had been before them."

"They were for a time."

"No. They remained so until the moment of death."

"I don't understand."

"I will explain everything, my son. High society was baffled when your grandfather asked my sister to marry him, and even that didn't shake the friendship between the three of them. They were inseparable. Everyone believed in that fraternal love between Randolph and Calantha, but not me. As a jealous and envious woman in love, I could see the way Seth's grandfather looked at my sister when she was already engaged to Obadiah, and even after they were married."

"How is that possible?" London asks. "There's no way Grandpa wouldn't have noticed."

"Oh, he noticed. Just as I was in love with Randolph, he was in love with your grandmother. Jealousy poisoned me from within. I created situations after their marriage and when your father was already born, to end that friendship because I was convinced that if I could distance Randolph from the couple, he would see me and fall in love with me. I was foolish and deluded. A man who had set his eyes on your grandmother would never see another. It was that way with your grandfather and his best friend, my love, Randolph. And it happened the same way with Ellington Bixby."

"What?"

"Ellington Bixby was in love with your grandmother, Dell. Calantha had three men madly in love with her."

"Grandma and..."

"No, she never cheated on your grandfather."

"She cheated on him; otherwise, the tragedy wouldn't have happened," Vernon interjects.

"No, she never betrayed Obadiah. She loved him, just as she loved Randolph, boys. Your grandmother lived a three-way love. They were completely in love. The two men for her. My sister for both. I caught them unaware, asleep after making love. The photo of my sister with Seth's grandfather was taken by me. But Obadiah was with them. Coming out of the bathroom, actually, and I almost got caught, but I managed to escape in time."

"You're telling me that our grandparents and Seth's grandfather formed a *throuple*?"

"I don't know if that's the term, but yes, there were two men with her, completely devoted and in love with my sister. Society at the time would never accept that, and that's why they kept it a secret, of course. In public, they were best friends. In the bedroom, they were three passionate hearts."

"What did you do, Wilma?"

"I tried to get Randolph's attention in every way I could. I offered myself to him even without a promise of commitment, which at that time would have disgraced me. He refused, and I knew the reason. His heart was already taken. If everything hadn't unfolded as it did, he would never have married, and the Seymour lineage would have stopped there."

"My God!" I hear Evelina say, sniffling as well.

"Baby, I think..."

"No, Dell. I'm staying. Continue, Wilma," she urges my great-aunt.

"My hatred grew with every appearance of the three together. With every smile they exchanged. It got to a point where I was going crazy. I didn't eat, I didn't sleep. My envy and madness knew no bounds, so I ran and told Ellington Bixby everything. I was sure he would create a scandal and put an end to that shamelessness because, like me, he would be jealous of Calantha being with two men at the same time and never having given him a chance."

"She loved them. Not Ellington Bixby, but Grandpa and Randolph," I say.

"Try to understand, Dell. I was a woman in love."

"Not in love, Wilma." Evelina steps closer to the bed. "I love Dell with every drop of my blood and every cell in my body. And even now, while I'm still hurt by him, I could never do anything to harm him. What you felt for Randolph was obsession."

She cries, but I can't be moved.

"You were the one who delivered the photo that Dad found over my grandparents' bodies to Ellington Bixby. He was the one who killed them. It wasn't a murder-suicide. How could you, Wilma? You destroyed my father's childhood, the boy who claimed to love!"

"I tried to atone. I raised him as if he were my own. I raised all three of you."

"*Atoned?* You played God with our lives."

I stand up, unable to believe what I'm hearing. All the certainties, everything I believed my whole life, were nothing but lies triggered by jealousy and envy.

"You tried to get close to Randolph again after Dell's grandparents died," Evelina asserts, her voice never sounding this cold.

"I tried because I loved him. And he rejected me again. He was distraught with grief, but he told me he had made a promise to his friends. He didn't know I was aware of the relationship among the three, so he said that he, Obadiah, and Calantha had a pact. If one of them died, the other would try to remain happy to honor the one who lost their life. That's why Seth's grandfather got married, but he never loved Seth's grandmother, or maybe he loved her a little. However, his life was over. I can't say for sure, but I think he killed himself in that accident."

I pull away from her, hating her as much as I've hated Seth my entire life.

"You knew the truth—that because I thought our grandparents were having an affair, Seth and I hated each other. In fact, all the Westbrooks and the Seymours did. My father lived his life suffocating in resentment towards the enemy family. Seth, with the certainty that Grandpa had stolen the woman Randolph loved. How could you live with yourself, Wilma? My God, you are a monster!"

"I am not. I loved you all with all my heart! I didn't tell the truth to protect you and Seth."

"You didn't tell the truth to protect yourself, because if Ellington Bixby were arrested, I doubt he would spare you. He would reveal who took that photo."

"I kept it a secret out of love for you."

"No, you let a murderer live among us. You allowed Dad to die filled with resentment. I lived my life immersed in hatred; still, I could grant you my forgiveness, Wilma, because as I said, you raised us. But by being selfish and not letting us know who Ellington Bixby was, you put my wife and our baby at risk. Evelina was drugged while pregnant! I will never forgive you for that."

"I knew you would never understand this, and that's why I decided not to continue in this world."

I watch her, astonished, bite something that was already in her mouth, and then, much faster than any of us had time to react, her eyes widen. It doesn't take long for me to conclude that Wilma is dead.

"She committed suicide!" Evelina says, shocked.

"No, she fled from the responsibility of her actions once again. And for that, I hope she burns in hell," London states, leaving the room.

Chapter 62

Evelina

After the death of my great-aunt, Dell called her doctor, who confirmed that she had ingested poison.

The farewell we gave Wilma was one of the saddest scenes that could have ever existed.

There was no feeling of loss or longing, but rather a latent pain from the three Westbrook heirs against the woman who raised them.

We did not hold a wake. It was a cremation, and everything was very quick and cold, to the point that Fantini made me promise that when she passed, I wouldn't allow her farewell to happen like this.

My friend asked me to celebrate her goodbye to Earth with good champagne, dressed in haute couture, made up and styled, sitting in a Michelin-starred restaurant in Marseille that she loves.

I don't like to think about that possibility. The idea that Fantini will leave at some point makes me very sad because I've truly grown fond of her, and I even asked her to move permanently to the United States.

She accepted but told me she might live in Manhattan, as she finds Ridgefield too quiet for her taste.

The Frenchwoman also mentioned that she is wrapping up her work as a convenience matchmaker once and for all. Now, she believes in true love, having witnessed my story with Dell, according to her own words.

"She was crazy," Fantini says as we collect memories from the Westbrook family from Dell's great-aunt's house.

At first, he said he didn't want anything related to that woman and that he could never forgive her. However, I argued that our child would want memories of the family's past, and the more I rummage through Wilma's boxes, the more I realize I was right, as there are various photographs from different stages of life not just of Dell and his brothers but also of their father.

I feel a nudge on my leg and bend down to speak with Dasy, the little dog that belonged to Wilma and that I adopted. She is very old, and I know she won't live many more years, so I can't bear the thought of putting the poor thing up for adoption.

"Hello, my beauty. I know you want attention, but we're almost done, okay?"

She wags her tail as if she understands my promise and then lies down on a cushion on the sofa to wait for me.

"I don't know if she was crazy," I finally reply to Fantini. "Or if she lied so much her whole life that she convinced herself that what she did was nothing serious. However, I believe the love she felt for Dell's father, as well as for her great-nephews, was genuine."

"You are a wonderful girl, Evelina. I'm not that generous. To me, she usurped her sister's family. She raised Calantha's child and also her descendants."

"My God, that's a horrible thought. If it's true, she didn't learn anything from her own mistakes."

"She didn't learn, Evelina. If she were truly remorseful for the sins she committed, she would have handed Ellington Bixby over to the police. She didn't do that. She kept secrets to protect herself, allowing that cruel man to play with Dell's hatred against Seth and vice versa."

"She destroyed an entire family, as well as three lives. I don't believe what she felt for Randolph Seymour was love."

"I don't think so either. It was madness, obsession, selfishness. Wilma displayed all the traits of a narcissistic personality. The biggest proof of this is that right after her confession, she killed herself. In her mind, I believe, the world always owed her something. Nothing was ever her fault."

Dell

"I'M WITH HIM AND HEADING home. The police have him in custody."

"It will be very difficult to prove he killed our grandparents," I say to Seth on the phone.

He now knows all about Wilma's involvement in the story of our ancestors and didn't seem surprised when I told him what she did, nor that Ellington Bixby was the murderer of my grandparents and also indirectly caused the death of his grandfather.

I realized, even from our phone conversation a few days ago, that he was relieved to learn the truth.

My grandfather, Obadiah Westbrook, was not a murderer or a suicide. His, Randolph Seymour, was not a traitor. They were, along with Calantha, three passionate souls who, in life, could not declare what they felt before the world.

"No, Dell, you're mistaken. I got a recorded confession, and now it's with the police."

"How?"

"He felt untouchable, after all, he survived years of evil hiding his crimes. He hid out on a farm in Mississippi, and it was easier to make him talk than I imagined. I found out where he was and called him. The police had set up a wiretap."

"Without probable cause? They agreed to wiretap him like that?"

"They had probable cause. I found out Ellington Bixby stole Tempus years ago, embezzling funds."

"How had he not been caught until now?"

"He might have an accomplice within the company. I'm not sure yet. We'll need to investigate. The fact is, my phone and his were tapped because of this embezzlement. I provoked him by saying he was an envious, petty man who always wanted a woman he couldn't have, but in the end, he would die alone, just like Wilma did."

"And he took the bait."

"Yes. He bragged that your great-aunt was a poor wretch, weak, and that he was the victor because he destroyed one by one those who stole what was rightfully his."

"Damn."

"He was so certain of his impunity that he confessed in detail the crime he committed, and that the cherry on top was knowing that my grandfather probably killed himself out of grief in the helicopter accident, for not being able to conceive life without Calantha."

"Bastard."

"It's over. He's in jail and will be tried."

"You know he probably won't live until then, right?"

"I do, but I want the whole world to find out what he did, especially, I want everyone to know the love story of our grandparents, if you agree."

"I don't like talking about my family, but in this case, I think you're right. It will be a way to honor them. What do you have in mind?"

"To pay for a documentary to be made telling details of their story, as well as the roles Wilma and Ellington Bixby played in this tragedy."

"I agree. It's not fair for the world to never know how much our ancestors suffered at the hands of two selfish demons."

"I think we've ended our story of hatred then. Too bad, Dell. It was fun fighting against you."

"I don't know if I'll ever like you, Seymour. I've gotten used to hating you," I joke.

"As always, I'm at your service, Westbrook. Start the war, and I'll be ready."

Chapter 63

Evelina

"Marry me," he whispers in my ear, settling in behind me on our bed in Manhattan. Tomorrow, we will return to Ridgefield, where we will look for land to build the house of our dreams, and for now, we will have to suspend the work on the pastry shop since we are handing over the apartment where we were staying.

I agreed with him that I need to focus on my health so that my pregnancy goes smoothly.

I turn in his arms.

"I'm already married to you, my love."

"Yes, but now I want a real marriage, with everything you've ever dreamed of, Evelina. This is a new beginning for us, so let's do everything right. I love you, Russian."

"I want it, Dell. You, a dream wedding, and lots of children. My shop and a cake studio. I won't give up anything more. I'm going to pursue the complete dream, my fairy tale."

London

Somewhere in Russia

"THEY SAY YOU CATCH rats with cheese, but some types of rats are driven by money and a good dose of stupidity."

"Who are you?" Pyotr Volkova, the worm who is also my sister-in-law's brother, pretends not to recognize us, glancing between me and Vernon.

"You know who we are. You researched my brother. Did you really think Evelina would fall for the mistake of meeting you again? And right here in Moscow?"

"She has a lot to lose." He shrugs, trying to show indifference, but I know he's scared.

"Evelina is no longer a Volkova, idiot. She's a Westbrook now," Vernon says. "We would never allow her to meet you. How stupid do you have to be not to realize that the emails we started, supposedly from your sister, were nothing but a trap?"

"They're not murderers. What do you think you're going to do with me? They're two rich kids who probably have never been in a fight in their lives."

He threatens to reach for something in the back pocket of his pants, and I have no doubt it's a weapon.

However, at that very moment, the door to a hotel room in a Moscow suburb, where we set up the meeting with him pretending to be Evelina, opens, and a man points a gun at my sister-in-law's brother's head.

Pyotr Volkova's eyes widen because he knows he's screwed.

Vernon and I rise.

"You're right, jerk," I say. "We're not murderers, but look, we know the right people, and those people found those you owe."

"What?"

He makes a move, and the man behind him wraps an arm around his neck and now points the barrel of the gun at his temple.

"Move again, and I'll blow your brains out right here."

"You can't leave me with him!" He panics when he sees us walking toward the door.

"We can and we will. Your days of wrongdoing against your sister are over, Pyotr. Have a nice trip to hell."

Chapter 64

Evelina

Day of Dell and Evelina's religious wedding

"I can never thank you enough for giving me the honor of walking you down the aisle, dear. I think we'll shock Manhattan society, but it'll be worth it."

"More than shocking them that I'm getting married in a religious ceremony already showing a noticeable baby bump? I don't care what they think, Fantini. You were the one responsible for my union with Dell, so it's only fair that you're the one who delivers me to him."

"I never dreamed of having children, Evelina, but make no mistake, if I did want one, it would be just like you. You are beautiful inside and out. I can't wait for my grandson to be born."

Now we know we're having a baby boy, although Dell and I haven't come to a consensus yet on the name.

During the months we spent organizing my religious wedding, a bond formed between the Frenchwoman and the Westbrooks. We've become an unconventional family, coming from different parts of the world, but with each passing day, we grow closer.

Even London has accepted Fantini into our midst.

"I'm also excited. The future looks bright. So many plans. Marrying the love of my life again. A dream honeymoon on a paradise island. Opening my shop in a few months! It feels like living in a fairy tale."

"I'm sure when the guests taste the wedding cake you made yourself, orders will come pouring in. Maybe your pastry shop will turn into a cake studio after all."

"I've thought about that. I'll keep the original idea of the café here in Ridgefield. As for the wedding cake studio, if the orders start coming in, I'll set it up in the shop Dell bought for me in Manhattan. Yesterday, when Katya and her husband arrived for the wedding, I asked her what she thought about being my manager at the studio, and she loved the idea. Dell said he can easily arrange a work visa for her and Juhani."

Fantini smiles.

"Of course he can, after all, he's the almighty Westbrook. Now enough thinking about the future. Your man is waiting for you, and it's time to live in the present."

A few minutes later, as I walk down the aisle of a charming chapel in my new town, I focus on the joy of about to marry the love of my life for the second time.

I promise my grandmother, who must be watching me from heaven, that I will be happy and honor all the sacrifices she made for me. I also vow to myself that I will never again speak my brother's name.

Blood isn't everything. In fact, when it comes to some people, like Pyotr for instance, blood means almost nothing.

He's left behind wherever he is in the world because I'm definitively cutting him out of my life.

"I don't like it when you get so introspective," Dell says after kissing Fantini on the forehead and pulling me into an embrace, indifferent to the fact that we're standing in the middle of the church aisle and the guests must be watching us.

"I'm a contrast, husband. Half light, half shadow."

"No, love. You are pure light. Some people tried to steal your joy, but I will work hard for the rest of my days to ensure that never happens again, Evelina Westbrook. You are my love and my north. Our contract may have started as a mistake, but our love is the best acquisition I've ever made in my life. Now, come make me a serious man in the eyes of God, my queen."

I smile, rise on my toes, and kiss him.

"I didn't need this religious wedding to be sure that I'm yours, Dell, but I'm very happy that we're here. Now, I have everything."

"I've always had everything since the moment I made you mine."

Epilogue 1

Evelina

Day of Jagger Westbrook's Birth

I was raised by a loving woman. Grandma knew what it was like to love without measure; proof of this was that she dedicated herself to two men who didn't deserve it: grandpa and my brother.

Thus, the feeling of love was not foreign to me. I grew up receiving hugs and kisses, hearing that I was precious, the best granddaughter she could have dreamed of.

I loved her back too and wished she were here, but only today, with my boy in my arms, do I understand what the feeling she dedicated to me was, the love of a mother for her child.

Unconditional, absolute, devoted.

I would give my life for Jagger without thinking twice.

"We created a work of art, Dell," I say, emotional as I breastfeed our boy, and when I look up, I see that he has bright eyes too.

"Because you are perfect, just like the fruit of our love. I want to fill our house with children, Evelina. I'm tired of pain and darkness. Jagger will be the first of many."

I stretch my hand to him, who tries as best he can to accommodate his large body beside me on the bed.

"Let's start the book from the beginning, Dell. Let's pretend that we are both the prologue. Each chapter of our time together, we'll write with four hands throughout our life. I want addendums and footnotes. Fill moments and highlight smiles and happy days in bold. Leave the sad ones only as a watermark. We've had our fill of unhappiness and hurt. I'm dreaming of the pot of gold at the end of the rainbow."

A Year and a Half Later

WE HEAR JAGGER'S GIGGLES as he runs away from the babysitter upstairs, and I swear I don't want to be the doting mom, but the sound is music to my ears.

"Good thing we got an eighteen-year-old babysitter this time," Dell says, stroking my belly where our second boy, Harlan, is being grown. "The other one couldn't handle Jagger. Our son seems plugged into a two hundred and twenty volt socket."

I roll my eyes.

"Who does he take after?"

"You, of course. I'm a saint. The best husband and father in the world."

"I can't deny that, my love, but your son has all your temperament. Bossy, hyperactive, stubborn. And still, I'm crazy about you as much as I am about your mini-me."

"It's good you continue like this, wife, crazy about us. Because you forgot to add two of our main flaws. We are jealous and very possessive too."

Epilogue 2

Dell

Twelve Months Later

"Seth did an excellent job," Evelina says, drying her tears as the credits roll on the documentary about my grandparents and Seth's.

I'm not one to get emotional easily. The only people capable of achieving that are my wife and my two children. I suspect that when the third, Bridger, is born, he will also steal another piece of my heart.

Today, however, I felt all the pain that the triad experienced for not being able to show their love to the world.

"Yes," I finally agree.

"Will you guys never be friends?"

"Isn't it enough that we're no longer enemies?"

"Maybe the next generation of Westbrook and Seymour will change that narrative."

"Only time will tell."

I hadn't watched the documentary until now. Evelina, who just viewed it with me, is watching it for the second time.

It seems life was telling me to wait to do so because today it had a different flavor. The unique taste of revenge.

"I didn't think Ellington Bixby would live this long," she says. "And yet, he was about to go to trial."

The charge that first landed him in jail, we discovered, was actually a minor one and had occurred over two decades ago when Seth and I were still children. A lawyer who helped him and who worked within Tempus was also indicted, but in the end, aside from having to return what they stole, they were not convicted.

Regarding the homicide of my grandparents, the son of a bitch, with the power and money he held, delayed the trial for as long as he could, using endless legal maneuvers.

Given his advanced age, it was granted that he could await the trial at home, free, as long as he accepted to wear a monitor, which he agreed to.

Last week, it was announced to the entire world that the story of our grandparents would come out in a documentary, along with that of all those involved in the tragedy, including Wilma and Ellington Bixby.

Both Seth and I knew the risk of being sued for accusing someone publicly who was presumed innocent, as the bastard's trial had yet to take place. However, we have plenty of money for a legal battle and teams of lawyers who could drag it out for years.

It wasn't necessary. After the documentary aired yesterday, detailing all the sordid facts and portraying the damned Ellington as the embodiment of evil, which he truly was, he hanged himself in his home.

I hope he burns in hell forever.

"He got away with it for years. Thought he could escape this time too."

"And do what? He was almost ninety!"

"Some people never change, Evelina. He never regretted what he did. He was not content just killing my grandparents; he bragged to Seth that he enjoyed watching us fight against each other."

"A true fairy tale villain. Now it's over, right?"

"Yes. It's over, and we won. Seth and I avenged our grandparents."

Five Years Later

I WATCH THE DOOR OPEN and my blonde beauty walk in, stunning in a halter dress that's short and green.

It's not common for my wife to come to Manhattan. She only works part-time at the café twice a week, more for pleasure than necessity, as she has a capable team of staff managing the place.

She remotely oversees the cake shop in Manhattan, trusting Katya, her manager, to handle everything there.

Evelina prefers being at the small factory I had built for her, testing her recipes on the land of the house we constructed in Ridgefield.

We've settled permanently in the small town, and Fantini, who initially planned to stay on the island, now lives in a property next door because she can't get enough of spoiling the three grandkids. My children adore her, and I'm happy they have a grandmother to play with, something that was taken from me.

"I didn't know we had made any plans and was about to call the helicopter to take me home."

She smiles and gestures me to come closer with her finger.

As I approach, she removes my blazer and tie, making me sit on the sofa facing a panoramic view of Manhattan.

"I have plans," she says with a cheeky grin.

"Plans?"

"Plans that involve teasing you but not giving you what you want, husband."

In a swift motion that catches her off guard, I pull her onto my lap, her beautiful bottom up. I give her a hard slap and soon leave her nude, except for her black stilettos.

She pretends to try to escape, but when I touch her while she's still over my lap, she's soaked.

"Don't lie. You came because you wanted to be fucked in my office."

I provoke her, adding another finger now.

"Ahhhh... yes, husband. I love being naughty with you because the reward is a delicious punishment."

Fim!

Did you love *Secrets Beneath the Vows*? Then you should read *Blame It on the Boss*[1] by Nora Kensington!

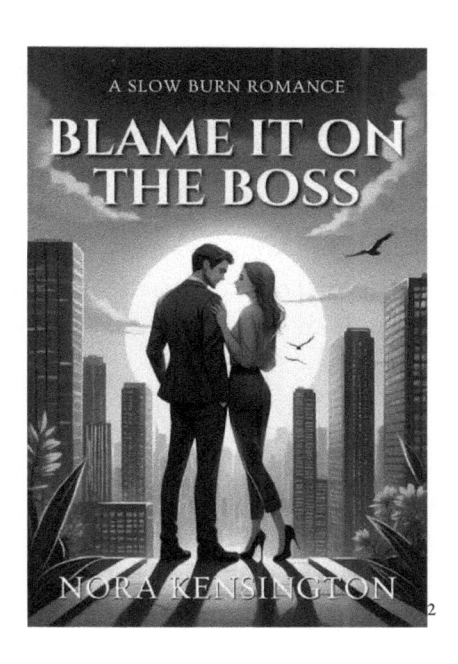

Blame It on the Boss

When Poppy left her small-town life behind, she had **big dreams** of making it in the city. But nearly broke and with her plans unraveling, she jumps at the chance to land a job as an assistant at one of the world's **top publishing companies**. The catch? Her boss is Liam, the **infuriatingly charming** son of the CEO and the company's hottest contender for the top spot.

From day one, Poppy realizes that working with Liam is no walk in the park. He's **demanding**, **arrogant**, and somehow manages to make every problem in her life worse. Yet, she can't deny the way he sets her **pulse racing**, even when they're bickering over deadlines.

---

1. https://books2read.com/u/bWAg77

2. https://books2read.com/u/bWAg77

Their office rivalry quickly spirals into a game of **cat and mouse**, where misunderstandings abound, and no one's willing to admit the undeniable **attraction** simmering just beneath the surface. As the competition heats up, so do their feelings, leading to a **battle of wills** over who will be the first to confess—or walk away.

Caught between love and a power struggle, Poppy and Liam are about to learn the hard way that when it comes to office romances, you can't always **blame it on the boss**... or can you?

Perfect for fans of enemies-to-lovers, slow-burn romance, and sassy, laugh-out-loud banter, *Blame It on the Boss* **delivers all the sparks and drama of an office love story you won't be able to put down.**

About the Author

Nora Kensington is an author known for her captivating blend of romance, suspense, and adventure. With a flair for crafting complex characters and heart-pounding plot twists, her novels transport readers into worlds filled with passion, danger, and emotional depth. Drawing inspiration from both everyday life and her love of classic literature, Nora weaves stories that explore the intricacies of love, courage, and resilience.